Book 5 in the Amber Ridge Series

unchained

NYSSA KATHRYN

UNCHAINED
Copyright © 2025 Nyssa Kathryn Sitarenos

All rights reserved.

An NW Partners Book
Cover by Deranged Doctor Design
Developmentally and Copy Edited by Kelli Collins
Line Edited by Jessica Snyder
Proofread by Amanda Cuff and Jen Katemi
Cover Photography by Briquelle Kayanne Photography

❀ Created with Vellum

He's her boss. She's too young for him. And lines are about to blur.

Taking a job at the newly opened Wilderness Adventure Park was supposed to be about gaining independence for Addison March. She wasn't supposed to find her boss so ridiculously good-looking. Or his smile so charming. Or his protectiveness such a freaking turn-on. The problem is, not only does he think he's too old for her—he also has a past. A past that makes him believe he's dangerous for Addie to be around. She disagrees. But convincing Noah is proving difficult.

Ex-Marine Noah Hayes has returned home to Amber Ridge not just because he wanted to…because he was forced. Medical discharge. Not physical—mental. Something he hasn't shared with his loved ones. But leaving the service doesn't mean his past has left him alone. The nightmares and flashbacks taunt him. And worse, they've touched the people around him…specifically, Addie, his newest employee. Ironic, considering she seems to be the only one with the power to soothe him.

For her safety, he needs to stay away from Addie. But when someone starts targeting her, making dangerous threats, Noah's forced to choose—keep his distance? Or protect her at the risk of exposing Addie to his own demons?

ACKNOWLEDGMENTS

Thank you to my team who helps me put out the best book possible—my developmental editor, Kelli. My line editor Jess. And my amazing proofreaders Amanda and Jen. You are all magic.

Thank you to my PA Alana and my ARC team. Your reviews and words of encouragement give me the confidence to release my book baby into the world.

And, of course, thank you to my amazing husband. It is you who creates the space and peace for me to be the best mom to our two girls, and an author at the same time. I love you.

CHAPTER 1

$\mathcal{A}$ ddie March clicked her pale pink fingernails against the oak desk, her eyes on the Wilderness Adventure Park homepage. Or more accurately, on Noah Hayes. On his bronze back as he bouldered up the cliff edge like a freaking Olympian. Was bouldering an Olympic sport? It should be, the way he did it.

She opened the photo of the zip line. Her second choice. There was no Noah, but that shouldn't influence her decision, should it?

Argh.

Of course it shouldn't. Noah wasn't her boyfriend. He wasn't even her friend. He was her boss. Not only her boss but also thirteen years older than she was. And sure, he was nice to look at. And kind and attentive. Or at least, he *had* been attentive before the *incident* last week.

A shudder rolled down her spine at the memory of Noah's flashback. One second, they'd been standing by the desk talking. Laughing even. The next, she'd nudged his shoulder and suddenly he'd been on top of her on the floor, looking at her like she was an enemy.

She shook her head. It had scared her, but also, it wasn't his fault. He'd just gotten out of the Marines. And he hadn't hurt her. He *wouldn't* have hurt her. Because he was a good guy. She didn't need to have known him long to know that.

So he didn't have to avoid her.

She lifted her gaze to the window behind her desk. To the thick line of trees that surrounded the adventure park. There were mountain bike trails, a zip line, bouldering and rock-climbing walls…even camping cabins.

None of which was her idea of fun. Not that Noah or his partner, Colt, knew that.

What had she said in her interview? The outdoors was her second home? Hell, she might even have thrown in a comment about mountain biking being a weekly Sunday event with her dad.

Ha. She'd never been on a mountain bike in her life. Her father had *tried* to get her to go with him once when she was twelve. She'd told him she'd watch from a log with a mug of hot chocolate. He'd never asked again.

But she'd wanted this job. She'd wanted to move from Bozeman to Amber Ridge because it gave her just that little bit of distance from her parents and her hometown. She loved her mom and dad but relied on them far too much.

And everyone said things that weren't entirely true to get a job…right?

She did have *some* hobbies. Starting books she never finished. Collecting cute coffee mugs she never used because she always used the same one with the weird-looking sloth on it. And chocolate. Chocolate was definitely a hobby.

She reached over and grabbed a mini Hershey's Kiss from her chocolate jar. Yes, an entire jar of chocolate, because running out was not an option. She had everything from mini Reese's Cups to Snickers Minis. She'd even picked up some huckleberry truffles because you couldn't live in Montana without loving their famous huckleberry chocolate.

She popped the Kiss into her mouth. But that was it—she was stopping after one because she was trying to curb this chocolate addiction. Or at least minimize it in the first half of the day. Chocolate after twelve felt more respectable.

She rose and stepped into the front desk area. The cabin had recently been renovated to include an airy reception area, a smaller office space with a million drawers and files, and a second office which had been converted into a kitchen. The place was perfect.

But right now, what she needed was fresh air. Tomorrow, this place would be open to the public and crawling with people, which meant today was the last day of peace. The team was doing their final day of training, and Jules was making sure the food van was stocked and ready to go.

Food van…hmm, that didn't sound like a terrible place to be.

The cool mountain air slipped over her skin as she headed outside to gaze over the mountains.

God, it was beautiful here. She'd been in Amber Ridge less than a month and she already didn't want to leave.

They'd situated the food van in a section that was flat and open and right in the center of the park. The guys had lain down some new grass and brought in picnic tables. It was great. The entire place was great. The fact that they'd been able to fix it up in just a couple of months was actually pretty amazing.

She was almost at the van when a crunching noise sounded in the trees behind her.

She stopped and turned her head.

A month ago, the small sound wouldn't have bothered her. But this last week…she'd been getting the creepy feeling that she was being watched.

It was hard to explain. A prickle at the back of her neck. The hairs on her arms standing on end. And right now, she was experiencing both those things.

Her heart beat faster as she scanned the trees. There was no one there. Because there was *never* anyone there.

She shook her head. She was being silly. After living in the same town, in her parents' home, for her entire twenty-two years, she was just nervous to be somewhere different. Which was exactly why she'd needed to move out for a bit.

When she reached the food van, the smell of freshly ground coffee hit the air. Oddly enough—well, odd to other people—she'd never been a coffee person. She liked the *smell* of coffee, but the taste? Absolutely not. She was a hot chocolate girl through and through, and she'd die on the chocolate-over-coffee hill.

Jules, the owner of the van, turned and smiled. "Addie, darling, good morning."

Jules was a short lady in her fifties with shoulder-length honey-blond hair. The second Addie had met her, she'd felt an instant connection. The older woman was warm and nurturing and exactly who you wanted to greet you in the morning with a hot drink.

Addie smiled back at her. "Hi, Jules. All ready for tomorrow?"

"Absolutely. I have all the coffee beans, hot dogs, and tacos waiting and ready."

"I hear those tacos have been pretty popular with the staff."

Jules chuckled. "I've had to emergency order more supplies. Coffee has also been a big hit. I was told I'm *almost* on par with The Tea House."

"That's quite the compliment." It was still shocking to Addie that the only place in Amber Ridge that sold decent coffee was a tea house. Although they could now add Jules's van to the list.

"Hot chocolate?" Jules asked.

"I am dying for one."

"Well, it just so happens I've ordered in some new salted caramel hot chocolate. Would you like to try it?"

Addie's belly growled. It was unbelievable really—she'd just had chocolate in her office, and she could still down a quart of chocolate in liquid form. "You are like the sun to my morning."

The older woman grinned as she heated the milk. "I'm still shocked you don't drink coffee. I thought that was a precursor to being an adult."

"Trust me, I know. My mother tells me that caffeine holds civilization together, and I must be an alien."

"Your mother sounds like a smart woman. Does she live close?"

"Bozeman, so not far."

"And your dad?"

"Same. Although, he's very supportive of the absence of coffee in my life. According to him, I value functioning adrenals. He says this right in front of my mother while she drinks her third cup of the morning."

The older woman threw back her head and laughed. "He sounds very pragmatic."

"It's the former Marine in him."

"Just like the boys who run this place."

Noah and Colt were *not* boys. They were men. The kind who could chop wood, start a fire, and break your heart before lunch. "Yes, just like Noah and Colt."

When Jules turned with the hot chocolate in hand, steam rolled into the air. "Would you like some whipped cream and caramel drizzle on top?"

Yes. Yes, she would. But she wouldn't. Dammit. "No, thank you. I'm trying to be at least semi-low sugar before midday."

She took her beverage, the cup warming her hands the second she held it. She had a tab with Jules and paid at the end of the week. Which was a bit dangerous, because it made stopping by for a drink or lunch far too easy.

"You're better than I am." Jules laughed. "I'm three coffees and a chocolate croissant down."

"Oh, don't temp me, Jules." They both laughed. "Thanks."

"You're welcome, Alison." Jules sighed and shook her head. "Sorry, Addie. You look like an Alison I know. Have a lovely day."

"Don't worry, my parents mix me up all the time and they have no other children, so I don't know what's going on there." She grinned. "You have a good day too."

As she headed down the path, she sipped her drink and immediately flinched.

God almighty, it was hot. But, man oh man, was it good. Sweet but also salty and kind of buttery.

It was official. She could never leave this town. Not when she and Jules worked at the same freaking site.

She took another sip. Good God, it just got better. She wanted to bathe in the stuff.

When she reached the cabin that doubled as the entrance to the park, she passed the reception desk and went into the office beyond. She'd just sat down and taken another sip of her hot chocolate when a knock sounded at the door.

She looked up and choked on the hot liquid.

Noah. All six foot three of him. Jesus, he basically took up the entire doorframe.

He stood there wearing a tight white shirt with Wilderness Adventure Park embroidered across the front. But it was the way his thick muscles stretched the material that really had her staring. Well, that and the bronze of his skin that made the shirt look glaringly white.

She forced her gaze up, and her breath immediately hitched. Because his eyes...they were gray like steel, and so intense she couldn't bring herself to look at anything else.

"Noah. Hi. Good morning." She swallowed hard. Tongue-tied. She was totally tongue-tied. It happened every dang time she saw him.

"Hi, Addison."

She used to correct him because no one called her Addison, not even her parents. But over time, her full name had started to grow on her. Maybe because it had started to feel personal. Like it was his name for her, and his alone.

There was no smile on his face today.

She frowned at the way he stood by the door, not coming any further inside the room. Usually, he came straight over to her. Leaned over her desk, sometimes stealing a chocolate from her jar.

But that hadn't happened since the incident.

She cleared her throat. "Is everything okay?"

"I want to talk to you about what happened last week."

Okay, she'd been expecting this…so why did her belly do a big roll? "Okay."

"I'm sorry I haven't talked to you sooner."

"It's fine."

"It's not fine." He shot his gaze over his shoulder. "Would you feel safer having this conversation outside? Or with a third person in the room? I could get Colt, or—"

"No." *Jesus Christ.* "I'm okay with you, Noah. I told you, what happened was not a big deal."

He cursed under his breath. "I threw you onto the floor and put my hands around your neck."

Her fingers twitched to touch the skin of her throat. Because yes, it had scared her. But only for the smallest fraction of a second. Then he'd blinked and come back to her. "You weren't in control. You were having a flashback of something." She stood and stepped forward, but he immediately moved back. "Noah, my dad has them too sometimes. And he's been out for a decade. I'm not scared of him, and I'm not scared of you."

Pain creased his brows. And she hated it. He was a soldier. He was used to protecting people. And last week, something had triggered him to get stuck in his head and it brought up bad memories, which made him do something that he was struggling to forgive himself for.

"You wouldn't have hurt me," she whispered.

"You don't know that. And if you don't feel safe with me, if you don't want to work here anymore—"

"Please stop. I *love* my job here. I feel perfectly safe around you. I think we should just let it go."

His jaw clenched. He wasn't going to let it go. She knew that just by the look in his eyes. The guilt. Maybe even some self-hate.

And that was how she knew she was safe with him. Because he hated himself for what he'd done. Because he was a good guy.

CHAPTER 2

*N*oah Hayes watched the deep blue of Addie's eyes darken. He'd avoided her for a week. An entire damn week and he *still* couldn't wrap his head around what he'd done. They'd been at the reception desk, talking, laughing, when suddenly he was having a flashback to the worst day of his life and he was ready to hurt her.

He flinched at the memory. He flinched *every fucking time*. Because he wasn't that guy. He didn't *do* things like that.

As though she heard the conflict inside him, Addie's eyes softened. "This doesn't have to be a big deal."

It did. It *was*. It was a huge damn deal. He could have hurt her. One more second stuck in his head, and he would have.

He retreated, as if her sheer closeness could push him to hurt her.

"You were always going to realize it was me," she said softly.

That was the thing—he wasn't sure that was true. "If you decide that you don't want to work with me—"

"I won't."

His hands tightened into fists. She didn't seem even a little bit fazed by what had happened, whereas for him, it had changed everything. Made him feel unsafe in his own skin.

She took another step toward him. This time he didn't move. But he did smell chocolate. This woman *always* smelled of chocolate. "Did you visit Jules?"

Her lips cracked into a smile. It was wide, and damn if it wasn't radiant. "How did you know?"

"I can smell it on you."

She chuckled. "I consider smelling like hot chocolate a compliment, so thank you. She has a new salted caramel flavor." She lifted the to-go cup and sipped before groaning. "It's un-freaking-believable. I'd offer you some but that would mean one less sip for me."

This woman… One second, they were talking about how he'd basically assaulted her, and the next, she was joking about not sharing her drink. "I thought you were cutting back on the chocolate."

"I told you that?"

"No, I heard you telling Jules on Tuesday."

"Oh. Well, I am. So far, I've only had one Hershey's Kiss. And this is liquid chocolate, so it doesn't count. Plus, I said no to the whipped cream and caramel drizzle. That's progress."

He was tempted to tell her that the lack of cream and caramel had nothing to do with cutting down on chocolate, and yes, liquid chocolate did count, but he kept his mouth shut.

"I should get back to the guys." He and Colt had been walking the team from the zip line to the bouldering wall when he'd seen her walk into the office. He'd forced himself to follow her in here because he'd *needed* to talk about the incident. It had taken him too damn long as it was.

"Do yourself a favor—get one of these." She held up the cup.

"I'm not really a hot chocolate kind of guy."

"Everyone is a salted caramel hot chocolate kind of guy unless they're a salted caramel hot chocolate girl."

His lips twitched. And this was why he was drawn to the woman. She was the only person who could make him smile in what felt like a fucking hurricane.

He cleared his throat. "Have a good day, Addison."

"You too, Noah." She smiled before turning back to the computer.

And fuck, even the way she said his name held him hostage.

He forced himself to turn and move. But the second he passed the front desk, the memory popped back into his mind. He could still feel her skin beneath his fingers. And the nightmare...the way it jolted him back to the hell in which he'd almost died.

He shoved outside, ignoring the anger that pulsed through his veins. Anger at himself. That he would allow himself to get pulled so deep into a memory that it caused him to cross a line.

He scrubbed a hand over his face as he hurried down the path. He'd thought he was okay. That leaving the Marines, coming here, would push all the shit that had happened on that last mission to the back of his mind.

It wasn't the case.

A hand touched his shoulder, and he flinched and spun to find Rhett, one of the new hires, behind him.

He lifted his hands. "Whoa, sorry, boss."

"Why aren't you with the group?"

"Had to take a leak. Is that allowed?" There was a grin on Rhett's face. At only twenty-three, he was one of the younger new employees, but he was fit and had experience in all the activities offered at the park.

Noah nodded toward the path. "Come on."

"Everything okay?" Rhett asked as he walked beside him.

"It's fine." If *fine* involved being on the brink of losing his damn mind.

Rhett shot a look over his shoulder. "I saw you coming out of reception. Did Addie say something? She's got some fire in her, doesn't she?"

Noah's muscles stiffened. Was Rhett interested in her?

If he was, it was none of Noah's business. Rhett was a lot closer in age to Addie than he was. She was twenty-two and Noah was thirty-five, so even if that damn incident hadn't happened last week, he shouldn't be interested. He was too old for her, and he was her boss.

"How are you feeling about the park opening tomorrow?" Noah asked, because yeah, he was avoiding any talk about Addie.

"It'll be a piece of cake. This place is tiny compared to Geronimo."

Was Rhett cocky or confident? Maybe a bit of both. But probably for good reason. Rhett had spent the last couple years working at Geronimo Adventure Park near Houston, which boasted a twenty-four-foot outdoor rock-climbing wall, four climbing trails, and a huge zip line canopy tour—exactly why Rhett was the most experienced of the new staff.

"Glad you're confident," Noah said.

When they reached the group at the base of the granite cliff, Cass, Flint, and Buck were setting up the crash pads while Colt rifled through the equipment box. It was a great spot for both bouldering and rock climbing, since it was fifteen feet of rugged rock formations.

Noah crossed over to Colt, who looked up and immediately paused. "You okay?"

No, he wasn't. But he hadn't told Colt what had happened in the office a week ago, because then he'd have to tell him everything else.

"I'm fine." He grabbed the bag of chalk and turned to the group now standing around, waiting. "We ready?"

When everyone looked up, he tossed the bag to Buck, who fumbled it. While Rhett was the most experienced, Buck was the least.

"This is the last session before you have people depending on you," Noah said loudly, so the whole group could hear. "Bouldering can be fun, as long as safety measures are adhered to. You are there to *instill* those safety measures. We open in less than twenty-four hours and people will be climbing this rock with only a foam pad to save them. What's the most important thing to remember on the bouldering wall?"

"Give clear commands and if someone panics, stay calm," Cass answered. She was usually the one to respond.

Noah nodded. "Correct. Pair up."

Rhett went with Cass, while Flint and Buck partnered.

He watched them prepare. Cass and Flint were the first climbers.

Colt joined Cass and Rhett, while Noah went with Flint and Buck. This was where Buck's inexperience really became evident. Luckily, he was better at mountain biking, where he'd mostly be scheduled to work.

Buck was halfway up when he hesitated. He had one hand gripping a sloping hold while his foot searched for the next step. It was a hard move, a blind heel hook over a slight overhand.

Noah shifted his gaze to Flint, who was barely paying attention. Hell, he looked like he was half asleep. "Flint, you watching?"

Flint shot his gaze back up. "Buck, reset your left foot."

"I can't see where it goes," he called.

"You don't need to see it," Flint said.

"Remember your training," Noah called.

When Buck still wasn't getting it, Noah stepped forward and calmed his voice. "Feel for the ledge with your left heel. It's there."

Slowly, Buck started feeling for it with his foot until he finally located it. Then he pulled himself over the lip.

"There you go," Noah called. He turned to Flint. "That's the kind of feedback you need to give."

Flint nodded. "Yeah, sorry, I know that. I just hesitated."

"Next time, don't."

When they were finished with the bouldering wall, they started toward the mountain bikes.

Colt came to stand beside Noah. "You're *not* okay."

"Why do you say that?"

"I can tell, and so can they."

"If you're talking about Flint, he looked half asleep and people will be depending on him tomorrow."

"He took your feedback on board though."

So he should.

When Noah remained silent, Colt frowned. "Noah—"

"How I'm doing isn't as important as you and Indie after everything you've both been through. How is she?" Colt was married to Noah's sister, Indie, and just two weeks ago, she'd been kidnapped. Hurt. Almost killed.

Noah still saw red just thinking about it.

"She's good," Colt said slowly. "She's been resting a lot."

Another thing…after years of infertility, she and Colt were finally expecting a baby.

Noah dipped his head. "I'm glad she has you to look out for her." He really was. Colt was a good guy. One of the best. His sister was safe with him.

The rest of the day went quickly. The staff was good and Noah was confident that the opening weekend would go smoothly.

When they were finally done, Colt told everyone to get an early night.

Noah could have laughed. He barely slept anymore. And when he did, the nightmares riddled his dreams.

Once the team was gone, he stepped into the office to see a small group of teenagers inside, Addie in front of them.

"It *said* the park was open today," the tallest kid said, looking frustrated.

Addie shook her head. "No. As I already told you, the park opens *tomorrow*. You're welcome to come back then."

"We traveled an hour to get here."

Addie lifted a shoulder. "Well, check out the town, the food—"

"We don't *want* food. We came for the park."

"Is there a problem here?" Noah asked, moving to Addie's side.

"Yeah." The tall kid looked up at him. "Last I checked, your website said you were opening today."

Frustration thinned Addie's lips. "The website says we're opening tomorrow."

The shorter guy shoved his friend. "Good job."

The tall kid turned. "I didn't see *you* doing any research." He pushed him back.

"Hey," Noah started, but the kids didn't listen, just shoved each other harder.

Noah grabbed one of them as the other lunged forward. Addie tried to step in between them and got pushed to the floor.

Fuck.

"Enough!" Noah growled.

The shorter kid, who'd pushed Addie, looked down at her and his eyes widened. "Shit! Sorry."

"Get out. *Now,*" Noah barked.

The kids scrambled out, and Noah knelt beside Addie. "Hey. You okay?"

She laughed. She actually *laughed*. While he was ready to follow the kids and fucking rage at them for what they'd done.

"Yeah, I'm fine." She lifted a shoulder. "They're just kids with too much testosterone."

"They shoved you."

"If I'd been in any real danger, I would have put that kid on the floor."

Damn. Why did he find that so attractive? "Have you done that before?"

"Only when my father was teaching me how to defend myself. In his words, self-defense isn't a luxury, it's a necessity."

"I like him already." He held out a hand and helped her up. The second she slipped her fingers around his, something shot up his arm, hitting him right in the chest. It was so strong it almost stole his fucking breath.

Her eyes flared, as if she'd felt it too. "Thanks."

Even her quiet voice soaked into his skin. What the hell was going on? No woman had ever affected him like this.

He cleared his throat. "Next time, call me if there's trouble."

"I had it handled—"

"Call me."

She did a half eye roll. "Fine, I'll call you."

"Good. Are you heading home now?"

"Yeah."

"You deserve an early night. You've been working too hard. I'll see you tomorrow." He moved toward the door, only to stop at Addie's voice.

"Noah."

He turned.

"We're good now, aren't we? We're leaving what happened last week behind us?"

His fingers tightened around the handle. "We're good."

He stepped out, knowing he hadn't answered the second half of her question. What had happened *wasn't* behind them. Because he had no idea how to do that, and if he didn't work out his triggers, and fast, it could happen again.

CHAPTER 3

Noah pulled at the chains around his wrists, desperation to get free, to help Boone, tearing at his insides. Every thud of a fist hitting his friend felt like a punch driving into Noah's own body. Bruising him. Killing him. Making him want to claw his way out of his own skin.

"Leave him the fuck alone!"

But Noah's shouts did nothing, and his throat was so dry his voice was coarse and ragged.

They were going to kill Boone, and he could do nothing to stop them.

Noah shot up in bed, his heart thrashing against his ribs.

It was just a nightmare.

But it wasn't. It was a memory. One that felt like a chain around his neck, choking him. Holding him hostage to that day.

He dropped his head into his hands and scrubbed them over his face. His fingers shook. Hell, all of him shook. He could still smell the dampness of that room. Could still feel the helplessness coursing through him.

When would it end? Or maybe it wouldn't end. Maybe this was his new reality. His new life. One where he was forced to relive his worst moments again and again, forever waking in a pool of sweat, feeling like he was trapped.

He threw the covers off and climbed out of bed. It was early. Even with the curtains closed, he could see it was pitch black outside. Most of Amber Ridge would still be sleeping.

How much sleep had he gotten? Two, maybe three hours? He was used to it.

In the early days, he'd tried to get back to sleep after a nightmare. Bad fucking idea *that* had been. The sleep rarely came. And all lying in a dark room had ever done was make the memories play over in his head again and again. Boone's pain…Noah's rage.

In the bathroom, he turned the shower on hot before stepping under the stream, then he closed his eyes.

He was drowning. Yet he hadn't told anyone. Not a single soul. How could he? Indie was pregnant after years of infertility, and she and Colt had just gone through a hell of their own. He didn't want to dump this on his cousins or his aunt Pam. He'd only just reconnected with his youngest sister, Bonnie, and there was no way he'd share this shit with her.

Would he have talked to his parents about everything if they were still alive?

He'd never fucking know.

He scrubbed his hands over his face, trying to push the heaviness of everything down.

Once he was clean and dry, he pulled on a white park shirt, black shorts, and a hoodie.

It was when he stepped into the kitchen that his phone rang. The first small smile of the morning pulled at his lips.

"Hey, Bon-Bon," he answered on the second ring.

There was a small pause. "You answered."

"You thought I wouldn't?"

"Uh, yeah, it's freaking early. What is it? Four, five a.m. there?"

He wasn't sure. He hadn't checked. But yeah, it was probably around that time. "It's early for you in San Francisco too. You're an hour behind us. Can't sleep?"

"No, I can't. I've been thinking a lot. Stuck in my own head. You?"

"Same." Although, not so much stuck in his head as stuck in the past. "Want to talk about it?"

"Not really. You?"

"Absolutely not."

Her laugh was soft and familiar. "Guess we'll stick with the weather."

"Or you could tell me how work's going?"

Bonnie left Amber Ridge thirteen years ago, and he'd only recently made contact with her again. Since reconnecting, he'd learned that his sister worked in a women's shelter as the program coordinator. He'd always known she'd find a job that helped people.

"It's hard but rewarding. These women have been through so much and they just want a fresh start, but it's so much work for them to find their feet."

Which had probably been the case for Bonnie when she'd left Amber Ridge at eighteen. "If anyone can help them, it's you."

"Some days I feel like I'm failing them, but I try." There was another pause. "So, opening day, right?"

"You remembered."

"Of course. It's why I called. I planned to leave you a message, but seeing as neither of us likes sleep, I can say it straight to you."

He chuckled, but there was a heavy truth to that statement. He'd started to despise sleep, because that was when the nightmares haunted him. "Thanks for calling."

"Are you all ready?"

"I hope so. We're expecting a busy day."

"Of course you are—who wouldn't want to visit the old adventure park, but this time run by two Marines?"

"People who don't like the outdoors or heights or fast-moving bikes."

Bonnie scoffed. "Wrong town to live in if that's the case. I hope it goes smoothly. And I hope whatever has you awake this early allows you to sleep tonight."

His fingers tightened around the cell. That wouldn't happen. "Thank you. You have a good day too, Bonnie."

He hung up and glanced at his coffee machine before grabbing his keys and phone. Jules put his coffee to shame anyway. He'd just have to wait until she got to work.

When he reached the park, the sun was only just rising. Good. It would be his slice of silence before the storm of visitors arrived. The activities were fully booked. Hell, they were fully booked every weekend for the next two months, and even weekdays were busy. People could still come to hike the trails or get a coffee at least.

Over the next two hours, he traversed the park, making sure the equipment boxes were fully stocked and ready to go. It was stuff he'd already checked before leaving yesterday. Colt arrived an hour before opening, as well as the rest of the staff.

He wasn't sure if Addie had arrived, because that would require him to go to the office and visit her. Jesus Christ, he was a fucking coward.

When people started showing up for their booked activities, Noah would get busy and find the peace he finally needed. Because when he was busy, he couldn't think about other stuff. The nightmares. The battle he faced every day to stay in the present.

Finally, he stepped into the cabin to see the front desk empty. Addie was in the office, bent over the desk. He tried not to stare at her ass. *Fuck*, he tried.

Then she turned, and her blue eyes commanded all of his attention.

"Noah! I didn't hear you come in."

"There's quite a crowd out there."

She grinned. "I know. Exciting, right?" She straightened and moved toward him. "Need help with anything before I let the crowd in?"

"No, I just wanted to check that you're all ready."

"I certainly am, but then, I'm just at the desk. You're the one hanging from a bouldering wall." Her smile widened—and suddenly she flung her arms around him in a hug. "Congratulations! Your park is finally opening and you should be *so* proud!"

Addie surrounded him. Her sweet scent. The softness of her body.

It took him a moment to move. To lift his arms and wrap them around her waist. The second he did, he felt it.

Silence.

Every loud, invasive voice that had been taunting him all morning just vanished. The anger, the fear of the nightmares…it was like touching her allowed lightness to overlap the darkness in his head.

But that was crazy, right?

She pulled back and that familiar smile still widened her lips. "It's going to be a good day."

Then she walked away.

And he stood there, realizing that in the couple of seconds he'd held her, he'd felt more peace than in the entire last year of his life.

* * *

FINALLY, a moment of quiet.

Addie closed her eyes and breathed her first deep breath since the office door opened for customers. She'd known it would be busy. And she was glad it was. But God, her cheeks hurt from smiling. And she'd needed to pee for, oh, only the last hour and a half.

Why there was a kitchen off the office but no bathroom, she had no freaking clue. She had to leave this cabin and use the block of restrooms outside, which meant she needed to wait for someone to take over the front desk.

Thank God for Cass, who was hired to work both the park and the office. But she only covered Addie for her breaks and days off. She was due to swap with her in—she glanced at her watch—five minutes.

She liked Cass. She wasn't sure the two of them would be best friends anytime soon, what with Cass being all about adventure sports and the outdoors, and Addie…well, not. But definitely a friend, regardless.

She tidied the desk and was just putting the last pen away when the phone rang.

"Hello, Wilderness Adventure Park, Addie speaking, how can I help you?"

No one answered, and as the seconds ticked by, the silence stretched out.

She frowned. "Hello?"

Then she heard breathing. A heavy, rasping kind of breathing that made the hairs on the back of her neck stand on end.

She slammed the phone down and yanked her hand back as if it had burned her. Her heart beat fast and the room felt too empty.

It was just a prank call. Businesses got them all the time.

So why did she feel a bit sick? And why was being alone in this office suddenly the last thing she wanted?

Because she'd already had the strange feeling that she was being watched?

The door to the cabin swung open. Addie jumped, her gaze shooting up before air whooshed from her chest. "Cass."

Cass frowned as she entered. "Hey. Are you okay?"

"Yeah, I just got this strange call."

"Strange how?" Cass crossed over to the desk and took a peanut butter cup from the chocolate jar.

"No one said anything and there was just this weird heavy breathing." A shudder coursed down her spine at the memory.

Cass rolled her eyes. "A prank call. When my brother was fourteen, he and his friend did that kind of shit all the time. Trust me, it was just some kid being an idiot."

"Yeah, I know. I shouldn't let it scare me." She rose and shoved a chocolate into her pocket because, who knew, she might get hungry on her break.

Cass dropped into the seat. "You're new to town, right?"

"Yeah, but only from Bozeman."

"Wanna go out sometime? CJ's does great cocktails."

She smiled. "Actually, I'd really like that. I don't know many people here."

"Great, let's do it." Cass's phone buzzed, and she looked at the screen before rolling her eyes.

"Everything okay?"

"Just Rhett being Rhett. The guy doesn't give up."

"Is he harassing you?"

"No. He just thinks he's all that when he really isn't. Go. I've got it covered here."

"Okay, be back in ten."

"Make it twenty. My next session isn't for half an hour."

"You're amazing." Addie stepped outside, immediately inhaling a lungful of fresh air.

This was absolutely what she needed. To get outside and forget about the call.

After using the bathroom, she didn't go straight back to the office. Instead, she walked around the park.

There were people everywhere. Every section was in use. And even though everyone seemed to be having fun, none of the activities were things Addie would ever be interested in doing. In fact, watching people on the bouldering wall just confirmed for her that was *not* the sport for her. It was far too high and far too athletic-looking.

When she reached the mountain bike area, she stopped to watch Noah helping his group with helmets.

Just at the dang sight of him, her heart thumped faster.

What was it about him that made her want to be close to him? It didn't even matter if she was talking to him, she just wanted to be near.

His gaze suddenly lifted to her.

Shit. She was staring. Not just staring. Watching from the freaking shadows like a damn stalker. Argh.

After offering the briefest smile of her life, she turned and headed in the other direction. She took a right then a left, not really thinking about where she was going.

She'd only been walking for a couple of minutes when she realized she was lost.

Crap. This place was too big. She looked left, then right. She didn't recognize anything.

It was fine. She'd work her way back.

She turned around and started walking. When a noise sounded behind her, she stopped and spun, but there was no one there.

Her pulse picked up speed and she started walking again. But almost straight away, the crunch of leaves beneath feet sounded again. She turned. Again, there was nothing there.

What the hell?

She looked back ahead—only to screech at the sight of Jules just feet away.

She set a hand to her chest. "Jules! Oh Jesus, you scared me."

Jules lifted her brows. "Sorry, honey. I was just on a walk for my break. Are you okay?"

No. She wasn't. She was at heart attack stage. "I'm fine. I think I got lost."

Jules frowned before she set a hand on Addie's back. "Come on, I know the way."

Addie joined the woman…but she glanced over her shoulder. A part of her wanted to believe the noises were all in her head. But the other part?

That part knew there'd been something in the forest with her. Or someone.

CHAPTER 4

ddie was exhausted. Stop-the-car-and-fall-asleep-on-the-side-of-the-road kind of exhausted. And the park had only been open for a bit over a week!

One week and two days, and every one of those days had been busy. Although they were closed on Mondays and she'd had Wednesday off, it still felt like a lot.

At least she'd kept up with the busyness. No, not just kept up—she'd kicked ass, and there'd been *a lot* of things to smooth out. Booking system errors. Late bookings. Twice the website had crashed, and she'd had to spend hours figuring out why and how to fix it.

But…she was glad the guys had a busy park. After all the work they'd put into it, they deserved it.

She took a right turn, her mind going to Noah. During her break today, she *may* have passed the rock-climbing wall because she'd known he'd be there. And she *also* may have watched him for a solid ten minutes. He'd climbed beside an older woman who clearly had a fear of heights.

Addie's heart fluttered at the memory of how gentle he'd been with the woman. At the way he'd leaned in close to keep her calm. Addie hadn't been able to hear what he'd said, but whatever it was, it had given the woman the confidence to keep moving.

Gah! Working with a man as good-looking and kind and capable as Noah was hard.

She pulled up outside the Chinese restaurant and climbed out of her car. The parking lot was busy. Certainly busier than she'd thought it would be for a Sunday night.

She was halfway across the lot when she felt it. That damn feeling of eyes on her.

God, what was that? It was a freaking constant lately, and she *hated* it. She'd never felt this in Bozeman, and the first few weeks in Amber Ridge were fine. But now? Now she literally felt like she was being watched *all* the time.

She sighed as she stepped inside the restaurant and stopped at the counter. "Hi, I'd like to pick up an order for Addie."

She'd ordered far too much food. Think, feed-an-army, get-sick-if-she-ate-it-all kind of too much, because leftovers were always a good idea. Plus, variety was nice too.

The lady turned away to find it when a male said her name from behind. "Addie."

She turned.

Crap.

"Hi, Rhett." Was it not enough that she saw this annoying man every day at work? He was the most arrogant person she'd ever met, and she was pretty sure half the time he was flirting with her. Not good flirting though, hence her uncertainty.

"Good opening week at the park, wasn't it?" He bumped her shoulder.

"Yeah, it was very busy." She tried to turn away, but he kept talking.

"I was talking to Cass. She told me you're new in town."

"That's right."

"You know, before I moved to Texas to work at Geronimo

Adventure Park, I grew up here. I could show you around. Let you in on all the secret hangout spots."

Was it awful that she couldn't think of anything worse? Mostly because she hadn't had a single conversation with Rhett where he wasn't talking about himself or inadvertently hitting on her. "That's kind of you to offer, but I've actually seen a lot already."

"Uh, but you haven't had Tour El Ferdinanze."

Ferdinanze being Rhett's last name. It took a lot to hold back the eye roll.

"Here you go."

Thank God. Addie turned back to the counter to pay and thank the woman before taking her bag of food.

"Wow, that's a lot of food for such a little lady." Rhett gave her a one-sided smile. "You planning on sharing with someone?"

"Nope. This little lady likes to eat. I'll see you later, Rhett." She walked around him.

"Wait, where did we land on that tour?"

"I really don't need a tour, and I'm a bit busy at the moment." Busy? Ha. Her plan for tonight was to eat copious amounts of Chinese food while watching *The Bachelor* and finishing it off with some Huckleberry Chocolate Swirl ice cream. Yep, her chocolate addiction was alive and strong.

In the car, she popped her takeout onto the passenger seat and was about to pull out when her phone rang. She smiled when she saw who it was. "Hey, Mom."

"Addie, darling, it's so good to hear your voice."

"It's nice to hear from you too. How was school today?" Her mother was an elementary school teacher, and you could tell. She was gentle and patient and so incredibly passionate about her work.

"It was wonderful. I brought Henry in, and their little faces lit up."

Addie grinned. Henry was her parents' Labrador Retriever.

He was getting old, but that made him perfect for classroom visits. "I bet Henry enjoyed it too."

"Oh, he did. He got a lot of cuddles, and I gave him some treats for being such a good boy."

That dog got so many treats, he had to be fifty percent oats and peanut butter. "Of course he did, because he's a cutie. How's Dad?"

"Oh, you know your father. He doesn't know what to do with all his free time."

He hadn't known what to do with himself since his retirement, and that was ten years ago. "I'm sure he's finding some things to keep him busy."

"Lots of fishing."

She chuckled. "Is he catching anything?"

"Nope."

She laughed again. It was funny because he *never* caught anything, yet it was his favorite hobby.

"So, darling, what about you? How was opening week at the park?"

"Exhausting. But also fun and busy and noisy."

"I hope you're not overdoing it. If you ever want to come home, you know you have a room here."

"Mom, you almost make it sound like you want the business to fail."

"Of course not. Just because you worked for one failed startup here doesn't mean that one will be the same."

The *startup* had been a drop-shipping company in Bozeman. It was her first job after studying IT, and she was lucky they'd given her a shot. But she'd known from the start that it wasn't going to last. "I'm happy here. And unlike the startup, the guys running the park have their shit together."

"*Addie.*"

She cringed. Her mother did not like cursing. "Sorry."

"So, these guys…are they single?"

"Mom."

"Or cute?"

"Mom."

"What? It's not illegal to ask."

"One is single, the other is married and expecting a child. And they're both adequate looking."

Adequate? Either that was the biggest fib that had ever fallen out of her mouth or pigs could fly. Both Colt and Noah could front firefighter calendars.

"Hm." Her mother didn't seem to buy the lie. "Well, I'm looking forward to meeting them when we visit soon."

"I'm looking forward to it too. I should go. I'm in my car."

"Your car? Oh, why didn't you say so? I'll call again soon."

She was sure she would. Her mother called frequently, and Addie loved it. Because she missed her parents. "Love you, Mom. Say hi to Dad for me."

"I will. Love you too."

She hung up and there was an immediate ache in her chest. Leaving her parents had been hard. They were her best friends. But it had also been necessary. She needed to plant roots somewhere new. Step out of her comfort zone and figure out who she was without them. Because to them, she'd always be their baby.

She pulled out of the parking lot. She'd just turned onto the next street when a car behind her came into view. She frowned because they were driving close. Maybe too close? Or was she being paranoid?

She took the next left, then another right.

The car was still there.

Her heart started to beat faster. Were they following her? She pressed her foot down harder and sped up.

She turned right onto her street, fully prepared to pass her house and keep driving if they turned with her.

The car went straight.

She sighed. Jesus. She was so paranoid.

When she pulled into her drive, she turned the car off, leaned her head back, and closed her eyes. A few months ago, she'd rarely left Bozeman. Yes, for family holidays and a few trips with friends, but that was it. Living somewhere new shouldn't be freaking her out so much.

She climbed from her car and headed to the door, where she searched her purse for her house key. Only, she couldn't find it.

Shit, where was it?

Most people kept their house and car keys together. She didn't because her father had drilled into her that if she ever lost her keys, the thief had access to both her car and home. But…was she supposed to be thankful now that she'd only lost her house key?

No. She hadn't lost it. It had to be here somewhere.

She crouched down and tipped the purse upside down so everything fell onto the porch. Jesus, how much crap did she need? Lip gloss. Tissues. A glitter pen. Why did she have a glitter pen but no house key?

She sorted through everything. Every. Single. Item. It wasn't there. And worse, the spare was *inside* the house, because she'd ordered a cute key-safe garden gnome, but it hadn't arrived yet.

Shit.

If she was in Bozeman, she'd have called her dad, the fixer of all problems. But she wasn't in Bozeman. She was in Amber Ridge. And the only people she knew were from the park. But she wasn't really close to any of them. She'd had the most contact with Noah. She kind of considered him a friend.

She lifted her phone, hovering her finger over his name.

But what could he do? *He* didn't have her spare key.

She nibbled her bottom lip, her gaze lifting to the street. And that's when she remembered the car that seemed to be following her, and the constant feeling of being watched. The footsteps behind her in the park the other day…

She hit Noah's number and he answered on the second ring.

"Addison?"

"Hi." Okay, now she felt stupid for calling. She was twenty-two. An adult. She should be able to solve her own problems.

"Are you okay?"

She scrunched her nose. "Actually, I locked myself out of my house. Or at least, I can't find my key. And usually I'd call my dad, but I don't want him to make the one-hour drive to Amber Ridge, and he doesn't have a key anyway. And I don't know any locksmiths. Heck, I don't even know why I'm calling *you*. Maybe because I don't have anyone else. Maybe because I'm losing my mind along with my key—"

"Addie…" There was a gentleness to his voice. "Send me your address."

"Really? You can help me?"

"I'm leaving now."

The relief almost weakened her knees. "Thank you."

She hung up and texted him her address. And the second she lowered her phone, she scanned the street again. The empty street. Because no one was watching her.

So why did she feel so uneasy?

Suddenly, her legs were moving. She crossed her front lawn and slid into her car before locking the doors.

She wasn't sure how long she sat there, but at some point she closed her eyes and leaned her head back. When she opened them, a shadow moved beside her house.

She straightened. What was that? An animal?

Or maybe it had been nothing at all. Maybe it was her eyes playing tricks on her.

But what if it wasn't? What if someone *had* been following her, she wasn't crazy, and they were here right now?

A smart person would stay in their car. But that wouldn't help her figure out if this was all in her head or not.

Quickly, she rummaged through her purse before pulling out a can of pepper spray.

Thank you, Dad. She received one from him every year for Christmas. Every. Single. Year. And she'd never used a single one…until maybe now.

Quietly, she slipped out of her car, the can clenched between her fingers. If there *was* someone following her, the asshole would regret it in about five seconds.

She walked down the side of the house, checking the bushes that would be easy to hide within. But no one was there.

A crunching noise suddenly sounded behind her.

She spun and lifted the can, but before she could spray it, the bottle was snatched from her grasp with one hand and her wrist was grabbed with another. The move was so fast and skilled, she barely recognized what was happening. But strangely, it was also gentle.

Then she was looking into a very gray, very confused set of eyes.

CHAPTER 5

𝒩oah frowned at the fear in Addie's eyes, fingers still wrapped around her wrist. "Are you okay?"

Her gaze shot behind her before she looked back at him. "I'm fine, sorry. I just…I thought I saw something but—"

"What did you see?"

"A shadow. But it was dark. You can't see a shadow in the dark." She slapped a hand over her eyes. "God, I feel stupid."

He scanned behind her, then back to the driveway. He would argue that in the dark, a shadow could still be the outline of a figure.

He slipped his hand from her wrist to the middle of her back, not even caring if the touch was too intimate, before nudging her forward. "Come on."

Awareness from where he touched her warmed the skin on his palm, shooting up his shoulder. He'd been driving home from the park when her call had come through. It had surprised the hell out of him to see her name on his screen, but in a good way.

"You always keep pepper spray on you?"

A hint of a smile curved her lips. "I could start an Amazon

store with all the pepper spray I own, courtesy of my father, so I may as well keep one in my purse."

Good. Noah liked that she had a way to defend herself. Not that she should have to.

When they reached the front door, he handed her the canister and pulled out the flathead screwdriver and slim tension wrench from his back pocket.

"What are you doing?" she asked.

"I'm getting you into your house, Addison."

"With a screwdriver?"

He slipped the tension wrench into the bottom of the keyhole and applied just enough pressure, as if he was turning a key. Then he worked the screwdriver into the lock and felt for the pins.

"You look like you've done this before," Addie said suspiciously.

"Many times, and not just as part of my SERE training. You'd be surprised at what we learn in the military, and maybe a bit scared."

"Yeah, my dad comes out with some crazy skills sometimes. Once, the power went out and Dad left the room. I thought he was getting a flashlight, but he came back with jumper cables, an old car battery and a ball of wire. I don't know how, but he turned them into light."

Noah chuckled. He probably would have gone with a simple flashlight, but her dad's method sounded impressive.

The lock turned with a soft click, and he stood and opened the door. "Done."

Addie's eyes were wide. "Wow. I've completely lost faith in door locks."

"Don't worry, this is a specialized skill your average house thief probably doesn't have. Although, I always recommend a house alarm."

"You sound like my father." She glanced at her car in the drive, then back to him. "Let me repay you with food."

"Food?"

"I have enough Chinese to feed a family of five. Maybe more."

Dinner with Addie. Alone. At night. That didn't sound safe, in more ways than one. "Addie—"

"And before you say no because of anything that occurred between us"—the muscles in his shoulders twitched—"we decided to forget about that. Remember?"

He'd never agreed to forget about it, because that would be fucking impossible.

She lifted a shoulder. "And it's just food."

But it wasn't…it was *her*. Her house. Her company. Her sweet scent that would surround him the entire meal.

"Sure." The word slipped out and he had no fucking idea how.

Her eyes brightened. "Great. I'll get it from the car."

Ten minutes later, the takeout was spread over the coffee table, and she was right. It was a lot of food.

He shoved his hands into his pockets and glanced around her small living room. It was a quarter of the size of his, but it felt cozy, and not just because of the size. The throw over the couch, the copious number of cushions, the fluffy purple rug that should look out of place but didn't…it was all Addie.

He cleared his throat as he turned back to the Chinese. "You ordered all this food for yourself?"

"Sure did. When people ask me what my hobby is, I tell them eating. They think I'm joking… I am *not*."

His lips twitched. This woman was a walking contradiction. Her hair was perfect, her nails always a different color, and she constantly wore heeled boots. She looked high maintenance. But she wasn't. She was as down-to-earth as they came, and she made him laugh more than anyone else. "That explains the chocolate you carry in your pocket."

She paused, mid-scooping a huge spoon of fried rice onto her plate. "How do you know that?"

"I saw you pull a peanut butter cup out of your pocket while you were waiting for your drink outside the food van today."

Anyone else might look embarrassed. Addie laughed. "I like food, but chocolate is king of the foods. And a day without chocolate is a day wasted."

Once Addie's plate was full, he filled his own. "Anything you *don't* like?"

"Pineapple on pizza. Yuck. I hate it so much that even the smell of hot pineapple makes me gag."

He leaned back with his plate. "You're not a pineapple-on-pizza kind of girl?"

"It doesn't belong there."

"A lot of people would disagree with you."

"A lot of people are wrong." She aimed a suspicious frown his way. "Do *you* like pineapple on your pizza?"

"I don't feel safe answering that question."

"Oh my God, you're one of *them*?"

"Them?"

"Pineapple-on-pizza-loving crazy people."

"Now I'm definitely not answering."

She almost looked angry as she shoved a forkful of Kung Pao chicken into her mouth.

"How are you finding it here?" he asked, a change in conversation topic feeling safest.

"I miss my parents, but it's good for me to have a little separation from them. My mom's my best friend, and I rely on my dad far too much."

"That's what parents are for."

She chuckled. "Yeah. And they're the best. They actually adopted me after they couldn't have biological kids, and they've always treated me like they're the luckiest two people to be chosen as my parents. I love them to pieces." She looked back at him. "What about you? Close with your mom and dad?"

"They died in a car accident when I was twenty-two."

Addie's fork clattered to her bowl, and she pressed a hand to her chest. "Oh, Noah, I'm so sorry."

"Thanks. It was a really hard time. I was in the military and couldn't get as much leave as I wanted. My sisters were a mess, and they struggled in different ways. Indie cried a lot. And Bonnie just left."

"Left where?"

"She went to San Francisco. She cut contact with everyone. I've only just reconnected with her."

Addie's eyes softened. "That would have been really hard to lose her *and* your parents."

"It was. Indie found it hardest. I have hope that Bonnie will come home when she's ready."

Addie nodded, but there was a tinge of sadness in her eyes.

For the next hour, they chatted and ate. They talked about anything and everything. Big stuff. Small stuff. Addie showed him the chipped sloth mug that she, for some reason, used over all her non-chipped mugs. He asked when her chocolate addiction had begun, which was so long ago she couldn't remember.

Addie was easy to talk to. So easy, he almost forgot that she was thirteen years younger than he was and that he was her boss. Hell, he didn't even think about what he'd done to her a few weeks ago, or the demons that lived inside him. And that was the biggest reason he liked her company—when he was with Addie, all he could think about was *her*. How good it felt to be in her presence. And the peace that came with it.

"So," she said, leaning forward once they were both finished. "I have ice cream in my freezer." He could have laughed. Or maybe he did, because she frowned. "What?"

"We just ate an entire family-size portion of Chinese food."

"That went into my savory stomach. My dessert stomach is still empty and ready for food."

Jesus, she said it with so much authority he almost believed dual stomachs were a thing. "How about I clean up while you eat what I presume is chocolate ice cream."

She shook her head. "No. That's not fair on you."

"Of course it is. You fed me, I clean up. It's how I was raised."

"Noah—"

"I'm starting now." He lifted plates and took them to the kitchen.

Addie sighed as she headed toward the freezer and pulled out a tub of Huckleberry Chocolate Swirl ice cream.

He'd nailed it.

She perched on the edge of the counter and dug a spoon in. He was about to glance away when her gaze went to the window, a flicker of fear crossing her face.

He followed her look, but nothing was there. Nothing that he could see, anyway.

"When I got here, you thought you saw someone," he said slowly, turning back to the dishes. "Do you know who it might have been?"

"No."

The answer came quickly. Too quickly?

"Has something like that happened before? Or has anything happened to make you scared?"

There was a pause, and even though he was rinsing the plates, he could almost hear her thinking.

When the silence stretched, he turned back to look at her. "Addie?"

"Okay. I've had this feeling like someone's been...watching me."

The *fuck?*

She shook her head. "But I haven't actually seen anyone."

"But you've *felt* them?"

"I'm just freaking myself out because I've never lived away from home before."

"Addie—"

"I shouldn't have said anything. Don't worry about me."

He *did* worry about her. Even though he'd barely known her for a couple of months, there was this strange need for her to be safe.

"What about you?" she asked quietly, concern in her eyes. "How are you doing with everything?"

The muscles in his forearms tensed. He didn't want to talk about him or the demons that plagued him. The ones she'd gotten a small glimpse of the day he'd thrown her to the floor beneath him.

Did she want the truth? That he couldn't close his eyes without returning to the day from hell? That he barely slept? That since the incident in the office, he walked around in fear that he'd have another flashback and do it again to someone else?

He cleared his throat. "I'm fine." Two words strung together to make a lie.

He went to step around her to put some of the Chinese into the fridge, but she grabbed his arm and tugged him close, the ice cream forgotten on the counter beside her. "Hey. You don't have to do that."

"Do what?"

"Pretend to be okay. I know we haven't known each other for long, but you can talk to me. Or if you want to talk to a professional, my dad has an amazing therapist who specializes in veterans suffering from PTSD."

Her words wove inside him. She wanted to help. But he'd done therapy. He'd had to after that last mission. It hadn't helped. Not at all. What it *had* done was get him a one-way ticket home. "You don't need to worry about me either, Addie."

"I know. But I do anyway." Her thumb brushed over his arm, making his skin fucking tingle.

His gaze shifted between her eyes. They were the deepest blue he'd ever seen, like the ocean when the water was really deep.

"Can I tell you something?" she whispered, her warm breath brushing his face.

He wanted to say no, because he was sure that anything she said would just drag him deeper into whatever the hell this was between them. "Sure."

"A part of me knows there are all these reasons we shouldn't kiss…but I can't seem to bring myself to care about a single one of them."

His pulse thudded low in his throat. Not panicked. Just loud. "But we should care…shouldn't we?"

Was he asking or telling? He had no idea. But right now, he couldn't seem to give a single fuck about any of the reasons he shouldn't feel this woman's lips against his. Why he shouldn't tug her to the edge of the counter and let her thighs wrap around his waist.

Maybe that's why he inched closer. Why he didn't care that her hands eased up his chest, then his shoulders, then his neck.

Step away, Noah. Get the hell out of this house.

But he didn't listen to the voice of reason in his head. He was too focused on the warmth of Addie's touch. The way her soft palms made the roughness of his skin feel smooth.

"This is a bad idea," he whispered, his head lowering to hover over her mouth.

"The worst."

Then that space between them disappeared, and he was kissing her. He wasn't sure who made the final move. He didn't care.

He grazed his lips across hers, his grip tightening on her hips.

Her lips were just as soft as the rest of her. And Jesus Christ, they felt good against him. The kind of soft that made blood rush loudly between his ears and his cock turn to stone.

He pulled her hips to the edge of the counter, and at her gasp, he slipped his tongue past her lips. She tasted sweet like chocolate, and her tongue was cold from the ice cream. It was exactly how he'd expected Addie to taste—and he wanted more.

She moaned as she ran her tongue against his, her fingers now in his hair, grasping at the strands, her hips moving, grinding against his cock.

Every part of him reacted to her. Every part of him *needed* to be closer. To touch her. Make her need him like he needed her.

He slipped his hands beneath the material of her shirt and touched her soft, warm skin. Immediately, she wrapped her legs around his waist and pulled him closer to her core.

It sent him fucking wild.

When they finally came up for air, they both heaved, like the simple act of getting oxygen into their lungs was too much.

She touched her forehead to his. "Still think it was a bad idea?"

Honestly, he had no idea *what* to think. Nothing about that kiss had felt wrong or the least bit like a mistake. "I don't know."

One side of her mouth lifted. "Want to know what I think?"

"I'm not sure."

"I think that was the best decision I've made in a long time."

CHAPTER 6

$\mathcal{A}$ kiss…she'd freaking *kissed* her *boss*. And it had been a good kiss. No, not just good, amazing. Better than any kiss she'd had in her twenty-two years. Yes, *that* good.

Her fingers twitched to touch her mouth, because even though it was now Wednesday night, she swore she could still feel his lips there.

She pulled into the parking lot of CJ's Bar as her phone buzzed with a text.

Cass: I'm inside. I have a table for two.

Apparently, this bar did jugs of cocktails. *Jugs.* She'd never heard of that before, but hell, she'd try it. She sure as heck needed a cocktail after three days of working with Noah but barely seeing him.

She grabbed her purse before climbing out of the car. She'd gone with a light blue slip dress with spaghetti straps, and the cool wind made goose bumps pop up over her skin.

As she walked toward the door, her mind flicked back to her boss. At the way he'd been missing all week, like he was avoiding her.

But why was he doing that? Because he thought the kiss was a mistake? He shouldn't. It was only a kiss, not a marriage proposal. Although, if she had the chance, she would absolutely kiss him again because, well, he was Noah.

She pushed inside the bar and encountered a thick crowd of people.

Jesus, was CJ's always this busy, or just on Wednesdays?

She wove through the throng and found Cass at a standing bar table.

The other woman grinned at her. "Hi! You made it."

"I did. Is it always this busy?"

"Pretty much, but especially on Wednesdays, when they do two-for-one jugs."

Addie spotted the jugs of alcohol on the table and laughed. "You think we're going to drink all of that?"

Cass lifted a shoulder. "We can try. Besides, Rhett's been annoying me, so I need to blow off some steam." Cass poured some of the alcohol into an empty glass and pushed it in front of Addie. "Whiskey Apple Cider Punch. It's amazing."

"Thanks." She wrapped her fingers around the glass. "What's Rhett been doing?" If Cass said anything even slightly resembling workplace harassment, Addie was going to Noah and Colt. Yesterday, Rhett had tried to write his number on her hand. She'd yanked her arm away so fast, she'd given the man whiplash.

She lifted the glass to taste her drink.

Cass lifted a shoulder. "We had sex, and now he's being all distant."

Addie choked on her punch. "You had sex with *Rhett?*"

"Yeah. He was interested, and I hadn't been laid in a while."

Okay, *that* made her little kiss with Noah seem like nothing. "But you're not dating?"

"God, no. He's a man-child. But he was good in bed, so…" She shrugged before sipping her punch.

So, what? She'd have sex with him again?

Maybe it was the small-town girl in Addie, but this all

sounded a bit out there for her. She took a big gulp of her own punch.

"So…" Cass started. "What about you? Dating anyone?"

"No. Just getting used to the new town."

"Are you interested in anyone?"

Did Cass know? Of course not. She couldn't.

"Because," Cass said with a grin, "I've seen the way Noah looks at you."

Air stalled in Addie's lungs and heat bloomed in her cheeks. "What are you talking about?"

"Oh, come on, you *have* to have noticed. He does this thing where he looks at you and his eyes go this intense gray shade. It's kind of adorable."

"He's my boss."

"And?"

"And he's older than me."

"How much older? Ten years?"

"Thirteen." She knew that because she'd had to file a document for him. She hadn't been snooping exactly, his date of birth had been right there, so of course she'd peeked.

Cass scoffed. "That's nothing. I once dated a guy twenty years older than me, and honestly, I felt like I was the more mature one." Cass lowered her glass and her eyes locked on something behind Addie. "No way. Speak of the devil."

"What?" Addie turned her head and gasped.

Noah.

She blinked. Once. Twice. Nope, he was still there.

He wore a tight gray shirt that was almost the exact shade of his eyes, and jeans that, although not tight, still showed off the power in his legs. But then, there probably wasn't much that could hide that.

Colt and his wife, Indie—also Noah's sister—stood with him.

Cass blew out a breath. "Those men are *fine*."

That was an understatement.

Colt spotted her and Cass first. He waved before saying some-thing to the others. Indie smiled at them and started in their direction. Whereas Noah? The second his gaze collided with hers…he didn't look angry, but then, he didn't look happy either.

Well, that told her all she needed to know on his thoughts about the kiss.

The three of them stopped at the table, Noah beside Addie.

Colt smiled at them. "Hey. Good to see you guys here."

Cass dipped her head. "You too. Thought you'd be too tired after all that zip-lining today."

"Could say the same about you and your bouldering," Colt added.

Indie scoffed and rubbed her pregnant belly. "Peanut and I are tired just hearing about it."

As the three of them spoke, Addie looked up at Noah and lowered her voice. "I didn't see much of you today." Or yesterday. Or the day before that.

"I took a big group out for mountain bike riding."

She knew that. She'd made the booking. She also knew that the ride had only lasted two hours.

"Did you find your key?" he asked.

"Actually, no. I'm using my spare. I'm not sure what happened to it. I must have dropped it somewhere."

"At work?"

"Maybe. I'm sure it'll turn up." She nibbled on her bottom lip. Noah's gaze immediately lowered. And the way he looked at her made her lower belly pulse.

"Addie—"

"You don't need to say it," she cut him off, voice quiet so the words would only reach him.

His brows flickered. "Say what?"

"Tell me it was a one-time thing. Say something about how I'm a great person but for this and that reason, we can't repeat what happened."

"I wasn't going to say any of that."

"What were you going to say?"

"That you look nice."

Air caught in her throat. "Really?"

"Yeah." Then his eyes trailed down her body. "The blue matches your eyes."

Suddenly it was hard to swallow, but she sure was glad she'd gone with her slip dress.

"Don't you think, Noah?"

Noah looked back at the group as Addie's phone buzzed. She was still feeling ridiculously off-center when she looked down to read the text.

Unknown number: You've overstayed your welcome. Get out.

* * *

Something was wrong with Addie. She'd been fine when he first got to her table, but now she'd gone completely pale. And it was because of something on her phone. It was when she'd looked at her screen that everything had changed.

Why? He'd asked, but she'd said it was nothing.

It wasn't nothing.

Addie's lips curved at something Indie said, but the smile didn't quite reach her eyes.

Had she received bad news? From her parents maybe?

Whatever it was, if she didn't want to share, it wasn't his business.

So why did he care so fucking much?

He lifted his beer and downed a quarter of the bottle.

"We're going to the bathroom," Cass said, before the three women headed away from the table.

The second they were gone, Noah felt Colt's eyes on him. He looked at his friend. "What?"

"Why are you staring at Addie?"

Fuck. Had he been staring? "I'm not."

"You are. And what were you whispering about when we first got here?"

He should have known his friend would see that.

He hadn't told Colt what had happened on Sunday night. He hadn't told anyone.

"We kissed." The words fell from his mouth. They felt like little damn explosions.

Colt choked on his beer. "You *what?*"

"We kissed on Sunday night."

"What the hell do you mean you kissed on Sunday night? Where? At the park?"

"At her place. She called me because she lost her key and couldn't get into her house. I picked the lock, she invited me to stay for Chinese, and…"

"And you kissed." Shock tinged Colt's words. "Did you—"

"*No.* We just kissed, and I left." The *just* felt out of place though. It hadn't *just* felt like a kiss. Because the moment shouldn't have been so stuck in his head for just a kiss, should it?

There was a small pause, like Colt was trying to wrap his head around the information. "Okay. What now?"

"I don't know. I'm her boss. She's young. Too damn young for me. And…"

Colt frowned. "And what?"

Noah's jaw clicked. He also hadn't told Colt about the real reason he'd left the military. Was now the time? Hell, was there *ever* a time?

His fingers tightened around his beer. "There's something I haven't told you."

"Okay, so tell me now."

"My contract wasn't up."

Colt's frown deepened. "What do you mean? How did you leave?"

"I left on a medical. Combat-related PTSD."

Another silence, this one heavier.

He wasn't sure what he'd expected Colt to say. Maybe to ask about the specifics of the cause of the PTSD. Maybe ask why he hadn't said anything earlier.

He asked neither of those things. "How are you doing now?"

Noah swallowed. It was a good question. "Sometimes I'm okay. A lot of the time I'm not."

Finally, he looked up. There was no pity in his friend's eyes. But then, he shouldn't have expected it. PTSD was well-known by soldiers.

"What can I do?" Colt asked.

"I don't think there's much you *can* do. I'm the one who has to do the work."

"Are you talking to someone?"

"I was. But not since I got home. I didn't find therapy helpful."

"I've heard some people need to try a few therapists before they find one who works for them." Colt gripped his shoulder. "Tell me if there's anything I can do to help."

"I appreciate it."

The women returned to the table. And the second Noah saw Addie, he forgot about his shit and focused on her. On how pale her skin was. On the way she kept looking at her phone like she was waiting for something.

"Expecting a text?" he asked.

Her gaze shot up, eyes widening. "No."

"Addison, what's wrong?"

"Nothing."

A damn lie. "Addie—"

"I need to make a call. I'll be back in a second."

Then she was gone. He watched her find a quieter corner of the bar and put her phone to her ear.

"I don't know what's going on with her," Cass said. "She was fine when she got here, but she's gone really quiet since."

Fuck it. He was finding out what was going on. He didn't care that they hadn't known each other long or that he was technically just her boss. She was new to town. She didn't have many people. If she needed help, he wanted to be that help.

He passed a large group of guys who were drinking and being rowdy. He ignored them, reaching Addie just as she was turning.

She jumped. "Noah."

"What's going on?"

"Nothing."

"Bullshit."

She huffed. "You have your own stuff going on. I'm not going to pile my stuff on top."

So she *did* have stuff going on. "I can handle it."

"No." She stepped around him and got halfway back to the table before he grabbed her arm.

"Addison—"

"Noah, I don't need you to fix my problems. I'm an adult and can handle them myself."

"Does it have anything to do with feeling like someone's been watching you?"

Her eyes flared.

It did.

He stepped closer. "Has something happened between Sunday and now?"

She opened her mouth to reply, but she was shoved as a fight suddenly broke out behind her.

Noah cursed and grabbed her before she could fall to the floor.

"*Hey!*" he shouted at the assholes.

None of them appeared to hear him. The idiots were too busy throwing punches.

Great.

When one of them lifted a beer bottle, Noah shot forward and grabbed it out of his hand. "What the fuck are you doing?"

"Get out of my way." The guy slurred his words and tried to shove Noah.

A body suddenly hit Noah from behind. He turned as a fist flew toward his face. He dodged, grabbed the guy's wrist, and spun his arm behind the guy's back.

Colt and a bartender jumped in to break up the fight.

"Don't fucking move," Noah growled at the man, before pushing him to the floor. He moved toward two guys rolling between tables, throwing punches at each other.

He grabbed the guy on top and threw him to the side. From his peripheral vision, he saw another man get shoved into Addie as she was clearing away from the fight. She fell to her knees, and the man landed on top of her.

Fuck. Noah shot toward her and tore the guy off. The asshole immediately spun and pulled a fist back.

Noah saw the punch coming. He'd already received so many that he was close to blacking out.

But he couldn't black out. He wasn't dying today.

He dodged the hit, and the guy growled when his fist hit the concrete wall behind him. Even though Noah was bound, he lunged anyway.

Suddenly—he was free.

He grabbed the guy around the middle and sent them both to the floor. A hand tried to grab him, but he swung an arm back to shove them away before lifting a fist. Before it could land, stronger hands grabbed his arm and ripped him off the asshole.

No! He was going to kill him. He was going to kill all of them.

"Noah!"

Noah blinked. The music, the smell of beer and sweat—all of it pulled him back to the present. He wasn't in Iraq. He wasn't being held against his will.

He was in Amber Ridge. In a bar.

He turned to see Indie and Cass helping Addie to her feet. How'd she get to the floor?

Then he remembered. The first hand on his arm…it had been soft. Small.

It had been Addie's.

He stumbled back.

Shit. He'd done it again.

"Addie…I'm so sorry." Each word tore from his chest, choking him. Forcing the air to stall in his lungs.

"It's okay," she said, her words barely crossing the distance between them.

But it wasn't. This was the second time he'd put his hands on her. The *second fucking time*.

The fighting had stopped, but Noah couldn't concentrate on anything but her.

A part of him wanted to go to her. Make sure she was okay. But the other part? The other part wanted to run. To get as far from her and this place as possible. Because he couldn't trust himself around her. She wasn't fucking safe with him.

He was moving before he could stop himself. Voices called out from behind, but he ignored them. He was outside and almost at his truck when a hand grabbed his arm.

Noah swung around to see Colt.

He lifted his hands. "Hey. I'm just checking that you're okay."

"I shoved her."

"You didn't mean to. I saw you. You were somewhere else."

"I still did it. *Me*. No one else."

"Noah—"

"I have to go."

He wasn't sure where; just *away*. Somewhere to silence the fucking noise in his head. To learn how to live in a body that didn't feel safe to him anymore.

CHAPTER 7

*A*ddie wasn't sure what to focus on, the text she'd received from the unknown number last night, telling her she'd overstayed her welcome, or Noah and the look on his face when he realized he'd shoved her. She hadn't even been hurt. It had been *her* fault for touching him.

It had been a mistake. A huge, colossal mistake. But at the time, it had been a reflex. The second she saw the change in him, she'd been so scared about what he'd do. All she'd wanted to do was help him.

Yeah, well, she sure hadn't done that.

She glanced at the door leading to the park. It was a rare quiet moment. Which wasn't exactly optimal, because it gave her far too much time to get stuck in her head.

Her gaze shifted back to her computer screen. She was supposed to be updating the FAQ section of the website, but she couldn't concentrate.

She tapped the screen of her phone like she expected to see another text. There was none.

Someone wanted her to get out. Out of where? Amber Ridge?

Why? And was she actually being watched by someone, and *this* was that someone?

She'd tried to call the number. No one answered. Not a surprise. That was the entire reason to text, right? Because they wanted to keep their identity secret. Because they wanted her scared of the unknown.

Well, mission accomplished. And what was worse, she felt like she was just waiting now. Waiting for the next text. Waiting for them to do something to her. Because she wasn't leaving. This was her home right now. And she was not going to be scared away.

The door opened and Jules stepped in, her usual wide smile on her face. "Good morning, Addie."

Addie tried to return the smile, but it felt wonky. "Morning, Jules."

The food van had been so busy that Jules had hired help, which meant she was able to bring Addie's hot chocolate to the office some mornings. It was honestly a highlight of her day.

"Uh-oh." Jules stopped at the desk. "What's wrong?"

"Nothing." If nothing included a phone terrorist and a complicated relationship with her boss.

"I can see that's not true." She pushed a to-go cup across the desk. "A new hazelnut hot chocolate to brighten your morning."

"You're too good to me."

"Not too good. The perfect amount of good." Jules tilted her head. "Want to talk about it?"

"Not at the moment, but I appreciate you asking."

"I'm always here if you need someone."

Addie's smile softened. Another reason to love this woman… she cared. "Thank you."

Jules squeezed her hand before heading out.

Addie lifted the hot chocolate and groaned the second the sweet liquid hit her tongue. Holy Hannah, it was good. Really good. And *so* needed. She'd been in such a state this morning, she hadn't even touched her chocolate jar…not once.

What she *had* done was check her phone a gazillion times for a text from Noah. She'd messaged him last night to ask if he was okay, but he hadn't replied. Nor had he been in the office this morning.

She took the lid off her cup and went to pour the liquid into her chipped sloth mug, but as she did, her phone vibrated with a text. She looked up so quickly, she spilled hot liquid over her hand.

Shit! Crap! Hot! *Too hot!*

She set the to-go cup down on the desk and rushed to the kitchen, where she ran her hand under cold water.

Another reason to hate this damn person harassing her—she jumped every time her phone went off. And now she'd poured perfectly good hot chocolate all over herself.

She turned off the water and stepped out of the kitchen—only to stop. "Noah."

He stood in the office, taking up far too much space.

He frowned at her, eyes cautious. "Addie, is everything okay?"

"I thought my hand was a better place for my hot chocolate than my stomach."

He frowned.

She lifted her red hand. "I burned myself."

Two steps and he closed the distance between them before gently gripping her wrist. And holy hell, but his fingers on her skin felt good. Not just good, they made every fiber of her being shoot to life and her lower belly ripple.

"Are you okay?"

His deep, husky voice almost made her shiver. "I've had worse."

He ran his thumb over the burn, but surprisingly, it didn't hurt. Somehow, like the man's touch was magic, it took the edge of the ache away.

They both looked up at the same time, and suddenly she was breathless. The kind of breathless where her lungs forgot how to function because her body was too distracted by his closeness and how his eyes held her hostage.

She forced words out. "Are you okay after last night?"

"Not really."

She'd expected him to lie. To tell her something meaningless about being fine even though they both knew it wasn't true.

Was he being honest because he trusted her with just a bit of the darkness inside him?

She opened her mouth, not sure what words were about to come out, when the click of the door opening sounded from the other room.

His hand dropped and immediately her arm felt cold.

She cleared her throat. "I, uh, have something for you."

He gave her a quizzical look and she forced herself to step back. It took far more willpower than it should have.

In her bag, she rummaged for the folded piece of paper. When she found it, she handed it to him. "Here. It's the number of my dad's therapist. His name's Dr. Ted Burton and he's a clinical psychologist who specializes in treating PTSD. He works in Bozeman but does Zoom appointments."

Noah's frown deepened, and for a moment she wasn't sure if he'd take the slip of paper.

Crap. Was she overstepping? Was he about to tell her to mind her own business and walk away?

Instead, he slipped the paper from her fingers, and she released the breath she hadn't realized she'd been holding.

He dipped his head. "Thank you."

"You're welcome. I'll, um, get back to the desk."

She stepped back into the reception area to see a handful of people waiting. It would be Noah's zip-lining group that was due to start in a few minutes.

The first guy in line lifted his blue eyes. He had short brown hair and a kind smile. "Hi."

"Hi. I'm sorry to keep you waiting." She lowered into the seat behind the front desk.

"You didn't keep me waiting. I'm Toby. I booked into the ten a.m. zip-lining group."

"Addie, and your instructor is right here. But before you go, I'll get you to fill out these forms." She handed him a clipboard with the forms and a pen.

"Am I signing my life away?"

She chuckled. "You tell me."

He took the forms and sat down. She drew in a lungful of air before the next people stepped forward. Even though she smiled, far too much of her concentration remained on Noah. The way he'd touched her hand. The way her entire body reacted when he spoke to her.

* * *

NOAH STRODE down the path toward the zip-lining platform, his group following close behind. Their quiet chatter competed with the sounds of the park around him. But those intrusive fucking thoughts in his head were louder than anything. The ones he hated. The ones he wanted gone but had no damn idea on how to do that.

Damn, he was a mess. He told himself to leave Addie alone. Yet the second he was near her, the second he *saw* her, all he wanted to do was touch her. It was like a craving he had to give in to even though he knew it was bad for both of them.

They were halfway to the platform when one of the guys came to walk beside him. "Hi, I'm Toby."

"Noah."

Toby shoved his hands into his pockets. "You're one of the owners, right?"

57

"Yeah."

"You've done a good job. The place looks great."

"Thanks. We had a great team help us."

"You must have."

When the tower came into view ahead, Toby whistled. "She's tall. Should I be scared?"

"Depends, are you scared of heights?"

"I didn't think I was, but then, I've never climbed a tower like that and zip-lined off it before. But I'm trying to step outside my comfort zone."

"You'll definitely do that here."

Noah stopped in front of the tower and turned, then waited for the last of the group to arrive before he began.

"Welcome, everyone. I'm Noah Hayes, and I'll be your instructor. One of my guys will be waiting for you at the other end of the zipline. Before we get up there, I'm going to go through a few procedures and safety instructions."

He gestured to the gear he'd prepared earlier. "Everyone will be fitted with a harness."

He spent ten minutes going through the equipment and safety instructions before handing out lanyards for the belay cable. "Before climbing, we attach our lanyards to the belay cable so that we're secured."

He noticed one of the older women look up to the platform a few times, and each time, her skin paled a bit further. He made a mental note to keep an eye on her.

When the group was getting ready, he stepped over to her. "Hey, Cindy, right?"

She nodded quickly.

"Are you okay?"

She swung her gaze from the platform back to him. "Yes."

Scared of heights. She didn't need to say it for him to know. "You can stop or pull out at any time."

"No. I want to do this. I'll be fine."

He nodded, not sure if she would be, but if she wanted to give it a try that was her choice.

Noah checked that each lanyard was clipped correctly to the belay cable before climbing the vertical ladder. He liked to go up first so he could help them up onto the platform from the top.

"Make sure you keep in contact with the ladder at all times," he called behind him.

When he was on the platform, he turned and looked down. One by one, everyone headed up and he helped them in their final steps of the climb.

Cindy was last, and she was slow.

"You're doing well, Cindy," he called, once everyone else was up. "Slow and steady."

Suddenly, one foot slipped, and she screamed and grabbed the ladder in a bear hug.

"Hey, Cindy," he called. "You're safe. You're connected to the cable. You're not going anywhere."

"I-I can't move," she gasped, her words barely reaching him.

"You're doing great. Take as long as you need."

"No. I don't want to be here! I need help. I-I can't stop shaking."

Shit. He'd lifted his radio to call Rhett to come and help her down, when Toby lowered beside him. "Mind if I try?"

Noah looked the guy over and nodded.

Toby glanced down. "Hey, Cindy." His voice was low and calm.

She looked up, fear keeping her eyes wide.

"I'm Toby. Can I talk to you for a second?"

She gave a jerky nod.

"It might not feel like it, but right now, your brain's being really smart. It's spotting danger and trying to keep you safe. It's doing exactly what it's supposed to do."

The woman stared at Toby like he was a lifeline. Was the guy trained in this stuff?

"But," Toby continued, "your brain doesn't realize that the danger isn't real. It doesn't recognize that you're harnessed in and there's no way for you to fall. Can I help your brain catch up?"

She nodded again. "O-okay."

"Let's start with some deep breaths. In through the nose, hold, and out of the mouth."

Cindy closed her eyes and did exactly as Toby told her to.

"Slow and steady. That's good. Do you feel your body starting to relax and feel safe? It's coming out of its freeze. Let's breathe again."

Cindy breathed again.

"Good. Now, I want you to do something for me—one step up. That's your only job."

Noah didn't think she'd do it. But she lifted a foot and stepped up the ladder.

"That was really great, Cindy! Now the next one."

Toby continued to talk to Cindy and, one step at a time, the woman climbed the ladder.

When she got near the top, Noah pulled her up.

Toby smiled at her. "Amazing work!" His voice still held that calming undertone. "You ready for the next part?"

Who the hell *was* this guy?

It didn't matter. He was helpful.

Not only did Toby help the woman up the ladder, he used the exact same method to get her down the zip line, where Flint met everyone on the other side.

The group's hour and a half went quickly. Everyone had a few turns, and by Cindy's third time up the ladder and down the line, she didn't blink.

Toby was a damn magician. Maybe they should hire him.

At the end, Noah debriefed everyone and collected the gear before walking the group back with Flint. Even Cindy was smiling.

As people left, Noah turned to Toby. "Thanks for your help today."

"It's my job." Toby frowned and glanced toward the parking lot before stepping closer. "Look, I don't mean to butt into something that isn't my business, but I couldn't help overhearing a bit of your conversation with your receptionist when I arrived this morning."

Noah's jaw clenched. Great, now even strangers were finding out that he was a damn mess.

Toby shoved his hands into his pocket. "I'm a clinical psychologist. I'm very familiar with treating trauma. I don't use any fancy machines or do anything too crazy. I do a lot of cognitive processing therapy, which helps restructure traumatic thoughts, so they don't control you."

Noah had already had therapy before leaving the military. It hadn't helped. But he did *need* help.

Toby cleared his throat. "No pressure, but I'm in the process of setting up an office here in Amber Ridge. You've got my name and number. Feel free to reach out." He smiled before heading off.

Noah scrubbed a hand over his face, not sure what the hell to do with that information. He wanted to be okay. He *needed* to be okay. He couldn't let either of the incidents with Addie happen again. Because next time, she might not come out of it unscathed.

CHAPTER 8

Not. Enough. Sleep. Not *nearly* enough sleep.

Addie pulled the sheets over her head to prevent the sun that was already poking through the curtains from hitting her in the eyes.

The house was old and it groaned and creaked *all* the time. Add the wind and the animals outside and there were no peaceful, quiet nights. Heck, she might even have a racoon or something living in her attic, there was so much noise.

Of course, it probably didn't help that she'd been on the phone to her mom until far too late, and the woman had asked her three times—*three*—whether she was ready to come home.

Her mother meant well. But she didn't understand that Addie *needed* to do this. She needed to live somewhere different and have a bit of separation from her parents.

With a deep sigh, she crawled out of bed before stepping into the shower. It was a quick shower because she wanted to go for a run. She needed to do something to clear her head. And not just a run around the block. She needed trees and mountains. She needed open Montana air.

All of which she could get at work. The mountain bike trail

was perfect for running, she just had to get there before the place opened. She didn't usually work up too much of a sweat, especially with the cold air, but if she did, she could just sneak home and take a shower at lunch while Cass covered for her.

Back in the bedroom, she pulled on some leggings, a sports crop, and a sweatshirt. She'd just stepped back into the bathroom to pull her hair up when her gaze caught on something in the sink. She frowned.

What was that?

Slowly, she lowered her head to look closer. Were they... hairs? Short, black hairs...

No. That wasn't possible.

She had blond hair, and she was the only person who used this bathroom. Hell, apart from Noah, she was the only one who'd spent any time in this house.

Wait, no—a plumber had come yesterday while she'd been at work. It was from him. It had to be him.

Air rushed from her chest.

She was so shaken by that text and the feeling of being watched that she was scaring herself.

Quickly, she turned on the tap and washed them down the drain.

She hadn't received another text since the bar. And she was praying it stayed that way. Because she *was not* running home to her parents scared.

She'd considered going to the sheriff's station about it, but it was probably just some prank texter. At least, that's what she was trying to convince herself.

Quickly, she pulled up her hair in an elastic band, then grabbed her work clothes and shoved them into a bag before leaving. When she reached the park, the sun was only just rising. It almost looked amber and was beautiful. But then, all of Amber Ridge was beautiful.

The second she climbed out of the car, her first real smile of the morning stretched her lips. At the sound of the birds—maybe mountain bluebirds—in the forest. At the cool morning air on her skin.

In her office, she dropped her bag onto her desk before stepping outside again and going straight to the mountain bike path. Then she started running, her feet hitting the ground.

God, it felt good.

Why didn't she run more? She should. That, combined with the fresh air in her lungs, just made every heavy thought inside her feel lighter. Every worry about Noah, every fear about the person who sent the text... it suddenly felt like she could carry the load and not crumble.

She wasn't sure how long she ran—it had to be close to half an hour. It was enough time to let the endorphins kick in and her mind get lost in nature. It wasn't until she neared the end of the loop that the familiar crunching sounded behind her. The first time since the text.

She glanced behind her but continued to move.

No one was there.

She looked back ahead, a strange feeling now in her belly. A ripple that made her uneasy and even a bit sick.

The noise sounded again. She shot another glance over her shoulder. Again, nothing.

She ran faster, sprinting down the path, pushing to get to the office cabin. It was in view. She was almost there.

When the noise sounded again but closer, she turned her head for the third time. When she looked back in front of her, she saw the large rock too late.

Her foot hit it hard, and she toppled over, landing on the ground with a thud. Pain erupted across her side, making her groan.

Jesus freaking Christ, that hurt.

She tugged her sweatshirt up to see a nasty scrape. It wasn't bleeding, but her skin was red and raw.

Great. Just what her morning needed.

Her gaze lifted to the path behind her one more time. And nope, no one was there. Because no one was *ever* there. She was just losing her goddamn mind.

With a groan, she pushed to her feet. It wasn't just her side that hurt. Apparently, her entire body couldn't handle a fall.

At least no one had seen. The embarrassment probably would have hurt her ego more than the scrape.

In the cabin, she pulled the office door closed behind her. Facing away from the door, she quickly tugged off her sweatshirt and switched her sports bra for a lacy black one. After toeing off her shoes, she stepped out of her leggings and pulled on a high-waisted skirt. She'd just done up the back when a knock sounded at the door.

She turned but didn't have time to say anything before it was pushed open and Noah stood there, eyes wide as he took in her shirtless chest.

* * *

NOAH PARKED his truck beside Addie's black Jeep Cherokee.

She was early. Why? To get extra work done? Or did she suffer from the same kind of insomnia as him?

Yeah, right. He was pretty sure that kind of sleep was reserved solely for him.

He climbed out of his truck, his phone weighing heavy in his pocket. He was going to call Toby today. He'd almost called yesterday but just…hadn't. The guy had made it obvious he was good at his job, so Noah just needed to man the hell up and call him. Yeah, he hated therapy, but maybe Toby would be different.

His mind conjured the image of Addie on the floor of the bar where he'd shoved her.

Yeah, he needed help and he needed help fast.

He stopped inside the reception area. The desk was empty. Where was Addie? Maybe back in the kitchen?

He knocked once on the office door before opening it.

His jaw immediately dropped, blood burning in his veins. Addie stood a few feet away, shirtless.

His mind blanked of everything but her. She wasn't even naked, but it was like the sight of her short-circuited his damn brain.

Her ample breasts pushed up against the lacy material. Her skin was smooth and looked so damn soft that his fingers itched to touch her.

He bit back a curse.

He was staring. He was staring like a fucking scumbag. Great.

He was about to turn when something on her side had him pausing. "You're hurt."

She glanced down. "I had a little fall."

"That's not little."

He moved over to the cupboard and pulled out the first aid kit.

Addie shook her head. "Noah, it's nothing."

"Sit."

"Noah—"

"Either I clean it, or I call someone to do it. Either way, that needs to be seen to."

Her mouth opened and closed, like she was debating arguing some more. Then she sighed and dropped into the seat at the desk.

He knelt in front of her, and her breasts were right fucking there.

Don't look at her, don't be a scumbag, Noah.

He gritted his teeth before taking out the saline and cleaning the scratch. "How did you fall?" At her silence, he glanced up. "Addie?"

She didn't look at him while she answered. "I didn't see a rock in front of me."

"You don't seem like a careless person." He ran the saline-covered pad over the wound again before throwing it into the trash and taking out some gauze.

Addie lifted a shoulder. "I thought I heard something."

His gaze shot up, his hand holding the pad against her ribs. "Addie...this isn't the first time you've thought someone was there who shouldn't have been."

She squirmed, like she was uncomfortable. "Yes. But again, I didn't see anyone."

The muscles in his forearms flexed. Because that didn't mean shit, and she knew it. "Has anything else happened that I don't know about?"

Her eyes widened slightly.

There *was* something. "What?"

"I got a text."

Something hard and uncomfortable pitted his gut. "From who?"

"An unknown number."

"What did it say?"

"That I've overstayed my welcome. And to get out."

Jesus fucking Christ! "Have you reported it to Jesse?"

She shook her head. "I'm sure it's—"

"Don't say *nothing*. You can't put all that stuff together and still believe it's nothing. You need to report it to the sheriff's office."

"But—"

"No buts, Addie. I also want you to make sure you're not going outside alone. Let me or one of the guys walk you to your car. Don't get here before everyone else. No more runs by yourself."

"Is that really necessary?"

"If someone is following you and trying to scare you out of

town, then yes." He stuck the pad onto her ribs with surgical tape before leaning back. "Promise me, Addie."

She didn't want to. He could see it in her eyes. But then she blinked. "Fine. I'll call Jesse."

"And be careful."

This time she rolled her eyes. "Of course I'll be careful."

"Good."

For a moment, neither of them moved, he just watched those blue eyes like his gaze was fucking stuck.

Suddenly, the click of a door opening sounded.

Shit.

Addie swung around and grabbed her top, while Noah quickly went into the reception area and pulled the door closed behind him.

A family bustled inside.

He smiled at them. "Hi. Welcome to Wilderness Adventure Park. Addie will be out in a moment."

He waited for Addie to step out of the office. When she did, her eyes briefly met his, an emotion he couldn't place flaring within them, before she turned to the people on the other side of the desk. "Hi. Sorry to keep you waiting. I'm Addie."

Noah waited until he was outside to let the full weight of the anger bear down on him.

Someone had messaged her. Threatened her. And that same someone was probably following her around.

His hands fisted, the need to know who this asshole was raging inside him. Why did they want her out of Amber Ridge? And what would they do if she didn't heed their warning?

He stopped at the base of the bouldering and climbing wall, confused at the sight of Rhett rummaging through the equipment box.

What the hell was he doing? He wasn't even scheduled to work for another hour.

"What are you doing?"

Rhett jumped and swung around. "Noah."

"I'm going to ask you again, Rhett." He stepped closer. "What are you doing in the equipment box? You're not scheduled to work at this wall today, and your shift hasn't started."

"I lost my watch yesterday. I thought it might have fallen in."

Noah studied his bare wrist. "What kind of watch was it?"

"Garmin." Rhett shook his head. "I'm sure it will show up. Keep an eye out for me, would you?"

He started walking away, but Noah called out to him.

Rhett stopped and a couple of seconds passed before he turned.

"You weren't working on this wall yesterday. Why would it be here?"

The muscles in Rhett's shoulders visibly tensed. "I lost it a couple of days ago. Only realized this morning."

Noah didn't respond straight away. Instead, he let the silence stretch. It was usually the best way to make a liar break. Rhett didn't break, and eventually Noah nodded.

Once Rhett was gone, Noah studied the equipment box. Maybe he should do a little digging into the guy. He wasn't assuming Rhett was the person harassing Addie, but it didn't hurt to double-check his background.

But first, he needed to make the call he'd been dreading.

He pulled his cell from his pocket. If Addie needed help, then there was even more reason for *him* to get help. He needed to be okay, and that wasn't going to happen unless he actively did something.

He hit Toby's number.

CHAPTER 9

$\mathcal{N}$oah leaned back on the deck chair at the back of his house and watched the sun set over the mountains.

Fucking gorgeous. If there was anywhere to go to heal, it was Amber Ridge.

"She stole your burrito?" Jesse asked, beer in his hand.

"Swiped it from right under my nose," Becket confirmed. "I have successfully picked up terrorists sneaking up on me. Once, I even saw an asshole in the bushes five hundred meters away in open terrain without gear. Yet Bella's able to steal my burrito from the middle console while she's in the back seat. She'd be a better soldier than all of us."

Noah laughed, and damn, it felt good to laugh with his cousins. "How does that happen?"

"Sky was on speaker, so I got distracted. I found the wrapper under the passenger seat when I got home."

The guy was a former Navy SEAL, trained to have the best tactical awareness in the world. But one phone call from his woman and he missed a dog eating his food.

"But...I wasn't even mad," Becket said, lifting his beer to his mouth. "I said 'well done,' and then I went and bought a taco."

Noah shook his head. "You're becoming a softy."

"Tell me about it." Becket looked at him. "We've been doing all the talking. What about you, Noah?"

"What *about* me?" He was deflecting because he did *not* want to talk about himself.

"How are you doing being home?" Jesse asked, all hints of humor leaving his eyes. "The transition back into civilian life isn't easy."

He glanced down at the beer in his hands. "Truth?"

"Always," Becket said.

"It's been tough. I'm here, but I don't always *feel* like I'm here. I thought being away from the military would...unchain me from certain memories."

Jesse leaned forward. "I know that feeling. When you live on the edge of danger for long enough, your nervous system takes time to find peace."

Time...was that all he needed?

"It took me at least a year to feel like I could sleep without waking every hour," Becket agreed.

They said it with such ease. But then, they didn't know the details of his last mission or why he'd left his team. And *that* was imprinted so deeply inside him it would be there forever.

His gaze moved over the mountains. "I loved my time in the Marines but sometimes...sometimes I feel angry that I signed up."

He'd never said those words out loud before. He'd barely allowed himself to *think* them. He wasn't sure why. Maybe because it was honorable to be a soldier. To fight for your country. So feeling anything but proud felt taboo.

"I've been there," Jesse said quietly.

"Same," Becket agreed. "The military changes you, and there are moments where that change doesn't feel for the better."

So it wasn't just him.

"It helps to move," Becket added. "Running or an hour with a bag does a world of good for your mental health. Have you tried the new gym? It's called The Pit, and the owner is former UFC."

"Colt told me about it, but I haven't gone."

"You should."

Becket was right. Noah worked out every day, but he hadn't hit a bag in too long. "Thanks. Now, onto a different topic, why haven't I seen you guys on my zip line?"

Both of them laughed.

An hour later, the guys were leaving, Jesse getting ready for his evening shift at the station and Becket going home to Sky and Bella.

He was just closing the door when his phone vibrated with a text.

A smile stretched his face when he saw who it was from.

Addie: I know what you did.

Noah: It wasn't me.

He didn't know what *it* was, but denying blame felt safest.

Addie: All my peanut butter cups are gone. Every freaking one of them. And I know it was you.

Noah: Do you have evidence to support your claim?

Addie: I have intel.

Noah: Have you considered that your intel is wrong?

Addie: I trust my informant.

Noah: What exactly did this informant say?

Addie: That they saw you rummaging through my chocolate jar. Now I am mysteriously all out of peanut butter cups. Which are my favorite.

Noah: Last week the huckleberry truffles were your favorite.

Addie: Things change.

Noah: Hm. This is a mystery.

Addie: I'm not joking, buddy. Theft is a very serious crime.

Noah: Would you like me to buy you some more peanut butter cups, Addison?

Addie: Are you admitting to the theft?

Noah: I admit nothing.

Addie: Spoken like a true criminal.

He chuckled before heading back out onto the deck and lifting the empty beer bottles to take inside.

Noah: Correct me if I'm wrong, but you still have half a dozen other chocolates in that jar.

Addie: None of them are peanut butter.

Noah: You'll find some peanut butter cups and a jar of peanut butter on your desk on Monday morning.

Addie: Okay. That helps.

Noah: Will it also make you feel better if I tell you that Jules got a new flavor of hot chocolate?

Addie: Depends…what flavor?

Noah: She calls it The Lumberjack. It's dark chocolate with cinnamon and maple.

The three dots popped up, then disappeared. Then they popped up again.

Addie: I did not know this. It does make me feel better.

He chuckled, but his smile slipped as he wrote the next text.

Noah: Have you been keeping safe?

It had been a week since her run. And he hadn't seen her nearly enough in that time.

Addie: No creepy shadows or noises or texts. I'm starting to feel optimistic that whoever the text was from was just messing around.

Noah wouldn't get too excited.

Addie: I'm going to take a shower and get ready for bed. Just needed you to know I'm disappointed in you.

Noah: I told you I'd replace them.

Addie: That didn't help me today when I was in the throes of my Peanut Butter Cup Withdrawal.

His lips twitched as an idea hit him. It was a terrible idea for a multitude of reasons. And his head told him not to do it. But for the first time in his life, he didn't listen.

* * *

ADDIE WAS STILL SMILING as she stepped into the shower. A huge just-texting-Noah-makes-me-grin-uncontrollably smile.

Hot water beat down on her shoulders, warming her cool skin. Yes, she really *had* wanted a peanut butter cup today. But honestly, the discovery that it was Noah who'd taken them had made her almost excited, because it had given her an excuse to text him.

That sounded pathetic, right? To need an excuse to text your crush? Argh, and she was referring to him as her crush. She was twenty-two years old, for Christ's sake.

She *shouldn't* be texting him. It was not smart to fall for Noah Hayes. In fact, it was probably as far from smart as she could get.

Yes, they'd kissed, and *yes*, that kiss had been the best freaking thing she'd ever experienced…but nothing had changed. He was still her boss, he was still thirteen years older than she was, and he was still working through his trauma from the military.

But there was no harm in texting, right? Or staring at him while he got onto the climbing wall, or remembering their kiss while letting her pulse take off at a million miles an hour?

Gah. She was screwed. And not in the literal way.

Fifteen minutes later, and after side-stepping way too many invasive thoughts of Noah, she got out of the shower and pulled on panties and an oversized shirt her parents had given her for Christmas. It said, "Powered by Chocolate," and it was the most honest piece of clothing she'd ever worn. They'd also given her one that read: "A day without chocolate is a day wasted," and she absolutely agreed with that one too.

Now she had a night of chocolate pudding and *House of Wax* to look forward to, because was there a better combination than chocolate and a horror movie? No. No, there wasn't. And Chad Michael Murray and Jared Padalecki just sweetened the deal.

She was just stepping into her living room when the creak of an old floorboard near the kitchen made her stop.

What was that? It sounded like it came from the laundry off the kitchen.

But then, this was an old house. It made noises all the time, so it could have been nothing. It *was* nothing. Of course it was.

She continued to the kitchen and grabbed the pudding from the fridge. She'd just set it on the counter when another creak sounded, this one louder.

She spun, heart thrashing against her ribs. That definitely came from behind the closed laundry door. Was someone in there?

Her gaze shot to the front door. Should she run outside? Drive to the sheriff's station? Or lock herself in the bathroom and call for help?

No. That was dumb. Why would she lock herself in a house with an intruder?

A sudden knock on the front door made her jump. Fear made a small tremble move through her fingers. They could be connected—the person in her laundry and the person at the door.

Quickly, she pulled a knife from the block and held it up as she crossed the living room, constantly checking behind her like she was waiting for whoever was in her house to jump out. This could be their plan, distract her with the front door so she turned her back on the person in the laundry room.

She looked through the peephole—and air immediately whooshed from her chest.

As quick as her trembling fingers allowed, she tugged open the door, not even caring that she only wore panties and a T-shirt.

Noah stood on the other side, a bag of Reese's Mini Peanut Butter Cups in one hand and a jar of peanut butter in the other.

His eyes flared at the sight of her. Then his gaze narrowed at the knife in her hand. He stepped forward. "What's wrong?"

"I think—"

The click of the back door opening and closing sounded, making her gasp and spin.

There *had* been someone here!

"Who's that?" Noah demanded, as he stepped inside and closed the door after him.

"I don't know. But they were in the house with me!" She felt sick. The kind of sick that gave her a rolling belly and stole her breath.

Noah cursed and flicked the lock on the door before pressing her against it. "Stay here."

"But—"

It was too late, he was already moving. Air caught in her throat when he stepped into the kitchen.

What if they had a weapon? A gun? Noah could get hurt trying to protect her.

Her fingers tightened around the butcher's knife. How long had the person been in her house? And how had they gotten in?

She wasn't sure how many minutes passed before Noah returned, maybe one, maybe five. He walked straight over to her and slipped the knife from her fingers before setting it on the foyer table.

"They're gone," he growled, veins popping out in his neck. "You only have split-rail fencing between you and your neighbors. They could have come and gone from any direction."

Addie swallowed. It was true. Her yard was ridiculously open and easy to access from any of her neighbors' properties.

He watched her carefully. "I called Jesse. He was in his patrol car and close, so he won't be long."

"Someone was in my house," she whispered, still not able to wrap her head around it.

He touched her arm. "I'm here, and I'm not going to let anyone hurt you."

She nodded, but it didn't change the fact that she felt violated and scared and sick all at the same time.

"We should get some more clothes on you."

Clothes? She hadn't even been thinking about clothes. But Noah was right, in a few minutes, Jesse would walk in. She should at least put pants on.

Gently, he gripped her arm and led her to her bedroom. She took out the fluffiest leggings she owned and pulled on an over-sized sweatshirt.

Ten minutes later, Jesse and a female deputy named Claudia stood in her living room.

She sat on the couch beside Noah, and that shake in her fingers had now trickled into other parts of her body. Her hands. Her knees. Even her jaw felt like it was trembling. Or maybe it was just cold combined with exhaustion. She was tired. Apparently, having someone break into your house did that to you.

"So you didn't see anyone?" Jesse asked.

Addie shook her head. "No. I changed after my shower and went into the kitchen. I heard the floorboard creak from the laundry. That's when Noah got to my door."

"I didn't see anyone out there," Noah said between gritted teeth. There was so much anger in his voice. "But we heard the back door open and close."

Jesse glanced at the back door before looking back at them. "Was the lock—"

"Unbroken," Noah said.

Jesse's attention shifted to her. "Did you leave it unlocked?"

"No. I always lock my doors. My father drilled that into me since I was a kid."

"Does anyone else have a key to your house?" Claudia asked.

"No—" She stopped and frowned. "But I lost my key a couple

weeks ago." Oh God, was that how they'd accessed her house? Had someone else had a key to her home this entire time?

Her skin started to crawl.

Noah slipped an arm around her side. He didn't say anything, but his strength and warmth were everything. She leaned into him, needing his support.

"Who would have had the opportunity to take the key?" Jesse asked.

She lifted a shoulder. "I realized it was gone after work one day. But I leave my bag in the office. I should have seen someone go in there."

"Who takes over for you when you have breaks?"

"Cass. But she wouldn't do this. Maybe she left the desk unattended at some point and someone went in there? That cabin doesn't have bathrooms, so she could have stepped out. Or sometimes we have to take groups outside and show them how to get to their activities."

That had to have been the case. Because this couldn't be someone who worked at the park. Statistically speaking, she knew it was most likely the case, but she didn't want to accept that.

"We can do a check on everyone who works there," Jesse said, as Claudia wrote something down on her notepad.

"Has anything else happened before this?" Jesse asked.

Noah stiffened beside her. He was right. She should have told Jesse. "I've felt like someone's been watching me. And when I got home a couple weeks ago, I thought I saw a shadow beside the house."

"And on your run," Noah added.

She nodded. "Last week, I went for a run along the trail before the park opened. I heard someone behind me." Something else flickered in her memory. "Someone also texted me telling me to get out of town, but it was from an unknown number. And I woke up to find hairs in my bathroom sink that morning. Short, black ones. I thought they were from the plumber who'd been by, but maybe…"

Oh, Jesus. She really *was* going to be sick. Because did that mean they had accessed her bathroom while she'd been sleeping?

Deep breaths, Addie.

She lowered her head into her hands, and it was only the gentle rub of Noah's hand across her back that kept her from completely losing it.

And what had been the intruders plan tonight? What would they have done if Noah hadn't shown up?

Jesse crouched in front of her. "Addie, it sounds like you have someone stalking you. Maybe trying to scare you out of your home. Until we find out who it is, you shouldn't be alone. Is there anywhere you can stay tonight?"

"She can stay with me."

Addie looked up at Noah. She wasn't sure if she was supposed to refuse his offer to help, or suggest she drive back to Bozeman. She did neither of those things. Because she wanted to stay with Noah. It was where she felt safest. "Thank you."

CHAPTER 10

*A*ddie stepped inside Noah's home, only to stop abruptly.

Holy crap…it was beautiful. But not in a modern, sleek kind of way. It was an old-style craftsman home that had clearly been renovated.

"Everything okay?"

She glanced at Noah beside her. "Yeah. I just…you have a nice place."

The corners of his lips lifted. "Expecting a bachelor pad with a gaming console in front of a sixty-five-inch TV?"

"Maybe." Definitely. And this was *not* that. It was warm and cozy and had character.

She stepped into the living room, where a fireplace centered the wall, with built-in shelving around it. Her gaze caught on the flames. "How is your fire on?"

"I texted my sister. She and Colt came by and put it on so the place would be warm when we got here."

Thoughtful…another ridiculously attractive trait to add to his seemingly endless list.

She turned to see him alarming the house, the small bag she'd packed strung over his shoulder. A deep frown was now etched on his brow. It was the same one he'd worn in her house the entire time Jesse had been there.

"Thank you for letting me stay here," she said quietly.

"You shouldn't be in your house if someone has a key. Hell, you shouldn't be alone while you have a stalker."

Her pulse kicked against her throat. Stalker. The word sounded big and dangerous and uncomfortable, and she wanted it nowhere near her.

"I don't understand," she whispered. "I haven't done anything to anyone. I don't have money or influence. I'm only twenty-two. There's no reason for someone to want me out of this town. And what was their goal tonight? What would they have done if you hadn't arrived when you did?"

In the blink of an eye, Noah closed the space between them and cupped her cheek. "Hey. There are some sick people in the world, and they need very little motivation to do sick shit like this. It's about them, not you."

It had to be a *bit* about her. And she wanted to know why.

Tears suddenly burned her eyes—tears that she *hated*. "I feel violated. They have a key to my home. How many times have they used it? I heard creaking the other night while I was sleeping. Was that them too? And the black hairs in my bathroom sink?" A shudder didn't just course down her back, it rolled through her entire body.

Noah cursed and tugged her into him. "You're safe with me."

She believed it. They may not have known each other long, but out of every place she'd been in Amber Ridge, Noah's arms felt safest.

She leaned into him, letting the tear that trickled down her cheek soak into his shirt. Letting the strength of his arms wrapped around her act like a protective shield.

When she pulled back, he gripped her hips, and for a second, her gaze caught on his lips, memories of their last kiss skittering through her mind. Of the rightness she'd felt in that moment. The safety that had enveloped her, and that she so desperately craved right now.

For a second, Noah's eyes darkened, desire swirling in their gray depths. Then his jaw clenched and he stepped back. "Come on. I'll show you where you're sleeping."

She followed him down the hall, only to frown when she stepped into a bedroom. There were dog tags on the dresser. A framed photo of Noah with a group of guys beside the bed. Even a shirt slung over a chair.

This wasn't a spare room. This room was lived in.

She turned to Noah. "This is your room."

"The spare's filled with boxes."

"I'm not taking your room." Not just his room. His bed. His space. She'd be sleeping between the same sheets he slept between every night. No way. That felt far too intimate.

"I'll sleep on the couch." He said it like it was already a done deal.

"No, *I'll* sleep on the couch."

He laughed. "If you think I'd let you sleep on the couch, you don't know me very well."

"Why not? I'm smaller than you. It would be more comfortable for me."

"No."

She frowned. Just no? "Noah—"

"I was raised a gentleman, and there is no way in hell I would let my guest sleep on the couch when I have a perfectly good bed for her."

She opened her mouth to argue more, but he got in first.

"It's also a safety thing. I need to be closest to the door." He lowered her bag to the bed. "Hungry?"

She sighed. "No." For once, she didn't even think she could

stomach chocolate. Apparently, the knowledge that someone had been in her house while she'd showered completely turned her off food. "I might just take another shower and sleep. Are you sure—"

"You're taking the bed."

Dammit.

He took a half step toward her, making her breath catch in her throat. He seemed to hesitate for a moment before cupping her cheek. "Are you sure you're okay?"

All she wanted to do was lean into that touch. And maybe she did, just a little bit. "No. But I will be."

"You will be. Call out if you need anything."

"I will."

Don't look at his lips, don't look at his lips. The words whispered on repeat in her head. Because every time he stood this close, every time he touched her or she felt his breath against her skin, all she wanted to do was lift to her toes and see if he tasted as good as he had the first time.

He swiped her cheek with his thumb before dropping his hand and moving back. "There are fresh towels in the bathroom cabinet. Call out if you need anything."

One more smile and then he was gone again. Suddenly, the room felt too quiet.

She wrapped her arms around her waist and scanned the room, wishing she had the courage to call him back. Or even ask him to sleep in the same room. But that was ridiculous. She was a grown woman and they weren't in a relationship. They'd kissed once, that was it. It was not appropriate for them to share a bed.

After a quick shower—her second for the night—she turned off the lights and slipped beneath the sheets.

And just like she'd known it would, the bed smelled exactly like Noah, a mixture of sun-warmed bark and crushed sage.

Okay, time to sleep, Addie.

She closed her eyes, but the second she did, she heard the creak of floorboards like she was still in her house. It wasn't real. It was in her head. But it *felt* real.

She scrunched her eyes, and this time she saw the shadow beside the house.

Stop thinking about it, Addie. It's not going to help you.

She rolled to her side.

A few minutes later, she rolled to her other side.

It had to be close to an hour later before she finally drifted off to sleep.

She wasn't sure how long she'd been sleeping when a sound woke her. At first, she wasn't sure what it was. A voice maybe? A growl?

She lay still, waiting to hear it again. A few seconds passed and she wondered if maybe it had been in her head.

She was moments from closing her eyes again when a loud growl rippled through the house.

She shot up.

Noah.

Was someone out there with him? Had her stalker followed them to his home and broken into the house? No. He had an alarm. So what the heck was going on?

Quickly, she scrambled out of bed and ran down the hall—only to stop at the sight of Noah on the couch. His head swung back and forth, pain and rage melding together on his face to create an emotion so dark, she almost didn't recognize him.

He was having a nightmare.

She inched closer, not sure what to do. It would be smartest to leave him. Let him wake from the dream in his own time.

He growled again, another scrunch of his face showing utter agony.

God. He was hurting. And she couldn't physically force herself to step away. No part of her felt capable of that.

"Noah."

Nothing. His head continued to move from side to side, his chest heaving, his breathing loud.

"Noah, wake up."

It was like he couldn't hear her. And it was getting worse. His growls were getting louder. The pain—Jesus, it just leached out of him.

His head flew back and for a moment, it looked like he wasn't breathing. "Noah, you need to—"

"No!" The shout was loud and fierce, and in a split second he was standing and grasping her arms in such a tight grip that her muscles burned.

* * *

PAIN PULSED beneath Noah's skin, relentless and hot.

He hurt. Everything fucking hurt. His wrists from the chains breaking his skin. His cracked ribs from the boots pounding into him. And his head...Jesus, it pounded. A mixture of beatings and dehydration and exhaustion.

He tried to peel his eyes open, but one was so swollen it wouldn't budge.

The darkness...fuck, it was everywhere. It was all he'd seen for days. He could just make out the concrete walls. Then there was the cold, but he'd kind of gotten used to that. Hell, he almost welcomed it because it eased the burning heat of his injuries.

It was the smell that really fucking hit him. The mixture of blood and sweat and this stagnant air that made him want to be sick.

Dizziness spun the world around him, and he lowered his head to his chest, but the chains connecting him to the wall refused to let his hands drop.

He was in the depths of hell and his captors knew it. Had designed this place to be hell.

The assholes had tried to break him. They hadn't. And they wouldn't. They wouldn't get a single piece of intel from him about his unit or their allied forces.

He just had to survive until the rescue team came. Because they would *come. And if he cracked before then, he was as good as dead anyway.*

He sucked in a lungful of air, which made the ache in his ribs cascade through his body.

His mind flicked to Jay, and the pain suddenly turned to rage.

Dead. Jay was dead. Killed in the ambush. It still didn't feel real. But that bullet that hit Jay in the skull had played over in Noah's mind again and again. Even though they'd been in the middle of a fucking ambush, time had felt like it stopped. Noah had felt paralyzed. It was only Boone pulling him into the irrigation shed that had saved him from the same fate.

But that hadn't been the salvation either of them had hoped for.

A new wave of fury rolled through him at the memory of the stun grenade. At waking up here in the depths of hell.

He tugged at the binds around his wrists, not caring that his skin was red and raw.

Where was Boone? What had they done with him? No one would tell him.

Another wave of dizziness swamped him, almost dragging him back under, but he forced his eyes to remain open.

Survive. That was his goal.

The creak of the door opening had his head shooting up.

Then the already dark world blackened further.

Boone.

He looked like he'd already gone through the same torture yet was still fighting the assholes who stood on either side of him. The second he looked up at Noah, they both knew what was about to happen...they were going to be pitted against each other. But only one of them would make it out alive.

Make it Boone. He wanted to die so that Boone could live.

A man came to stand between them. He was the only one in this godforsaken place who spoke English. The fucker who'd been trying to get information from Noah before he lost consciousness.

The asshole looked at him. "It's time for you to speak, soldier."

No. They'd chosen to try to crack Noah...which meant Boone was the one who wouldn't make it.

"He's not telling you shit," Boone spat. "So you may as well kill me now."

He punched Boone in the face.

Noah growled and pulled against the chains, not feeling the pain in his wrists anymore. "I'm going to kill you. I'm going to kill all of you."

The guy laughed before turning to one of his men and nodding. The blows hit Boone hard and fast. And all Noah could do was watch. He couldn't give them the information they needed. As a Marine, he had a code of honor and duty. He was trained to never compromise a mission or their unit.

But even if he wasn't, giving these assholes information wouldn't save Boone. It would just kill him faster.

Even though he was chained to a damn wall, he fought. He tugged and growled, the burns and aches gone, his body now numb.

The guy in front of him raised a brow. "Noah, you need to—"

"No!" Noah lunged, wanting to tear the fucker apart. The chains suddenly disappeared, and he grabbed the guy by the arms. But it was wrong. His arms were too slim. His skin too soft.

The room suddenly changed. It wasn't cold or made of concrete. The floor wasn't hard. The person beneath him wasn't one of the assholes who took him.

It was Addie.

He was home, in Amber Ridge, and he'd been a second away from hurting Addie—again.

He released her and jumped back, the space between them too small. "Addie, I'm..."

"I know." Her soft voice was gentler than he deserved. He wanted her to fucking rage at him. Tell him what a scumbag he was.

"Are you okay?" she whispered.

What kind of question was that? *He'd* scared *her*. He'd *grabbed* her. Probably bruised her.

"I'm *fine,*" she repeated before tilting her head. "Now I need to know if you are."

He shook his head, his fingers running through his hair, pulling at the damn roots. He wasn't close to fine. He didn't even know what fine felt like anymore. "You shouldn't be around me."

"I'm not scared of you, Noah."

"I could have *hurt* you, Addison."

"But you didn't. You pulled yourself back to reality."

Reality. What even *was* reality anymore? Every time those dark memories pulled him in, they felt real. Like he was there again. He could smell that place. Feel the cold on his skin.

Shit, he needed to get out of there.

"Do you want me to call Jesse?" Noah asked.

She frowned like the idea was absurd. "No. I'm not pressing charges, if that's what you're asking."

"You should."

That frown on her face deepened. "Noah—" She stepped toward him and he leapt back.

"I'm going to go."

Before she could respond, he was moving.

"This is *your* house," she said, following. "*I'll* go."

"No. I have a good security system. Lock the doors after me and turn the alarm on once I'm out. I'll text you the details. I'll also call Jesse and get him to put a deputy on the house." He went to his room, grabbed a bag, and packed his shit. He'd go to Indie and Colt's for the rest of the night.

"Noah, don't do this. It's *my* fault. I shouldn't have gotten close to you. It's the middle of the night."

He lifted the bag and moved toward the front door. In the hall, he pulled out a spare key from a drawer and set it on the table. "Lock up in the morning when you leave. I'll wait until there's someone outside so you won't be unprotected."

Then he stepped out of the house, guilt so heavy on his shoulders, his knees almost caved from the weight of it.

He'd done it again. She hadn't even touched him this time, yet he'd almost hurt her. And there was nothing about that fact that felt forgivable.

CHAPTER 11

$\mathcal{A}$ddie glanced down at her phone. He hadn't messaged all morning. Granted, it was only nine, but she'd woken at three a.m. to Noah's nightmare and hadn't gone back to sleep, so it felt later.

She was tired. And frustrated. And it felt like there was this band around her chest, tightening with each breath.

Yes, she'd felt a flicker of fear when Noah had grabbed her. But he *hadn't* hurt her.

Mrs. Gerald set a mug on her table. "Here you are, dear."

"Thank you." She wrapped her fingers around the hot mug, letting the warmth slip into the cool crevices inside her.

Before the older woman walked away, she frowned. "Are you okay?"

"It hasn't been a great morning." Understatement of the century.

"Is there anything I can do?"

"You've already done it by making me this steaming-hot cup of cocoa. Thank you. And thank you for checking in."

"Let me know if you need pie too."

Despite everything, her lips twitched. "I just might." Heck, she might need two pieces of pie.

When the other woman walked away, Addie lifted her mug, but even the sweetness of the drink didn't help.

"Oh my, it must be bad if the hot chocolate isn't making you smile."

Addie looked up to see Jules slide into the booth opposite her, a piece of pie in her hand.

"Jules, hey."

"You should be smiling. It's Monday, the park's closed, we all have the day off, and the sun's shining."

"After the twenty-four hours I've had, smiling is not high on my to-do list today."

Jules's brows flickered. "Is this about Noah?"

"Noah?"

"Addie, I've seen the way you two look at each other. Has something happened?"

Cass had said something similar. Was it that obvious to everyone? "It's complicated."

Jules seemed to consider that for a moment. "Well, if there's anything I've learned in my fifty-five years on this earth, it's that there's no problem that cannot be solved with pie." She pushed her slice across the table.

"Oh, no, it's yours."

"You look like you need it more than me." Julie tilted her head. "Want to talk about it?"

Ha. If she told this woman about everything that had happened in the last twenty-four hours, heck in the last *month*, her eyes would probably fall out of their sockets. "Trust me, you do not want me to spill all my problems on you."

"I've had my share of problems, and talking has always helped. In fact, my therapist is possibly my best friend."

Addie chuckled. "You seem far too happy to need therapy."

Something flickered over the other woman's face. It came and went so quickly, Addie wasn't sure what to make of it. Was it sadness? Maybe a bit of regret?

"Trust me," Jules said slowly, "my life has not been all sunshine and roses."

Addie frowned. "Are you okay now?"

"Actually, I'm in the best place I've been my entire life."

"That's good."

"It's amazing. I'm glad I saw the job at the park advertised and it brought me to Amber Ridge. It's a beautiful town. You're new here too, right?"

"I am. I only lived an hour away though. My parents are still in Bozeman."

"You said you were close with your parents?"

"They're my best friends. But then, I'm an only child, so I had no choice."

Jules's smile softened. "I'm glad. Do they work?"

"My mother's a teacher who will probably work until the day she dies because she loves those kids more than anything else. And my father's a retired Marine, although I think he's regretting the retired part because he doesn't know what to do with all his spare time."

"Wow, a teacher and a Marine. They must have given you a very safe upbringing."

"The safest and the best. I'm very lucky."

The café doors opened, and Addie almost rolled her eyes at the sight of Rhett stepping into The Tea House, closely followed by Buck. Buck wasn't so bad. Maybe slightly vacant and hard to talk to, but Rhett was just annoying. Although, he was flirting with her less, which maybe had something to do with all the time he was spending with Cass, since apparently Rhett was done avoiding *her*.

"Great," Addie muttered under her breath. Just what her morning needed.

Jules glanced over her shoulder before looking back to Addie. "Not a fan of the guys?"

"Not a fan of *Rhett*."

Right on cue, Rhett stopped at their table. "Hey, hey, it's like a team meeting."

Addie offered a small smile. "Hi, Rhett. Hey, Buck."

"Mind if we join you?" Rhett asked.

Oh, hell no. She opened her mouth to say just that, but Jules got in first. "Actually, we're talking woman things."

Rhett grinned. "Well, it's your lucky day, because I'm an expert on all things women."

Oh, brother.

Jules straightened. "Great, you might be helpful then. I was just telling Addie about my ovarian cysts."

Rhett blinked, and Buck made a face that could only be described as horror.

"They're large," Jules continued, "and one's kind of twisted. I actually have a photo from my doctor that I was about to show Addie, so now I can show you guys too." She pulled out her phone and unlocked it. "To me it looks like a dismembered fish, but—"

"You know what?" Rhett stepped back, hands raised. "We, uh, were… We're going now."

The guys left. Well, basically *ran* from the table.

Addie burst out laughing. "Okay, that definitely made my terrible morning feel just a bit better."

"Men act tough but most will run the second you throw out any words concerning a woman's anatomy."

"I feel like I could learn a lot from you."

"Honey, stick around, and I'll give you fifty-five years of wisdom."

* * *

THE COUCH WAS HARD. Noah didn't care—he'd sat in worse places. But for some reason, he'd expected a therapist's office to have a comfortable couch. His last therapist's couch had been so soft you could have slept on it.

And not only that, the walls were bare. Weren't there supposed to be framed degrees or certificates or something?

Lucky he'd looked the guy up on the internet to confirm his credentials, because otherwise he might question if the guy was a real therapist.

The door to the office opened and Toby stepped in. "Sorry to make you wait. There are fires left, right, and center today." He lowered to the armchair across from Noah.

"You don't need a laptop or notebook?" Noah asked. His therapist in North Carolina had looked at that damn notebook more than he'd looked at *him*.

Toby shook his head. "No, I like to be present with my clients. Besides, I have a good memory. I write my notes up after."

Notes… Noah had been offered a copy of his notes from his last therapist. He'd declined. What the hell was he supposed to do with them? Read about the therapy that hadn't done shit for him?

"I noticed on your form," Toby said, "that you spoke to someone before returning to Amber Ridge."

"It didn't help. Probably why he signed off on a medical discharge. Pretty sure he saw me as a lost cause."

"How did that make you feel?"

"It was expected." Didn't really answer Toby's question and, of course, he would know that.

Toby's smile gentled. "Well, I'm glad you're giving me a chance. We don't have to start with anything heavy. We can talk about the weather or the park."

Noah bit back a scoff. "I don't want to talk about the weather."

"What would you like to talk about?"

"How to unchain myself from what happened to me." The words felt heavy, like rocks in his gut.

Toby nodded, a neutral expression now on his face. "Would you like to tell me what happened?"

The first time someone had asked Noah that, he'd barely gotten the words out. Now?

"My team was on the Syrian and Iraqi border region. Our job was to conduct surveillance on a suspected insurgent smuggling route. We got bad intel though. The town was supposed to be abandoned. It wasn't. It was actively used as a militia transit hub. We were ambushed."

Toby nodded, his brows tugging together. He didn't say anything, just waited for Noah to continue.

"They started shooting from rooftops. Some of the guys got away. But Jay was killed. And Boone and I were taken. I woke up in a concrete-walled room. I wasn't given any food or water, and they tried to beat information from me. When that didn't work, they used Boone against me."

"What happened next?" Toby asked quietly, when Noah paused.

This was the part Noah hated. His heart started to race like it always did and sweat beaded his forehead. "They beat him. Shot him. And I watched him die."

There was so much missing from that story. The hours of agony. The utter devastation that he was about to lose his second teammate. The feeling of hopelessness.

He swallowed but it did nothing to wet his dry throat. "An hour after he died, the rescue team breached the compound and saved me."

Another small nod from Toby. "Thank you for telling me. I'm sorry you went through that."

"I didn't just go through it. I'm *still* going through it. I relive it every day. I see Boone dying *every fucking time* I close my eyes. I feel the chains around my wrists. The rage and hopelessness live inside me all the time. I'm *tired* of reliving that day."

"Only when you close your eyes?"

"Sometimes when I'm awake. I hate it. All of it. I want to sleep. I want to have a relationship and be healthy and happy."

Long beats of quiet passed. Toby didn't fill the space with empty reassurances. There was just the sharp tick of the clock on the wall. A car engine outside.

Finally, Toby leaned forward. "First of all, what you're experiencing is normal. The nightmares. The feeling of being connected to a moment in your life that changed you. It's your brain's way of telling you that it was hurt. Your brain isn't weak or broken though. It's just communicating with you."

"It feels pretty fucking weak sometimes."

"If your arm broke, no one would question you when you couldn't lift something. If your leg was shattered, no one would expect you to walk like it was fine. It's the same with your mind. It was wounded, and now it needs to heal."

"*Can* it heal?"

"Yes. Trauma is like any weight. At first it's so heavy it's impossible to move because it's weighing you down. But you put in the work. You get stronger. And eventually, it's not so hard to carry. But it won't be exactly the way it was before the injury."

Noah scrubbed his hands over his face. "I need to be good enough that I'm not a danger to others."

"Do you think you'd hurt someone?"

His jaw tightened. "When I have flashbacks, I don't feel in control of my actions. They make me feel...dangerous."

"It's good that you can recognize that. To begin, you need to understand your triggers, then we can work out how to ensure you stay in control. I believe that once we get further into these sessions, once we really put in the work, you'll feel more in control."

Fuck, he hoped so. He was *depending* on this working.

CHAPTER 12

$\mathcal{A}$ddie smiled and waved goodbye as the last park visitor left for the day. Her cheeks hurt. She didn't realize how much effort it took to smile when smiling was the last thing she felt like doing.

Six days. She'd been living in Noah's house for six whole days, yet she'd barely seen him. She'd thought that if she stayed in his home like he asked, they'd have an opportunity to talk or move on from what had happened, but instead of coming home, he'd been staying with Colt and Indie and there'd been a deputy on the house.

It was silly because it was *his* house. He should feel like he could spend time in his own home, but he clearly didn't because she was there.

Well, not any longer. She'd changed the locks on her front and back doors, so she could finally go home. Did she want to live by herself? No. But she was basically doing that now anyway, so nothing would really change.

And that wasn't the only thing on her mind right now. The park was closed tomorrow, but the staff was doing a team bonding day of rock climbing. She'd thought—hoped—that because she worked in the office, she wouldn't have to do it. Apparently, not the case, so she was rock climbing tomorrow, and everyone would find out that she was not the outdoorsy adventure person she'd marketed herself as.

Great.

With a sigh, she turned off the laptop and packed her bag. Once everything was locked up, instead of going to her car, she went down the trail to the campsite. A group of schoolkids were there for a few nights, and Noah had been with them all day *and* the day before. He was actually really good at staying busy and far away from her.

Her heart gave a little squeeze because, yes, it made her sad. She liked spending time with him.

Jules rounded a corner, empty trays in her hands. "Addie! Everything okay?"

"Yeah, I just need to talk to Noah." Or talk some sense into him, at least.

"Is it to make sure he goes home? Because that boy's been here far too much this week. He's a step away from setting up camp and living here."

Oh, she was absolutely aware of that. "Actually, it is."

"Maybe you'll have better luck than me." The older woman patted her shoulder. "I'll see you tomorrow, honey."

At the campsite, the fire was lit and there were kids everywhere. Some roasting marshmallows. A lot running around.

But where was Noah? There were a few adults around, probably teachers. But she couldn't see—

Her gaze zeroed in on Noah's broad shoulders. He was standing with his hands in his pockets, talking to Rhett.

Gotcha.

She crossed the campsite and tapped him on the shoulder.

He turned, and the second his gaze fell on her, a dozen emotions passed over his face all in the span of one second.

Surprise. Frustration. And maybe some desire. But that could be in her head.

"Addison…is everything okay?"

"Are you returning to your house tonight?"

His brows pulled together. "You walked down here to ask me that?"

"Yes." Absolutely yes. She already felt bad enough for stealing his home.

He ran his fingers through his hair. "I'm not sure. I have some stuff I need to get done here, then it will be late, so I'll probably just stay with Colt and Indie again."

"What?"

He paused. "What do you mean, what?"

"What do you need to get done here that's going to make you late?"

"I need to check the tire pressure on the bikes. Make sure the disc brakes aren't rubbing and replace any thin brake pads."

"And it all needs to be done after work instead of tomorrow?"

His frown deepened. "What's going on, Addie?"

"It's your house."

"What?"

"It's *your* house, and you're avoiding it because I'm in it."

Noah grabbed her arm and tugged her to the side. Because he didn't want Rhett to hear?

"I'm doing what's safest," Noah said, the second they were out of earshot.

"Look, I was going to move back home tomorrow, but I'll leave tonight so you don't have to avoid your own house anymore." She started to turn, but he grabbed her arm a second time and pulled her back.

"No."

Her brows shot up. "No?"

"You're not going home until we find this person."

"I have new locks."

"I don't care. My house has more security."

She tilted her head. "Noah—"

"I'll come home tonight. I'll sleep on the couch. I won't be home too late. Just...don't move out."

She swallowed. She felt like she should push, but there was something about his pleading gray eyes that made her want to give him anything he asked for. Did that make her weak? Or just a bit infatuated with the guy? "Are you sure?"

"Yes."

"You need to stop avoiding me at work too."

"You think I'm avoiding you?"

"I *know* you're avoiding me."

He swallowed hard. "Okay. I'll stop avoiding you."

"Good."

A lock of hair escaped from behind her ear and fluttered across her face. Before she could flick it away, Noah reached out and tucked it back.

Her skin tingled where he touched her.

That...that was her reaction to him. And that was what she was chasing...and he was running from.

"I'll try to be home at a reasonable time tonight," he said softly.

"G-good." Oh, Jesus. One touch and she was stumbling over her words. "I guess I'll see you later then."

"I guess you will."

One quick nod and she turned.

"Wait. I don't want you walking alone." He looked over her head. "Rhett, you're finished now. I need you to walk Addie to her car."

She just held in the cringe.

"Sure."

She turned and gave Rhett a forced smile. "Thanks."

As they headed down the path, she felt his eyes on her.

"What?" she asked, finally looking up.

Rhett's grin was wide. "So…you and the boss, huh?"

"I don't know what you're talking about." She was *not* in the mood for this guy's company.

"If I heard correctly, you're sleeping in his bed?"

She rolled her eyes. "He's letting me stay at his place while I go through something."

"I'm sure you're going through *something*."

She shot an annoyed glare his way. "What are you insinuating?"

"That I finally understand why you turned me down."

She laughed, but it was less out of humor than absurdity. "First of all, you never asked me out. But if you had, I would have turned you down without needing any other reason than I don't like you like that."

The cockiness slipped, replaced with…annoyance? "What does that mean?"

"It means what I said."

When they reached the parking lot, she stepped toward her car, but his fingers suddenly wrapped around her wrist and he pulled her back. "Are you saying you think you're too good for me?"

While Noah's touch had been gentle, Rhett's was rough. "Let go of my arm, Rhett. *Now.*"

He didn't. His fingers were like iron bands around her. "Answer my question first."

"You have two seconds to release me before I *make* you."

Footsteps crunched from somewhere off to the side before Jules's voice sounded. "Hey, what's going on?"

"One second left," Addie pushed, not answering Jules.

"I told you, answer my question first." His fingers tightened.

She moved quickly, turning her wrist toward Rhett's thumb, then pulling her arm back and up sharply, using her body weight for momentum.

When he was off-balance, she shot her palm into his nose.

He released her and grabbed his face, blood now pouring between his fingers. *"Fuck!"*

"You touch me again and I'll do worse."

She turned and reached her car just as Jules ran up to her. "Addie, honey, are you okay?"

"I warned him."

"I know you did. I saw." Jules shot a glance at Rhett, who was still leaning over, holding his face. "Should we call Noah or Colt?"

"I'll let Noah know tonight."

Jules's gaze flickered between her eyes. "Are you sure you're okay?"

No. She was shaking. But she didn't feel bad. The asshole had gotten what he deserved. "I'm fine, really."

Jules's frown deepened before she nodded and stepped back.

Addie slid behind the wheel and drove away. She'd just pulled into Noah's drive when her phone vibrated with a text.

Unknown: You're still here, which means you're either stupid or you don't get it. Leave before you make me do something you won't like.

* * *

Noah parked in his driveway, his gaze going to his front door.

He was late getting home. Later than he'd wanted to be. He'd tried to get home earlier, but every time he'd attempted to leave the park, he just wasn't able to.

He'd had another therapy session yesterday, where he'd told Toby about his fear of being around Addie. Toby had suggested that a bit of space might actually be good.

But Addie was in trouble. He didn't want her alone at her place. His house was safer, especially when he was there at night to protect her.

So what the hell was he supposed to do?

He leaned his head back and closed his eyes. Fuck, he was tired. He'd been tired for so damn long.

Eventually, he forced his body up and out of the car.

Inside the house, he keyed his code into the alarm before locking the doors. Just like every other night, he snuck a peek into the master bedroom. Addie was asleep beneath the covers, and she looked so peaceful.

A yearning pulled at his chest. One that called for him to cross the space between them. Wake her up.

Tell her that she was his.

He forced it down. Forced himself to close the door with a quiet click and move into the second bathroom. He took a long shower, letting the water get so hot that his skin burned.

He was just climbing out when a text came through from Jesse.

Jesse: Hey. Heard about the second text. Sorry we haven't made any progress on the case, but know that we're working on it.

A second text? To Addie?

He stepped into the hall and called Jesse.

He answered immediately. "Noah—"

"What the hell are you talking about?"

There was a small pause before Jesse spoke. "Addie didn't tell you? I thought she was staying with you?"

He scrubbed a hand over his face. "I got home late."

"Okay. Well, she called the station. She got a second text tonight. It said that she needed to leave before they did something she wouldn't like."

Noah cursed. Damn, he wanted to kick his own ass. He should have been here. She'd needed him. "I should have been with her."

"Why weren't you?"

"I just have some…stuff going on." It didn't come close to describing what he was going through.

"Anything you want to talk about?"

He was shaking his head before Jesse finished speaking. "Not right now."

"Let me know if that changes. I'm happy to listen."

"Thanks."

"And we're going to find the jerk who's messing with her."

"I know." He trusted his cousin. Jesse was good at his job and he would find them. But when?

Noah hung up, but instead of going to the couch, he stepped into the bedroom and crossed over to her bed, like every part of him was pulled toward her. Unable to stop himself, he crouched beside the bed, and just like he'd done that afternoon, he slipped a lock of hair behind her ear.

Her eyes fluttered open. "You're late."

"I'm sorry. I should have been here."

"Are you okay?"

"Jesse called. Why didn't you tell me about the text?"

"I was going to when you got home."

Yeah. His fault.

"Will you do something for me?" she whispered.

"Anything." And he meant it. In that moment, crouched in front of her, surrounded by her sweet scent, he would have agreed to anything she asked.

"Lie with me. Just for a little bit."

A voice inside him told him it was a bad idea. Told him to step out. Wait until he was safer for her to be around.

But her gaze chained him to the spot. Before he knew what he was doing, he rose and moved to the other side of the bed. The second he was beneath the sheets, he tucked her against him.

And Jesus, she felt good. She was soft and warm, and the sound of her sweet sigh was fucking music to his ears.

For the first time in months, his body relaxed. The feel of her against him silenced the voices in his head that had been deafening him for so long. It unraveled the rope around his chest and just let him feel that thing he hadn't felt in so long—peace.

CHAPTER 13

*L*ight hit the back of Noah's eyelids, making him frown.

Shit, what was the time? Usually he woke before the sun. Hell, he usually woke in the dead of night after a couple hours of broken sleep. But right now he felt rested, something he hadn't felt in a long time.

A small mound of warmth covered his chest, making his frown deepen. It was only when he felt the weight rise and fall, followed by air brushing against his skin, that he realized what it was.

Addie.

His eyes shot open, and he looked down.

He'd fallen asleep with her. *Shit.* He'd only meant to hold her until she fell asleep, then go.

But he couldn't remember waking. Not once. Did that mean there'd been no nightmares? He couldn't remember any.

He lifted a hand off Addie's back. It wasn't shaking. And his heart wasn't racing. There was no pit in his gut that simultaneously made him want to be sick and claw his own skin off.

That hadn't happened since *before*.

A small feminine groan filled the air. Then Addie lifted her head. The second her gaze landed on him, he fell into the deep blue of her eyes. They were still hazy with sleep and so fucking beautiful that they almost took him hostage. Paralyzed him in the best way.

A slow smile curved her lips. "Hey."

"Good morning, Addison."

Her lips twitched. "So formal. How did you sleep?"

"Good, actually. No nightmares." The words were so foreign that they didn't feel like his. Because the nightmares had just become part of his life and who he was.

Her eyes softened. "That's good."

It was better than good. It was kind of unbelievable.

She trailed a finger down his chest, and it sent spirals of warmth somewhere deep inside him. "Maybe you didn't need therapy. Maybe you just needed me."

She was joking. But there was a truth behind her words, because one night of holding her had achieved what countless therapy appointments hadn't. "You might just be right." Without his permission, his thumb grazed her hip. "Did *you* sleep well?"

"I would say 'like a baby' but my mother told me that I was a terrible sleeper as a baby. She prefers the term 'like a father.'"

He chuckled. "Your mother sounds very knowledgeable."

"Hence why I need to learn to live without her voice in my ear." She nibbled her bottom lip. "So…because last night wasn't terrible, maybe you can get home a little earlier from now on?"

He wanted to say yes. He wanted to spend every waking moment with this woman. But there was still uncertainty there. A shit load of it. "It was one night, Addie. I don't want us to get too relaxed. I would never forgive myself if something happened to you by my hands."

"Nothing's going to happen to me. But you're right, it was only one night. We should try another."

"That's a risk."

"I like to think of it more as an experiment." Her gaze lowered to his mouth.

And the combination of the heat of her body, the feel of her bare legs tangled with his, and her warm breath over his skin…it stole the air from his lungs, and he had to remind himself to breathe.

"Addison." But even as he said her name, his fingers curved around her neck and slid into her hair. Her head started to lower…

And he tugged her down that final inch and kissed her.

Fuck, she tasted good. Like oxygen he'd been deprived of for too long. Like everything good he'd been missing this last year.

Her lips separated and he slipped inside, tasting her. Exploring.

She moaned, a low, deep sound that vibrated against him. He wanted to bottle it up, listen to it again and again. Because this woman…she was color in a world that had turned too black-and-white lately. She felt like everything he'd been missing.

Gently, he rolled them over and pressed her to the mattress, his cock hard as it pushed into her core. She hummed and wrapped a leg around his waist, urging him closer.

Somehow, she still tasted damn sweet. Like honey in tea, warm and comforting, but also exciting enough to set his blood roaring through his veins.

He shifted his lips to her throat. All of her tasted the same, so infinitely Addie. When she cupped his cheek, he turned his head and kissed her palm, then her wrist.

He only opened his eyes for a second. A flicker of his eyelids.

But that was all he needed to see it.

The heat in his gut turned cold as he lifted his head and gripped her arm. "What's this?" But he knew what it was. Bruises. Bruises in the shape of a damn hand. Someone had grabbed her.

She blinked once. Twice. The desire in her eyes shifted to confusion. "What's what?"

Gently, he ran his thumb over the small dark circles. "Someone hurt you." The desire of moments ago twisted into something harder. Darker. "Who?"

Her mouth opened and closed. "I was going to tell you last night, but I fell asleep before you got home."

"Okay, so tell me now." It was hard to keep a shred of calm in his voice. He wanted to fucking rage. "Who did this, Addie?"

Her chest rose. "Rhett."

The *fuck*? "Tell me what happened."

"When he walked me to my car, I made a comment about not being interested in him. He grabbed me. I told him to let me go. He didn't, and so I slammed my palm into his nose."

Noah flinched. "He did this last night? When I asked him to walk you back to your car?"

"Did you hear the part about my palm and his nose? I was pretty badass. I'm pretty sure I broke it."

He'd grabbed her, *bruised* her, because Noah had asked him to walk her to her car instead of doing it himself.

He climbed out of bed, anger simmering in his chest as he pulled clothes from his dresser. Anger at Rhett. And anger at himself.

"Where are you going?" she asked quickly, sitting up in bed.

She knew exactly where he was going—to fire the asshole. "We need to get to work."

After a quick shower in the second bathroom, he threw on clothes and grabbed a couple of bagels. He wasn't hungry, but he forced himself to eat while he waited for Addie.

When she finally stepped out of the bedroom, her eyes were cautious. "Noah—"

"Come on. We don't want to be late."

She sighed before taking the bagel he offered and stepping outside.

He trailed her car the entire way to the park, his fingers so tight around the wheel that his knuckles were white.

When they arrived, half a dozen cars already filled the lot. Which meant everyone was probably already at the rock-climbing wall, and they'd all see what was about to happen.

Good. Let them.

Addie looked at him as they walked down the trail. "I'm scared about what you're going to do."

"I'm going to handle the situation."

"Okay, that's not very specific and doesn't exactly fill me with confidence."

"You don't need to worry, Addie."

"I *am* worried."

When they reached the base of the cliff edge, every staff member was already there, setting up equipment for the climb. Rhett stood at the end, a bandage on his nose.

Colt looked up from the equipment box, only to frown. Yeah, Noah probably wore the rage on his face like a mask.

He was moving before he could stop himself.

"Noah—"

He heard Addie's voice, but he didn't stop. Rhett was all he saw.

Rhett had his back turned to Noah when he grabbed his arm and yanked him around.

"Hey, what are you—"

"Get your shit and get out," Noah growled.

Rhett frowned. "What?"

"You heard me. Get. Out. *Now.*"

"Why would I..." His gaze shifted around Noah to Addie. Then he scowled. "What did she say?"

"She told me what happened." A silence fell over the group.

"Yeah? Well, did she tell you she broke my fucking nose?"

Noah stepped closer, the extra few inches of height allowing him to tower over the guy. "She told me you grabbed her. That she asked you to release her, but you didn't."

There was a small gasp from someone. Cass maybe?

Rhett actually stepped closer. "I barely touched her—"

"You *bruised* her."

"Bullshit."

"I saw the marks. Get out before I lose the last scrap of self-restraint I have left and murder you."

Rhett's jaw clenched, and he glanced at Colt. "I'm your most experienced staff member. You're really just gonna let him fire me?"

"We don't assault people here," Colt said, as he stepped beside Noah. "If you don't leave, we'll call the sheriff, who'll get a report about what happened last night."

"This is *bullshit*! I should have reported *her* for assault! You're gonna pay for this." He looked over at Addie. "*All* of you."

* * *

Everything was a mess. A complete and utter mess. She should have told Noah about Rhett when he'd gotten home last night. At least then he would have had the night to calm down, and this morning might not have turned out the way it had.

Yes, Rhett deserved to be fired, but she hated that every member of staff had seen. Well, not every member. Jules was sick.

Addie should have told everyone she was sick.

She looked up at the wall. Had it gotten bigger in the last few minutes? Because it looked bigger. And to make matters worse, she'd been so preoccupied about everything that had happened with Rhett, she'd barely heard a word Noah or Colt said to the group. They probably hadn't gone through all the how-to stuff anyway because everyone else could climb a freaking wall.

This was bad. Really bad.

And guess who was first on the pre-arranged climbing rotation? She and Buck were. Because a week ago, silly Addie had thought that going first would mean getting her turn out of the way.

She was regretting *all* her decisions.

"Ready?"

Her head shot up at Noah's voice. "What?"

"Are you ready to do some rock climbing?"

Absolutely not. "Yep."

His lips twitched. Did he know she was lying?

He touched the small of her back and led her to the second pile of equipment.

Oh, and something else she hadn't told anyone…she wasn't a fan of heights. She wasn't phobia-level scared, but she'd once stood on the edge of a cliff and gotten so nauseous that she'd almost been sick right then and there.

Noah helped her into her harness.

She studied the dark gray of his eyes. "Are you okay?"

"Better now that he's gone."

She nodded quickly, her gaze once again returning to the wall before going back to him. "So, I know that this morning's already been a lot, with my confession in bed and you and Colt firing Rhett, but I have another one for you."

"You've never rock climbed before."

Her jaw dropped. "How did you know?"

This time when he looked at her, humor played in his eyes. "You told me a story one time about how you went for a walk, ate a fly, then didn't go outside for an entire week. And you once referred to this harness as 'that safety thing.' There have been other signs too."

Of course he knew. "I'm sorry I lied."

"I'm not. I'm glad you wanted the job. And I wanted you to have it."

Her bottom lip disappeared between her teeth before she glanced down at Noah's strong, capable fingers as he cinched the strap on the harness. The combination of his closeness and the way the muscles in his arms flexed almost had her forgetting about the climb.

"I'm sorry about Rhett too," she said.

His smile dropped. "I'm not. He hurt you."

"I hurt him back."

Not even a small lift of the lips.

Once the harness was in place, Noah reached for her wrist, and just like he'd done that morning, he swiped his thumb over the bruises. "He shouldn't have touched you. No man should ever touch you if you don't want them too. Especially not like that."

Her breath caught, the touch and his words feeling intimate and warm over her skin.

She swallowed hard. "Any tips on climbing this wall?"

He grabbed the rope and threaded it through the carabiner of the harness. "At first it will feel unnatural to hang on the wall and trust the rope. But remember, you're safe. Your legs are strongest, so let them do the heavy lifting. Your arms are more like poles than anchors. Look before you move and keep your hips close to the wall."

She nodded, not sure how much of that she'd taken in, but hopefully she remembered at least part of it.

"And most importantly," Noah added, stepping back. "Don't panic if you slip. The rope's got you—and so do I."

"Don't panic if I slip. Got it."

If? Ha. Just last week she'd slipped on perfectly non-slippery asphalt for no reason at all. None. Slipping on a vertical wall was inevitable.

When she was all harnessed in, he looked at her, his smile almost calming her racing heart. "Ready?"

"It's too late to say no, right?"

"It's never too late to say no."

She sighed and looked up. She wasn't going to back out…even if her brain shouted at her that she was going to die. She worked at a freaking wilderness park. She needed to at least give rock climbing a try. "I'm ready."

He touched her hips. "Remember, I've got you."

She nodded and turned to the wall. Okay, this time it definitely looked bigger.

Beside her, Buck was already a few feet up. He seemed to be struggling a bit. Though, when she started climbing, Buck was going to look like a freaking professional.

She chalked her hands before reaching for the first hold. She took a step up, then looked behind her to see Noah's eyes on her gear. Her harness. The rope.

Safe. She was safe. And her rope would catch her if she slipped.

She found an edge for her foot and stepped up again, the click of the rope sliding another reminder that Noah was there, holding her and making sure that she was okay.

She took another step up, then another.

She was doing it. She was actually rock climbing! Yes, the rock bit into her fingers and the muscles in her thighs were already burning, but she was almost halfway up the wall. She was doing a heck of a lot better than she'd expected. She should have asked someone to take a photo so her parents believed her when she told them.

She reached up and found another hold with her left hand.

She was just pulling herself up when Buck grunted beside her.

Addie glanced over to see the rope catch him as he slipped off the rock. She was about to turn back to the wall when someone shouted. Her gaze shot back to Buck to see him drop to the ground, part of the snapped rope falling with him.

Everything narrowed to a single sharp point of disbelief.

The rope had snapped. How was that possible? Would *hers* snap?

She jerked her gaze up, but as she did, her foot skidded and she fell off the wall.

Chaos sounded from below, but she singled out one voice. Noah's.

"Grab onto the wall, Addison. Quickly!"

Heart thundering, she reached for the wall, getting it with her fingertips before pulling herself toward it. It took a second to find her footing, but as soon as she did, she looked up again—and this time she saw the thinning of her own rope.

Oh, Jesus…it was almost at the snapping point. That hadn't been like that at the start of the climb.

Her breathing shortened. One wrong step, one slip of the foot and she'd fall, and the rope wouldn't hold her.

She looked down to see Colt and Flint working on Buck. He'd fallen onto crash pads but he wasn't moving. Maybe he'd hit them at a bad angle. She had no idea.

Oh God, oh God, oh God.

She looked back at the rock and closed her eyes, fear making nausea swell in her belly.

"Addison, don't move. I'm coming," Noah called.

She barely heard him. His voice competed with the roaring of blood between her ears.

She tried to focus on her breathing, knowing if she focused too much on what *could* happen, her grip on the wall might loosen.

It was fine. She'd be fine. Noah said he was coming and she trusted him.

She wasn't sure how long she waited, just breathing through the panic, but the shuffle of movement sounded beside her. She turned her head to see Noah. He was so close that the warmth of his side penetrated her own.

"I can't move," she whispered.

"You're doing great. You're doing exactly what I asked you to do."

She inhaled a long shaky breath. "Is Buck okay?"

"Don't worry about Buck. Colt and Flint are taking care of him."

She nodded quickly, but the move was jerky. "I'm scared."

"I'm not going anywhere, and I'm not going to let anything happen to you."

She wasn't alone. Noah was here. She was safe with him. She just had to keep reminding herself of that.

"I'm clipping us together, okay?" Noah reached across and clipped her harness into a locking carabiner on his belay loop so that they were tethered together. He also unclipped the rope she'd been attached to. "You're riding with me, honey."

He smiled, and the small action thawed just a bit of the panic that crawled through her belly.

"Now, I need you to do something for me," he said gently.

She wasn't sure if she could do anything, but still she nodded.

"I need you to slide between me and the wall, wrap your arms around my shoulders and your legs around my waist."

Move? He wanted her to *move*? "I don't know if I can."

"You can. Trust me." He curled an arm around her waist. "I won't let you fall."

"I trust you." There was so much truth in her words. Despite the fear and the panic, something about Noah made her okay with putting her life in his hands. But also, she didn't really have any other options.

Letting go of the wall was hard, but she forced her fingers to uncurl. Her right arm trembled as it locked around his neck.

"That's good, Addison. Now the other."

The other hand was harder. It was her last grasp on the wall. She took one deep breath before turning her body and wrapping her other arm around his shoulders.

"That's good. Now wrap your legs nice and tight around my waist like this." He gripped her right thigh and gently guided it around his waist. "Feel safe?"

It was crazy, but she did. "Yes."

"Good. Let's get the hell off this wall."

He began to climb down, his moves slow and deliberate. She clung to him, feeling the muscles straining in his back. He wasn't connected to anything, but he probably didn't trust the equipment anymore. She certainly didn't.

"Almost there," he whispered. "I've got you."

She closed her eyes and dug her head into the crook of his neck. Her eyes were still closed when there was a soft thud. She opened them to see that Noah stood on the ground.

They'd made it. They were safe.

But she didn't release him, and he didn't set her down. She just held him, letting the power in his body chase away that last bit of fear.

CHAPTER 14

*A*ddie pulled on an oversized sweatshirt. It was Noah's but it had been sitting on his chair, and it looked big and warm, and she needed both those things right now. Even though she'd just broken a record for the longest, hottest shower, she somehow still felt cold.

Someone had tampered with the rock-climbing ropes today. Someone had tried to hurt her.

She still couldn't wrap her head around it. If Noah wasn't the former Marine that he was, she could have been seriously hurt, just like Buck. Not that she'd received an update on Buck—all she knew was that he hadn't regained consciousness before the ambulance had arrived.

Her breathing was shaky as she left the bedroom. The second she stepped into the hall, she heard him. Noah was shout-whispering over the phone, and the anger in his voice…God, she could almost feel it.

"It was Rhett, Jesse, I know it was. The asshole helped set up the equipment. He had access to the climbing rotation, so he knew Addie and Buck were going up first. He was trying to hurt her. Hell, he already bruised her arm last night. He also had the means to steal her key from her bag. All it would have taken was telling Addie or Cass at the desk that he needed to use the kitchen while they were at the front desk."

It was true. All of it. But her question was—why? Why would Rhett want to scare her? *Hurt* her?

Noah turned when she walked into the kitchen, and the second he saw her, he scanned her from head to toe. He seemed to take in her bare legs. His sweatshirt over her body.

She stopped at the kitchen island and lifted herself up to the edge.

Noah poured dark liquid into a mug before handing it to her.

Hot chocolate. Thank God. It was exactly what she needed.

"I know." Noah sighed. "I just…I want him in your custody. I want him off the streets so that he doesn't have the opportunity to hurt her or anyone else again."

She sipped the hot chocolate, closing her eyes as the sweet liquid warmed her belly. What the heck had Noah put in this? She scanned the counter behind him, but he'd already cleaned up.

"Thanks, Jess." Noah hung up and turned to her, gaze intense. "How are you feeling?"

"Like I will never rock climb again in my life. In fact, count me out of all semi-dangerous, could-fall-to-my-death outdoor activities."

He growled like he didn't find it the least bit funny before gripping her thighs and stepping closer. "You should have been safe up there."

"Does Jesse know what happened?"

There was a small pause when Noah's eyes darkened to the color of coal. "Battery acid. Someone coated the middle of the rope with it. When it evaporated, the rope didn't look any different, but because the rope's made of nylon, it weakened the internal fibers."

"Which made it break when weight was applied," Addie whispered, her skin suddenly cold again. "So it had to be whoever set it up, right? They needed the middle part of the rope to be coated in the acid so that no one smelled it."

"Colt said Rhett, Cass and Buck were the first ones there, and they set up the rope. Cass said she didn't see Rhett do anything wrong, and we haven't been able to ask Buck yet."

"How is Buck?"

"The crash pad saved him from any serious damage, but because of the angle he hit, he has a concussion and a broken wrist. He'll spend the night in the hospital."

Jesus.

"Why?" Addie whispered, the question one that had popped into her head so many times. "Why would Rhett do it?"

"I don't know. But one way or another, we're going to find out." His hands slid up her bare thighs, making the hairs on her arms stand on end. "The important thing is, you didn't get hurt today."

"What does this mean for the park?"

"We'll close down for a week or two. Have all the equipment checked and make sure it's safe before we reopen. Hopefully in that time, Jesse can find the evidence he needs on Rhett."

Thank God they'd been closed to the public today.

She focused on Noah. He was close, standing between her legs, hands on her thighs… It was the best kind of distraction. *He* was the best kind of distraction. "Thank you for saving me."

"When I saw your rope almost snap, everything else disappeared." His fingers tightened on her hips. "You scared me."

"You didn't look scared."

"I was terrified. Of you being hurt. Of me not being able to get to you in time. And I just kept thinking…I shouldn't have run from us."

Her heart lurched then stuttered, the beats wild as she played his words over in her head. "What should you have done?"

"This."

He lowered his head and groaned as he kissed her. The kiss

wasn't fast or rushed or desperate. It was slow. Gently coaxing her lips apart before he slipped his tongue inside her mouth.

Then she was tasting him. And God, he tasted good. Whiskey and a hint of mint.

She ran her hands up his chest and around his shoulders. Strong shoulders that, just a few hours ago, had been all that stood between her and a fall that would have hurt her.

She curved her legs around his waist and tugged them closer together. Then she felt him everywhere. In front of her. Around her. Flush against her body.

His hands moved higher, pushing up the sweatshirt. She liked his touch. It made her feel alive and feminine and wanted.

A small gasp escaped her lips when she was lifted off the island. Then they were moving, walking through the house and only stopping inside his bedroom.

Gently, he lay her flat on the bed, his body hovering over hers. Covering her. Warming her.

"Do you want this?" Noah whispered, his words like gravel. "If you don't, I'll stop."

"I want this. I want you. I've wanted you for so long."

A deep growl rumbled from his powerful chest before his head dropped, his mouth latching onto her neck so he could taste her skin.

Oh, God, yes. Yes to him and this and everything he made her feel. She wanted all of it. And she didn't care if that made her desperate.

She was so absorbed in the feel of his mouth on her neck that she barely felt him grip the edge of her sweatshirt until cool air hit her belly. She lifted her arms to help him before the soft thud of fabric hitting the floor cut through the room. Then she lay there in panties.

"Beautiful," he whispered, as his sweet kisses trailed down her chest.

When he took one nipple between his lips, she couldn't

breathe. She arched as his teeth grazed her hard bud. Then his tongue ran over it, flicking it back and forth and running in a circle.

It was torture. All of it. This man and the way he made her belly pulse like nothing and no one ever had before.

He sucked hard and she felt it everywhere. It made her writhe and bow her back.

He shifted to her other nipple and started the same slow torment. But this time, he also played with the breast he'd just released. Rolling the bud between his thumb and forefinger, pushing his thumb into the center.

She was drowning in Noah. The desire was wrapping around her lungs, keeping her head beneath water. But she didn't want to come up for air.

When he lowered his hand between her thighs, she stilled. Then he slid inside her panties.

Her thighs instinctively parted, giving him space to touch her. He took it, swiping across her clit.

A gasp cut from her throat, and she grabbed at his hair, tugging and pulling.

"Every sound you make drives me crazy," he whispered, before kissing up her chest and taking her lips again.

She kissed him. A deep kiss where their tongues tangled and any world beyond him and what he made her feel just ceased to exist. His thumb continued to move over her core, and she ground into him.

"You have too many clothes on," she whispered, the words barely leaving her lips before she yanked at the hem of his shirt.

He chuckled and slid to the side so he could remove his shirt and his jeans.

Her heart jumped at the sight of him in just briefs. Every inch of the man was power and strength.

She ran a finger over the scar on his shoulder, then another on his arm. He'd been through so much. And yet he was still here, trying to be better. Trying to overcome all his demons.

Slowly, she lifted her head and kissed the first scar. Then the second.

The air hissing through his teeth was loud. He gripped her wrist, the one that was still touching the scar, and kissed the inside. The second his mouth found hers again, she ran her hand down his chest and beneath the waistband of his briefs.

When her fingers wrapped around his length, the muscles in his chest expanded, his head dropping to the crook of her neck.

She slid her hand up until she reached his tip, then she ran her palm over him.

A shudder rolled down his body, and he groaned as she ran her palm back down to his base.

His reaction to every touch made her feel powerful and wanted and his.

"Addie." There was something dangerous in the way he said her name...like it was a warning.

She didn't listen. She wasn't finished touching and exploring him...learning what drove him as wild as he drove her.

But when he lifted off the bed, it was too soon, and she groaned in frustration.

He chuckled before pushing down his briefs. Then he stood in front of her completely naked. Her mouth went dry, her belly doing something between a somersault and a clench.

God, he was beautiful. If he stood still long enough, he'd almost look like one of those perfect sculptures.

He reached for the side drawer and pulled out a foil that he tore open with his teeth. Before he could slide it on, she sat up and took it from his fingers. Slowly, she rolled it down his length, her lower belly throbbing at the feel of him.

He growled, a long, deep sound, then gently pushed her back and dragged her panties down her legs.

Finally he lay between her thighs, and she could feel him right there at her entrance. It was intoxicating.

His gaze bored into her as he whispered, "Last chance to walk away?"

He thought she could walk away from this? He was already under her skin, deep inside her chest… He was everywhere.

She hooked a leg around his waist and tugged, feeling his tip slip inside her. "I've never walked away from something I've wanted. And I'm not going to start now."

Her name hit the air like a flare, before he dropped his head and kissed her while sinking deep inside her.

* * *

NOAH BURNED FOR ADDIE. She was like a flame that never died. And right now, the feel of her walls wrapped around his cock lit a fire in his blood.

He tangled his tongue with hers, forcing his body to remain exactly where it was, to ignore the urge to drive into her.

She groaned and rolled her hips, testing his self-restraint.

Shit, this woman killed him.

Slowly, he lifted his hips and pushed back inside.

Oh, Jesus, she felt good.

Her nails bit into his shoulders, her breath running over his mouth as she gasped. Even the fucking scent of her made him lose his mind.

He kissed across her cheek, then behind her ear, sucking her delicate skin as he continued to thrust in and out. Every moan, every time her body did that thing where her back arched and her nails raked over his skin, he was pushed that much closer to the edge.

He gripped her knee to lift it higher, hitting a new point inside her. The need to see her had him lifting his head. He watched the desire play over her face. The scrunch of her eyes. The separation of her lips as air panted out of her.

Perfect. She was fucking perfect. And she was *his*.

He lowered his head and kissed her while reaching for her breast and holding the small mound in his palm. When he found her nipple, he rolled it in a circle.

She gasped. He did it again. Her hips began to lift, meeting him thrust for thrust, drawing him deeper inside her.

Fuck, he was almost at the tipping point.

He thrust harder. Faster. And when he shifted his hand from her breast to her clit, he ran his thumb over the spot that made her entire body tremble. He did it again.

"Noah…" Her voice was almost a plea. And he knew exactly what she needed.

Simultaneously, he sucked her neck and rolled her clit, his movements fast and hard, before finally she cried out, her head flinging back as her walls pulsed around his cock. She broke beneath him, and it was fucking glorious.

He continued to move, but he didn't have much left. Everything that was his now belonged to her.

He dropped his head and kissed her, sinking his tongue deep into her mouth. Three more thrusts and he finally broke, growling deep in his throat as his entire body shattered.

Then the room shifted into silence as he lowered his head into the crook of her neck and breathed her in.

Her softness, her sweet scent, all of it called to him.

Her fingers ran down his back, her chest rising and falling in quick succession. "If there's any way to turn a shitty day around, it's that."

Despite everything, he laughed and lifted his head. "You're something else. You know that?"

"Something pretty?"

"No. Pretty is a drop in the bucket compared to what you are."

The smile disappeared and a hot intensity burned in her eyes.

"What we just did…it wasn't a reaction to what happened today, was it? It didn't happen out of fear of losing me? You're not going to wake up tomorrow and tell me it was a mistake?"

He fingered a lock of hair from her cheek. "I'd be lying if I said the fear and doubt weren't there. I'm only a week into therapy and I have a lot of work to do. But I want you. And maybe that makes me selfish."

"It doesn't. It makes you human. I want you too."

"Good." He lowered his head and kissed her, one soft kiss before dropping beside her and tucking her into him. "Do you need anything?"

At her pause, he frowned.

A half smile played at her lips. "I might have seen some peanut butter cups on your counter."

She was thinking about chocolate right now? "You're hungry?"

She lifted a shoulder. "I don't need to be hungry to want chocolate."

He laughed. Jesus Christ, Addison was like no one he'd ever met. He kissed her forehead before climbing out of bed. "I'll be back in a sec."

He stopped in the bathroom to clean up before pulling on some briefs and heading to the kitchen. But the second he was away from her, his mind shifted back to what had happened earlier that day. To Buck's rope breaking and him falling. To Addie almost experiencing the same fate.

That same fear he'd felt in the moment returned.

He wanted to kill Rhett. Because that was who'd done this. Noah was sure of it. Now he needed to work out why.

CHAPTER 15

The tick of the clock on Noah's living room wall was driving Addie crazy. The kind of crazy where she couldn't work or even concentrate.

Okay, maybe the clock wasn't the only reason she wasn't being productive. But how was she supposed to work when someone had tried to hurt her yesterday?

She looked at the time on the laptop screen.

Shit. Three hours. She'd been working for three freaking hours and all she'd done was reschedule a couple of bookings and order some new equipment. That was it.

Jesus.

She scrubbed a hand over her face. Maybe she should take up coffee drinking. The stuff was supposed to help focus, right?

Ha, the last time she'd forced coffee down her throat, she'd felt sick for the next four hours. Yes, she disliked it that much.

Maybe Noah's living room couch was too soft?

Or maybe, she needed to stop blaming everything else and just work.

Focus, Addie.

Her phone rang.

Thank God.

The relief quickly evaporated though when she saw who it was.

Her mother. Possibly both her parents.

Crap.

She'd called this morning to let them know what had happened. *But* she'd intentionally done it at a ridiculously early time, knowing her mother's phone would be on silent so that she could very cowardly leave a voice message.

She set the phone to her ear. "Hey, Mom."

"Are you okay?" Her mother's words were sharp and rushed.

"I'm absolutely fine."

"How the hell did the rope break?" her father growled.

"Um, someone actually put battery acid on it." She wrinkled her nose at what was about to come.

Her mother gasped, but it was her father who yelled, "*What?*"

"But I'm fine," she rushed to add. "And Buck only broke his wrist and got a concussion."

Only? Not only. It was awful.

"Who's Buck?" her mother asked, almost sounding like she was crying.

"The other guy who was climbing. His rope snapped and he fell. I grabbed the wall before my rope completely broke, and Noah climbed up to save me."

There was a long silence, and yeah, she knew she was leaving a lot of gaps.

"Addison Marie March." She cringed at her father full-naming her. "What is going on over there?"

She wanted to lie…but she didn't. "I've received a few…texts."

"Texts?" her mother asked, sounding confused.

"Someone's been messaging me from an unknown number, telling me to leave Amber Ridge or else."

"Come home." Her father's response was immediate. It was also hard and unyielding. It was the former Marine in him who was used to people following his orders. "We didn't want you to move out anyway."

"Your father's right," her mother added. "It's too dangerous."

There was such a big part of her that wanted to make her parents happy. She loved them so much that she almost needed to give them what they wanted. But with this, she just couldn't. "I'm not coming home. I'm sorry. I like it here. I enjoy my job. And there's someone I care about."

"You're dating someone?" her mother asked.

"Yes." Or at least, she was pretty sure that was what they were doing. Living in Noah's house, sleeping with him…that was dating.

"Who?" her father asked.

"His name is Noah, and he's—"

"Your boss?"

She cringed against her mother's sharp question. "Yes."

"The Marine," her father added. "How old is he?"

"Thirty-five."

There was a sharp gasp from her mother.

Okay, this conversation was not going the way it should. "Look, I know I've just given you a lot of information. The short version is this: someone has sent a couple of texts telling me to get out of town. The sheriff is aware. I'm staying at Noah's house, and he has a great security system. Yes, I almost got hurt yesterday, but Noah got me out of the situation without so much as a scratch."

"Darling." Her mother was crying, or at least on the verge of it. "Please come home."

She swallowed hard, closing her eyes. It hurt to say no. But she couldn't give up this life. "I'm sorry, Mom. I can't. I'm building a life here. But you don't need to worry about me. I'm being smart, and I have really good guys looking out for me." She glanced back at her laptop. "I have to go because I'm working, but I'll call again tomorrow, okay?"

They didn't sound happy, but finally her parents let her go.

Guilt swirled in her belly. She hated feeling like she was disappointing them. And more than that, her mother was a worrier. They were getting old, and she didn't want to stress them out.

But she liked the life she was creating here. She couldn't let some random person scare her away. She felt safe with Noah. Besides, she needed to get to the bottom of what the heck was going on. If she left and the threats stopped, she'd never know.

She looked back at her screen, and if it was possible, she felt even *less* motivated than she had before the call.

What she needed was one of Mrs. Gerald's frosted chocolate creams from The Tea House. And maybe pie. Yes, pie was the fixer of all problems.

She snapped the laptop shut.

The second she stepped outside, her eyes scanned the street and her fingers hovered inside her bag, where her can of pepper spray sat. Quickly, she crossed to her car, breathing a sigh of relief when she dropped inside and locked the doors.

Maybe she didn't have a reason to be scared anymore. Maybe Jesse was questioning Rhett right now, Rhett was confessing to everything, and she was about to get a call that she was safe.

Ha. When did things work out that smoothly? Plus, Rhett didn't seem the type to just confess to attempted murder or whatever it was he'd done yesterday.

When she reached The Tea House, she'd just climbed out when her phone rang, Noah's name on the screen.

Her cheeks heated at the sight of his name. At the memory of what they'd done last night. Then this morning, waking up naked in his arms.

How was she supposed to leave him and them and what they were creating?

She wasn't.

She answered as she crossed the parking lot. "Hey."

"Hey." There was a small pause. "You're outside?"

"I'm about to step inside The Tea House to get a drink and some pie."

Noah cursed. "You shouldn't be alone. I could have come with you. I'm just around the corner. I'll be there in less than a minute."

"I don't intend to stay long. I—" She stopped just inside The Tea House. *Oh no.* "Rhett." His name was a whisper on her lips. He stood by the counter, but even from behind she recognized him.

"*Rhett's* there?" Noah growled.

Rhett turned, and the second he saw her, his eyes narrowed.

Shit. Not good. She lowered the phone. "Rhett—"

"You blamed me?" He got so close, she could almost feel his breath on her face.

"I—"

"They questioned me for *hours*. Made me feel like a fucking criminal!"

"Look—"

"No, *you* look." Another step forward. Now he was crowding her. "I—"

"Is there a problem here?"

Addie looked up to see a tall, dangerous-looking man beside them. He had dark hair and blue eyes.

Rhett scowled at him. "Mind your own fucking business, man."

"When I see a woman being yelled at by an asshole, I *make* it my business."

Addie opened her mouth, not sure what words were about to come out, when the door opened behind her.

* * *

"WHAT DO YOU MEAN, you couldn't hold him?" Noah snapped, frustration heating his breath.

Jesse sighed from behind his desk at the sheriff's station. "It's an open criminal investigation and we didn't have the evidence to arrest him. Yes, he set up the equipment, but so did two other people, and none of them admitted to seeing any wrongdoing. He consented to us checking his car, and we didn't find any battery acid."

"So, because he's good at covering his ass, he gets to walk free?"

Jesse leaned forward and said each word slowly and deliberately. "We're paying him another visit today under the pretense of a routine follow-up. We're going to look for any inconsistencies in his story. We'll also ask to search his home."

Noah laughed. "Even if there *had* been something incriminating, it'll be long gone now."

"We're doing everything we can, Noah."

It wasn't enough. Buck had already been injured yesterday, and Addie easily could have been hurt too.

He pushed his seat back and rose to his feet.

"Where are you going?" Jesse asked.

"To Addie. If this asshole's still out there, then she's not safe."

He knew he wasn't being fair to his cousin. Jesse was good at his job, and of course he was doing everything he could to keep his town and the people in it safe. But fuck, Noah was angry.

He was halfway to the door when Jesse grabbed his arm. "Listen." Jesse waited for him to turn before finishing. "I'm working on this, okay? I'm not going to stop until we've nailed the person responsible."

"I know. I appreciate what you're doing."

Jesse squeezed Noah's arm, and he left his cousin's office. He'd just reached his car when Colt called. He waited until he was inside the vehicle to answer. "What's up?"

"Have you spoken to Jesse?"

"They didn't have enough evidence to hold him." Even saying the words out loud made him furious all over again.

There was a small pause. "Is it possible it wasn't him? Yes, he grabbed her the night before, but that doesn't mean he'd go so far as to want her or Buck to fall off the cliff."

"If not him, then who? Buck wouldn't have done this to himself. It could be Cass. That's something Jesse's also looking into. But it still brings up the question—why? Addie's adamant that she doesn't have any enemies here. Who would have something to gain from her leaving town?"

"Maybe we should do some more digging on everyone at the park, just in case. Cass is coming in today. I can talk to her."

"Addie and I can visit Buck and see if he remembers anything that he forgot to tell Jesse."

"Good." Colt was quiet for a moment. "Do you need anything?"

Yeah, he needed to figure out what the hell was going on. "You're already doing what I need by helping with this."

"Of course. Talk again soon."

When the call ended, Noah pulled onto the road and used the car Bluetooth to call Addie.

She answered on the second ring. "Hey."

He frowned at the wind blowing over the line. "Hey. You're outside?"

"I'm about to step inside The Tea House to get a drink and some pie."

Noah cursed. "You shouldn't be alone. I could have come with you. I'm just around the corner. I'll be there in less than a minute." With Rhett or whoever the hell this was still out there, she shouldn't be alone *anywhere*.

He took a right, The Tea House already in view.

"I don't intend to stay long. I—" Addie stopped mid-sentence. "Rhett."

"*Rhett's* there?" Noah growled.

Fuck.

He sped down the street, then slammed his foot on the brake outside The Tea House.

When he crashed through the door, he saw Rhett crowding Addie. But there was also a second guy there. He was tall and standing beside them.

Noah walked straight up to Rhett and shoved him back. "What the hell are you doing?"

"What am *I* doing? I'm explaining to your girlfriend that because of *her*, I had to sit through hours of questioning."

"Did you do it?"

The younger man scowled. "Fuck you!"

Noah went to step forward, but the stranger grabbed his shoulder. "Not here."

A hollow laugh burst from Rhett's chest. "I'm done with this anyway."

He stormed out, and every part of Noah wanted to follow him. Grab him. Force him to admit to what he'd done.

But Jesse would kick his ass. He had to trust Jesse to get the information they needed.

"Who are *you*?" Noah asked the other guy, the words sounding like more of a bark.

"Just someone trying to get a coffee." He glanced at Addie. "You good?"

She nodded, and the guy headed out of The Tea House.

Noah closed the bit of distance between him and Addie. "What happened?"

"He didn't do anything. He was just angry that he got called into the sheriff's office for questioning." She shot a glance over her shoulder, like she was looking for Rhett. "I would have thought he'd be at the station."

"Jesse didn't have enough to hold him." Second time saying it, and it sounded just as fucking ridiculous as the first.

Her brows flickered but she nodded.

Damn, he hated how sad she looked, especially after the night they'd had.

He cupped her cheek, forcing the tension in her face to ease. "You know what you need? Chocolate."

She laughed. "I *always* need chocolate, no traumatic week necessary."

"Well, let's allow Mrs. Gerald to make this morning a bit better."

They stepped up to the counter and were waiting for the café owner to reach them when Addie's phone beeped with a text.

At her gasp, he looked over in time to see her face pale. Then he glanced down at the text on the screen.

Unknown: You know, Buck would be okay if you'd done what I asked. I suggest you get out before another person gets hurt.

CHAPTER 16

Something brushed across Addie's cheek, tugging her out of sleep. She didn't want to wake up though. Her dream had included Noah and chocolate and a lazy day on the couch.

Another stroke of her cheek. A finger maybe? She squeezed her eyelids tight before slowly opening them to see a wide chest and broad shoulders. *Clothed* broad shoulders. Noah was fully dressed and perched on the edge of the bed, while she was completely naked beneath the sheets.

A slow smile curved her lips as she rolled to her side, making sure to keep the sheet above her chest. "Hey. Where are you going?"

"I have a therapy session."

She frowned. "That's at nine."

Amusement twinkled in his eyes. "It's eight thirty."

What? She'd slept in until eight thirty? Crap. "I promise I will be ready to start my workday at nine on the dot." Maybe nine thirty.

One side of his mouth lifted. "You start whenever you're ready."

That was a good perk of dating the boss. "How did you sleep?"

"Good, actually." He frowned. "It's strange. It's only when I sleep with you that I *actually* sleep."

She reached out and braided her fingers through his. "That's good."

"I don't understand how that works."

"Maybe you feel safe with me." She wanted him to feel safe with her. As safe with her as she felt with him.

"You're right, I do." A slow heat gathered in his eyes. "Are you going to be okay here by yourself?"

"Without you here to distract me, I might actually be able to get some work done." Yeah, freaking right. She'd come to the realization that productivity and working from home did not come hand in hand for her. At least not while so much else was going on.

"You think I'm a distraction?" he asked, far too innocently.

She could have laughed. "Yesterday, I was fixing a broken link on the website when you picked me up, carried me to the bedroom, and threw me onto the bed."

"I didn't hear any complaining."

"Well, of course not. You took off your shirt. Have you *seen* you without a shirt?"

His smile widened, and he lowered his head and kissed her, his lips lingering before he finally lifted again. "I'll lock up after myself. Keep the house locked and alarmed."

"Damn, there goes my idea of having an open-house rager."

He shook his head. "What am I going to do with you?"

"I can think of a few things."

He laughed, and the second he stepped out of the room, she missed him. It was instant and it made the room too quiet.

Gah, she was becoming far too obsessed with the man. She pulled the pillow over her face.

What she needed was a shower. A long, hot shower.

After a full thirty minutes in the shower, she dressed in black leggings, an oversized sweater, and wooly socks before popping two pieces of bread into the toaster.

She'd just lowered to the couch with her toast and laptop when her phone rang, Jules's name on the screen.

"Hi, Jules."

"Addie, honey, I'm just checking in to see how you're doing."

A small smile touched her lips. Jules had been checking in regularly, and Addie was so grateful for that. "I'm okay. I'd be better if they arrested the person who tampered with the ropes, but I keep reminding myself that it will take time."

"I know you haven't said it, but you think it's Rhett, right? After he grabbed you the way he did in that parking lot?"

She squirmed uncomfortably on the couch. She'd intentionally not said his name to anyone because they had no proof of it being him. "I'm not sure."

"Well, I'm glad those boys fired him anyway after the way he treated you."

"Me too. Have you heard from Buck?"

"I'm taking him a big container of pasta this afternoon."

Of course she was. "He'll love that."

"I'm bringing you one too."

"Oh, you don't need—"

"Of course I do. Feeding people is my love language. And what about a slab of chocolate brownies? The recipe I make is divine. My secret ingredient is walnuts."

"Walnuts?"

"Yes, ma'am. I'll drop both off this afternoon."

"Jules, you really don't have to do that. I'm okay."

"And you'll be even better with my chocolate brownie. Text me your address. I'll see you later, honey."

Jules hung up before Addie could protest a third time, but honestly, would a third protest do anything? Doubtful.

Addie had just set her cell on the coffee table when the doorbell rang.

Good God, the universe really didn't want her to start work today.

Slowly, she crossed to the front door and looked through the peephole to see Indie, Noah's sister, holding a tray. Had Noah known she was coming?

She opened the door. "Hi. I'm sorry, Noah isn't here."

"That's okay. I can drop this casserole off to you."

"A casserole?" Was feeding her an Amber Ridge thing?

"Noah told me about your scare on the rock-climbing wall. I just wanted to help in some way."

It was official, she was never moving back to Bozeman, because people here were too nice. What would have happened if she'd actually been hurt? Food for a week? A month?

Addie stepped back. "Come in."

"Thanks." Indie crossed over to the kitchen, where she set the casserole down. "Man, I love Noah's house. Isn't this butcher-block countertop just amazing?"

After locking and alarming the door, she joined Indie in the kitchen. "The house is really beautiful. He mentioned he did some of the work himself."

His sister chuckled. "Yeah, because completely tearing the old park apart and putting it back together wasn't enough for him. That man doesn't know how to stay still."

"I think staying busy helps with everything."

Indie frowned. "Everything?"

Shit. She'd just assumed Indie knew. They were siblings. And they were close. Indie visited the park all the time, plus she was married to Colt.

"Um…" *Shit. Say something, Addie.* "I'm just referring to transitioning back into civilian life after being in the Marines for so long."

Indie's frown deepened before she stepped closer. "Addie, did something happen to Noah?"

Oh, gosh, she'd really put her foot into it. "You should really talk to him about it."

Indie seemed to consider her words for a moment before nodding. "I've kind of had a feeling something was going on with him, and I kept waiting for him to open up to me. But so far, he hasn't."

"Sometimes it's hardest to share things with those we're closest to."

"Maybe. Or maybe he thinks he's protecting me after what I've been through." She shook her head. "Sorry, I shouldn't be dropping this on you."

"It's absolutely fine. It's nice to have someone to talk to. And it's good to have a distraction from work, which I've discovered I am not good at doing from home. Why don't you stay for a coffee?"

"I thought you didn't drink coffee?"

"*I* don't. But *you* do. Plus, I don't have a lot of work to do while the park's closed anyway. You'll be doing me a favor." She moved to the coffeemaker, and over the next hour, she sat and talked and laughed with Noah's sister. She hadn't spent a lot of time with Indie, but the other woman was easy to talk to.

When it was finally time for Indie to go, Addie stepped outside with her and waved goodbye. She was about to close the door when a sound came from the side of the house. Almost like a foot against ground. It could be an animal.

It could also *not*.

Quickly, she closed the door and flicked the lock.

Then she got angry. Angry that she was living in fear. Angry that something as small as a quiet sound beside the house could make her heart rate shoot up.

This person needed to be found, and they needed to be arrested *now*.

* * *

"How did you feel when you saw the rope almost snap?"

Noah's hands balled into fists at Toby's question. "Scared. Really fucking scared. Then I was relieved after I helped her down. Then angry again that it happened." Hell, angry barely touched the surface of what he'd felt.

"Angry at who?"

"The person who did it."

"But you don't know who that was?"

"I have a pretty good idea. But the asshole not being behind bars doesn't help the anger."

Toby nodded, his face neutral like always. "Is this person the only one you're angry at?"

Did Toby see it that easily? "I'm angry at myself too."

"Why? You didn't hurt her."

"It happened on my watch. I should have checked all the equipment myself." It was his damn park. And he was her boss. He was the reason she was up there.

"That sounds like guilt."

"Yeah, maybe it is."

Toby's brows flickered. "Are you two dating?"

"Yes." They hadn't given what they were doing a label, but hell, there was no other word for it.

"Did seeing someone you care about almost get hurt bring back what happened on your last mission?"

The muscles in his forearms twitched. "It was different. She's different."

"*I* know that."

He ran his fingers through his hair. "Yeah, maybe it did bring stuff back up. But the second I held her last night, that stuff quieted like it always does."

Another nod from Toby, like he was considering everything Noah said. Then he leaned forward. "There's something else going through your mind though, isn't there?"

He scrubbed a hand over his face. "The more I care about her, the more I wonder if I'm being…"

"What, Noah?"

"Selfish. She's good for me, but I'm not sure if I'm good for her. Not yet anyway. I'm getting better, but I'm not completely there yet. And even though I haven't hurt her, it's not an impossibility."

"Are you saying you want to break things off with her?"

Fuck, even thinking about that hurt. "I'm saying there's this voice in my head that keeps repeating to me that the only way I can truly keep her safe is by putting some distance between us."

There was a heavy pause. "It might not be a bad idea…for now. At least until you've put the work in to make yourself better."

Frustration twisted in his gut. At the idea of being separated from her. Of her not being his. "But I also can't leave her unprotected."

"What if she wasn't in danger? Would you still be dating her? Or would you give yourself more time to heal first?"

How the fuck would he know? "I don't know. But I do know that I care about her."

"Okay. But I want you to really ask yourself if it's fair to her *or* you for you to start a relationship with someone just because she's in danger. And what if next time, something worse happens to her? Will it set you back? And will that in turn hurt *her*?"

"You think I should break things off with her."

"I think you're still struggling with your past. That could put both of you at risk in different ways. And she deserves the best version of you. Sometimes, healing is about doing the hard work when the comfort isn't there."

A band wrapped around Noah's chest. Because nothing Toby said was anything he hadn't already thought himself.

"Let's leave it there for today," Toby said gently. "We've covered a lot and there's a lot for you to think about."

"A lot" being Addie. He was supposed to *think* about leaving her.

He drove straight home after the appointment. He still needed to go to the park today and do a couple of things, but he wanted Addie with him for that. Yes, she was in his locked and alarmed house right now, but with him, she was always safer. Exactly why the thought of breaking up with her felt fucking crazy.

Yet at the same time, she *did* deserve the best version of him.

He'd just pulled into his drive when his cell rang, Bonnie's name on the screen. A smile tugged at his lips as he answered the call. "Bonnie. I was starting to think you'd forgotten about me."

A soft chuckle sounded over the line. "Forget about my older brother, who used to grab me in a headlock and mess up my hair? Impossible. How are you?"

He glanced out the window, a lie on the tip of his tongue. But the lie didn't fall. "Not great."

"How come?"

"I've got some shit I'm working through from the military. And I've also just started dating someone. Everything feels… complicated." An understatement.

"And you're not sure if the timing is right."

"Yeah."

"Is she pretty?"

Noah chuckled because of course Bonnie asked that. "She's beautiful."

"What do you like about her?"

"She makes me laugh. I feel like I can't breathe around her, but in a good way. Her chocolate addiction is kind of cute. And when I'm with her, I just feel this peace that I don't get anywhere else."

"It sounds like she's helping you."

His fingers tightened around the cell. "Yeah, but maybe I'm not helping *her*."

"Noah…you're the best guy I know. Even a slightly injured version of you is in the top one percent of guys."

"You have to say that. You're my sister."

"Not true. Most would say the opposite."

He laughed. "Thanks, Bon." He spent another few minutes talking to her before finally hanging up and heading inside.

And the second he saw Addie, his heart did that thing where it squeezed and ached. Ached to touch her. Hold her. Breathe in her sweet scent.

She turned and looked at him, and her mouth stretched into the most beautiful smile he'd ever seen before she crossed the space between them and stepped into his arms. And it was only while he was holding her that those words whispered back to him.

Maybe he was being selfish. But was he even capable of giving her up?

CHAPTER 17

*N*oah ran his fingers over the harness as he studied every inch of it. The waist belt. The leg loop. He was looking for frayed stitching or signs that something wasn't right.

There was nothing. Good.

The park was reopening tomorrow, even though no one had been arrested. But who the hell knew how long that would take?

He was damn frustrated. Hell, frustrated didn't even touch the surface of what he felt.

He tugged at the buckles, making sure they cinched smoothly before checking that they released without catching.

Everything was exactly as it was supposed to be. But then, the equipment had already been checked a dozen times by both him *and* Colt. Yet he'd still gotten here early to check it again this morning.

When he reached the carabiners, he clicked them open and closed, listening for that clean snick.

Leaves crunching beneath shoes sounded from the forest behind him.

"We've checked all that."

Noah didn't bother looking over his shoulder at Colt. "I'm checking it again."

More footsteps sounded before a hand touched his shoulder. "Hey. The equipment's fine. It was a targeted attack. It's not going to happen again to the public."

"We don't know that. And it shouldn't have happened in the first place."

"You're right. But it did. And we can't change that."

Finally, he rose to his feet and looked at his friend. "I should have checked the equipment that morning."

"You can't do everything yourself. It's why we employ other people. Our only crime is that we trusted the wrong person."

"What if we trust the wrong person again?" Because Rhett had to be the person responsible. They'd done the check on Cass, and there were no red flags. Buck wouldn't have done this to himself.

"It could happen." Colt lifted a shoulder. "But what are we supposed to do? Not trust anyone?"

Yeah, that was exactly the way Noah was leaning. "Can I ask you something?" It wasn't on the topic of the park, but the question had been in his head every damn second of every day since that appointment with Toby.

"Anything."

"Do you think it's fair to Addie to start a relationship with her after what happened to me?"

Colt frowned. "Why wouldn't it be?"

"My therapist thinks I should do more work on myself first. And I keep going back and forth on whether he's right. On one hand, she helps me. And fuck, I care about her so much. But there have been a couple of times where..." He stopped, his heart suddenly thumping violently in his chest at the memories.

"Where what?" his friend asked quietly.

"I almost hurt her during flashbacks. I thought I was back in the military. The first time, I put my fingers around her throat. At the bar, I shoved her. Then the first night she stayed at my place, I was having a nightmare, and I just jumped up and grabbed her. She didn't even touch me."

A rustling noise sounded near the trees, and Noah and Colt shot their heads up as Jules stepped out.

The older woman cringed. "Sorry. I, uh, was just looking for a photo of mine. I lost it. I think the wind blew it out of my van into the forest. Have you seen anything?"

Noah shook his head. "I haven't, sorry, Jules."

"Me neither," Colt said.

"That's okay. Thanks." Jules gave them a tight smile before walking away.

"Can I tell you what I think?" Colt said, once it was just the two of them again.

"You probably will anyway."

"When you're with her, you're more relaxed than you are with anyone else."

"Yeah, she's good for *me*. But am I good for *her*?"

Colt lifted a shoulder. "That's her choice. It sounds like you haven't scared her away just yet. Maybe she can handle you."

Handle him…like he was a weight. A burden. Colt hadn't meant it like that, but it didn't make the thought any less real.

His phone vibrated with a text.

Addie: Don't kill me, but I was going crazy at home so I decided to pop into work for a bit. Just got here. But don't worry, I'll lock the doors.

"Dammit."

Colt stepped closer. "What?"

"Addie just got here."

"Why?"

"She doesn't like working from home." He shoved his cell back into his pocket.

"Come on, let's get this stuff packed away and you can go see her."

Noah lifted the harnesses. When he dropped it back into the box, a wooden plank at the bottom rattled.

What the hell?

He looked closer to see that the edges were warped. Then he reached inside, and sure enough, with a tug, it lifted off.

He cursed when he saw what was underneath.

"What?" Colt glanced over his shoulder. "Shit!"

Noah pulled his cell from his pocket and hit Jesse's name.

His cousin answered immediately. "Noah, hey, I was just going to call you."

"Colt and I found the battery acid."

There was a heavy pause. "Where?"

"Under a plank of wood in the storage box beside the climbing wall. It's a small container, a couple ounces."

"Jesus." Wind blew over the line. "Okay. I'm coming down there now. Also, I was calling to tell you that we can't find Rhett."

Noah straightened and put the call on speaker. "What do you mean, you can't find Rhett?"

Colt stepped closer to the phone before Jesse continued. "We went to his house this morning. He wasn't there, and his room-mate told us he hadn't come home last night."

"Why were you looking for him?" Colt asked.

"Buck called us because he remembered something."

Noah's chest tightened. "What?"

"The morning he, Rhett, and Cass were setting up, the chalk bag was missing. He and Cass left Rhett alone with the equip-ment for about ten minutes to find it."

The fuck? "Why didn't Cass say anything?"

"According to Buck, the two of them have been in an on-and-off relationship. So, she—"

"Could have been covering for him," Colt finished, scrubbing a hand over his face. "What a fucking mess."

Another staff member they couldn't trust. Just what they needed.

Noah opened his mouth to respond when a sudden scream

pierced the air. It sounded far away, but both Noah and Colt's heads jerked up.

"What the hell was that?" Colt asked.

"Addie." Her name had barely left Noah's lips before he was running.

* * *

ADDIE SHOVED her phone back into her pocket. There was no way Noah was happy she was here and not locked in his house. But she'd been going stir-crazy at home. Literally, if she'd sat there and looked at the same four walls a second longer, she would have completely lost her mind.

It sounded dramatic. It wasn't. It was an accurate account of what would have happened.

A few other cars were scattered throughout the lot. Noah's truck. Colt's Audi. Jules's red convertible. Even Cass's Ford.

With Buck injured and Rhett no longer an employee, everyone was going to have to pull longer hours. Addie had already canceled quite a few sessions.

It sucked. But it wasn't forever. They'd find the person behind the tampering. They'd hire more staff. Everything would be okay.

She crossed the parking lot to the cabin.

Even though there were people around, the door was locked. Not a surprise. Noah and Colt were the only ones who might need access to bookings and computers.

She stepped inside and locked the door behind her. The second she entered her office, a stench thickened the air. It wasn't strong but definitely noticeable, kind of like spoiled meat.

Argh. What *was* that? Had she left food somewhere?

She scanned the room but didn't see anything. Maybe in the kitchen.

Quickly, she dropped her bag to the desk before reaching for the window lock.

She frowned. It *wasn't* locked.

How long had it been unlocked? She never opened the windows, because she didn't want to turn into an ice block. Which also meant, she rarely checked it.

Wait.

She ran her fingers over the lock. Broken. Someone had broken the lock.

The knock on the outer door made her jump. She gave one more glance at the unlocked window before she made her way into the front area to see Jules and Cass outside. She unlocked the door. "Hi."

Jules smiled and stepped inside. "Hey, Addie."

Cass followed, only to stop and wrinkle her nose. "What the heck is that?"

"You can smell it too?"

"Can I smell death warmed up? Yes."

Addie frowned. "Something must have been left to spoil in the kitchen." She turned and headed back into the office, the click of Jules's and Cass's steps close behind her.

She tugged open the door to the kitchen—only to freeze.

Every muscle in her body, every inch of skin, it all went cold, and a buzzing filled her ears. The smell was so thick now that, for a moment, she thought she'd be sick. Or maybe that was because of the vision in front of her.

Rhett.

Cass's horrified scream cut through the air like a blade, and Jules's gasp was nearly as loud. Addie opened her mouth but no sound came out. It was like her very voice had been stolen.

Rhett lay on his back and his sweatshirt was soaked in blood. Blood that had spilled onto the white tiles beneath him. But it was his eyes that made her want to lean over and throw up her breakfast. They were open and completely empty.

Dead. Rhett was dead.

"What's that?" Jules whispered.

Addie followed her gaze to the wall beside him.

That's when her knees buckled.

Someone caught her before she hit the floor, but she didn't look away from the sentence. Each word was written in blood. Rhett's blood.

You should have heeded my warning.

CHAPTER 18

It felt like something was sitting on Noah's chest. Weighing him down. Stopping the air from moving in and out of his lungs.

Rhett was dead. Not just dead—murdered in their damn park.

By who? And why? Just to scare off Addie?

No. You didn't murder someone just for that, especially not someone Addie wasn't even close to. There was more to it than driving a person out of town.

His gaze shifted to Addie. She and Jules sat on a large rock beside the parking lot, on either side of Cass, who'd been crying since they'd found Rhett. Addie was just as pale. *Really* fucking pale. He wanted to get her home and away from this, but Jesse and his team were still inside and hadn't questioned anyone yet.

"What a fucking mess," Colt said under his breath, staring at the cabin.

"I don't know what the hell's going on. I thought Rhett was the threat."

"There's obviously someone else," Colt said quietly. "Maybe someone he was helping?"

"Until he became a liability." That was the most likely

scenario. But *who* could he have been helping? And how did Addie pose a threat to this person simply by living in Amber Ridge? Noah looked toward the door. "Jesse isn't going to be able to tell us much."

"Yeah. Not with it being an open murder investigation."

The wounds on Rhett's front flashed back in Noah's mind. "There were a lot of stab wounds. Makes me think it was a crime of passion. Maybe he didn't intend to kill Rhett. Or maybe he did, then Rhett pissed him off and he got too excited."

"I thought the same. There were also defensive wounds on Rhett's hands."

"He didn't expect the attack. Which means he trusted his attacker."

Deputies knelt outside the cabin, investigating the ground. He already knew what they were looking at—blood. Noah had scanned the area before Jesse and his team had arrived. There'd been a few other drops throughout the cabin. "He wasn't killed in there."

"Nope. But he wasn't killed out here either—there's not enough blood."

"So they drove him here."

"And accessed the cabin through the window because the lock was easier to break."

"Opened the front door and dragged him through to the kitchen," Noah finished.

"But then relocked the front door and went back out through the front window." Colt's brows flickered. "That's a lot of work just to relocate a body."

Noah's back teeth ground together. "He wanted Addie to find it. That was the whole point. Scare her. Push her to get out of Amber Ridge." He looked back over at Addie. Her arm was still around Cass, and the anxiety on her face…fuck, it gutted him.

"We need answers," Colt said under his breath.

Jesse stepped out of the building and headed straight toward them, his usual smile nowhere to be seen. "We're going to start interviewing everyone," he said as he got closer.

Noah nodded. "The sooner we get this over with, the sooner I can get Addie home."

"My deputies will interview you guys. I'll start with Cass."

Noah was one of the last to be interviewed, and he was so ready to get the hell out of there that he barely paid attention to the questions.

"You were the first to get to the park today," the deputy said. "Is that right?"

Noah nodded as he watched Addie, who was now standing with Jules. They'd both already been questioned. "Yeah, I got here at six."

"And you were alone?"

"Yes. I didn't see the body because I didn't go into the cabin."

The deputy wrote something down. "Is it true you threatened to murder Mr. Ferdinanze last week?"

Noah's gaze swung to the deputy, the question catching him off guard. "What?"

"You publicly accused him of putting his hands on Miss March and then threatened to murder him. Is that correct?"

"Who told you that?"

"I need you to answer the question, Mr. Hayes."

"I said, 'Get out before I murder you.'"

The deputy wrote something down. "Is it also true that you've assaulted Miss March more than once?"

Noah flinched. "Where are you getting your information?"

"That's not relevant. I've been informed that you put your hands around her throat. You also shoved her. And you threatened to hit her. So you have a record of violence. Is that correct?"

Noah didn't just flinch this time, it was a whole-body jerk. Because it was true. All of it. And when said out loud like that, it made him feel like the scumbag he sometimes thought he was. "That has nothing to do with this."

"That's not what I asked you. I asked you if it was true."

"Yes," Noah growled between gritted teeth. "But it's out of context. I would *never* intentionally hurt her. And I didn't kill Rhett."

"But you do suffer from flashbacks from your time in the military, during which you lose control, right?"

Where the fuck was he getting this information? "That has nothing to do with Rhett's murder. This interview's over."

He turned and moved toward his car.

"Mr. Hayes."

He ignored the deputy, and from his peripheral vision, he saw Jesse look up from where he was talking to another officer before calling for him.

"Where are you going?" Jesse called.

"Unless I'm under arrest, I'm leaving." He went straight to Addie, who was looking at him now, concern on her face.

She met him halfway across the lot. "Are you okay?"

"I'm going to head home."

"I'll go with you."

A part of him wanted to say no. Because the deputy had been right. He'd done all those things. And it made every fear about Addie not being safe with him, every doubt about whether he should be with her, come to life.

She pressed her palm to his chest. "Noah—"

"Come on. Let's get you home." He pressed a hand to the small of her back and led her toward her car. But even touching her made something inside him want to retreat. To pull back. To put as much distance between them as possible to keep her safe from him.

* * *

"You're not safe," her father growled. "You're coming home, *now*."

154

Addie lowered her head into her hand, the phone feeling heavy as she ran her gaze over the bed sheet. She'd wanted time before telling her parents, but Rhett's murder would be on the news and she'd prefer they found out from her.

She'd expected the conversation to be bad...but this was worse. "I haven't changed my mind about staying here." She closed her eyes against the string of stern words from her father and the pleas from her mother that followed.

"Addie, darling," her mother said, sounding desperate. "We just want you safe."

"I know. I want to be safe too. And I will be. This person murdered someone. They had to have left some evidence, and Jesse will find it."

"That someone was killed in *your* office," her father pushed, a mixture of fear and rage in his voice. "They wrote you a message in the guy's blood."

Her stomach rolled. "I know. I saw it. But I haven't been hurt. Not once. I'm living with Noah, who's a former Marine. Colt, the other owner at the park, is also a Marine. Jesse, our town sheriff, was special operations in the military. I'm as safe as I *can* be."

"You'd be safer here with us," her mother pushed.

She swallowed before saying her next words, knowing her parents wouldn't like them. "I'm not running back to Bozeman scared. I'm sorry if that isn't the answer you want to hear, but it's not going to change. I'm going to go now. But please remember, I'm safe."

"For now."

She sighed at her father's words. "I'll call again tomorrow. I love you both."

Not doing what they asked felt so foreign to her. But even if she did want to heed the threat and get out of Amber Ridge, there was no way she'd go home. This person had *killed* someone. And there was no guarantee they'd just disappear because she made the one-hour move back to Bozeman. If she left, she'd go somewhere far away.

But she wasn't going anywhere.

Her gaze lifted to the closed bedroom door.

Where was Noah? It was getting late, and he'd spent the entire day since getting home avoiding her. He'd even gone so far as to eat dinner at a different time because he'd needed to "chop wood." Wood! That wasn't a time-sensitive task—there was a ton of wood piled up at the back of the house.

She needed to find out what was going on, and she needed to find out now.

Quickly, she climbed out of bed. He wasn't in the living room. Or the kitchen. She checked every room off the hall.

Nothing. Where the heck was he? Outside again?

She opened the back door and, yep, that was where she found him. His back was toward her, and he was doing pull-ups on a bar that was bolted into two wooden poles. He was shirtless and the muscles in his bare back visibly strained.

Any other day she'd probably have fixated on how good those muscles looked as they worked. But today? Today she was worried. Something was wrong. Had Rhett's death scared him more than she'd assumed?

She moved outside and stopped beside him. "Hey."

He dropped from the bar and pulled out an ear pod. "Hey." He scanned her body like he was checking for injury, and it made a shudder roll down her spine. "Are you all right?"

No, she was far from all right. But that had nothing to do with finding Rhett this morning. "I just spoke to my parents."

"How'd it go?"

"Shocker, they want me to go home."

Something crossed his face. It came and went so quickly she couldn't place it.

He lifted a capped bottle of water. "Do *you* want to go home?"

How was that even a question? "No. *This* is my home. Amber Ridge. And I want to be here with you."

He drank the water, his expression unreadable.

She tilted her head. It felt like there was a barrier between them. A wall she couldn't push through. Why?

"What's going on with you, Noah? I know what happened today was…God, it was awful. But I don't understand why you're avoiding me."

"I'm not."

She could have laughed. Or maybe a half laugh escaped, because his focus shot up.

She lifted a brow. "Really? Is that why I've barely seen you all day? Why you couldn't even eat dinner with me?"

A few seconds of silence passed while his gaze shifted between her eyes. "I just want you to feel safe."

"I *do* feel safe. With *you*."

His frown deepened.

She stepped forward. "What aren't you telling me?"

"I don't blame you for telling them."

Okay, now she was really confused. "Telling who what?"

"You told the deputy about my flashbacks."

She frowned. "No, I didn't. Why would I do that? They have nothing to do with what happened today."

He studied her for a moment, like he was trying to work out whether she was telling the truth. "You're sure?"

"Of course. Did someone else say something?"

"The deputy who interviewed me mentioned it. He also brought up how I threatened to kill Rhett."

She gasped. "He doesn't think—"

"I don't know. But when you put it all together, it doesn't look good."

She touched his chest. "Jesse knows you. He knows you wouldn't actually kill Rhett."

"I don't care about that anyway. Right now, I just care about you. Us." His hands went to her hips. "If you ever decide that you want to be with someone else…"

"Someone else?"

"Someone younger. Someone who doesn't come with a shit-load of trauma. That's okay."

"You think we get to choose who we love?"

His fingers tightened on her hips. "Love?"

"Yeah. I'm falling in love with you, Noah. And you don't have to say it back. But you *do* need to understand that I'm not going anywhere. I *feel* safe with you." She stopped and swallowed. "But if us being together is affecting your business or slowing down your progress in therapy—"

"No. I don't care about the park right now. I care about you and your safety. That's it."

"Good. Then there's no problem."

There was still something in his eyes. Maybe a flicker of doubt? But before she could mention it, he lowered his head and kissed her. And just like that, every worry, every whisper of uncertainty inside her, just faded away.

CHAPTER 19

$\mathcal{A}$ddie scrunched her eyes at the ringing phone.

No. She did not want to wake up. She'd been in that deep sleep where even cracking one eye open was a challenge.

The ringing stopped.

Thank God.

She started to drift off again, only for the phone to start ringing a second time.

Holy Hannah. She was going to murder them. Yep, they were going to be dead, and she was going to be arrested.

Noah's arm tightened around her waist, and he nuzzled her neck from behind. "Want me to answer it?"

Yes. But that would require him to sit up and reach over her for her phone, when she could just stretch out a hand and answer it. Talk about lazy on her part.

"No, I've got it." With eyes still closed, she reached for the phone on the bedside table and put it to her ear. "Hello?"

"Addie?"

"Mom? It's early."

"Your father and I are at your house."

She frowned because she had to have heard wrong. It was Wednesday, and her mother had school. "What?"

"Your father and I are at your house. I know you said you're staying with Noah, but we don't know where he lives, so we came here."

Her eyes popped open. "You're at my house? Right now?"

"Of course we are. You didn't want to come to Bozeman, so we came to you."

She shot up to a sitting position. She wasn't dreaming. Her parents were here, in Amber Ridge, right now. "Mom—"

"No rush. We might go get a coffee. I see there's a diner in town."

She should have known this would happen. Geez, why hadn't she known they'd show up?

Noah sat up and frowned at her, questions in his eyes.

"Don't go to Rob's Diner," Addie said, scrubbing her eyes. "All the coffee drinkers I know say it's terrible. There's a place called The Tea House. It's on Fifth. I'll see you within the hour."

"Okay, darling, see you then."

She hung up and sighed before turning to Noah.

He slid a piece of hair behind her ear. "What's wrong?"

"My parents are in town."

"In Amber Ridge?"

"At my house. I'm going to get dressed and meet them at The Tea House."

"I'll come with you."

One side of her mouth lifted. "Meeting the parents. That's a big step."

"Too soon?"

"Not for me." Absolutely not for her. Heck, she'd already thrown the big L word out there.

She leaned over and kissed him, and the second she did, he threaded his fingers into her hair and slipped his tongue inside her mouth.

She groaned. Even first thing in the freaking morning, he tasted good. Rich like spices, but also so masculine.

He growled. "We don't have time for this."

"I disagree." But he was right. Dammit.

He pulled back, only to groan when he looked at her chest. The sheet had fallen and she was completely naked. "Get in the shower before I do something your parents would not approve of. I'm not going to be late for our first meeting."

"But—"

"No buts."

She groaned and dropped back onto the bed.

Her eyes were just closing again when Noah shouted, "Get out of bed, Addison."

She chuckled as the sound of the shower turned on in the other bathroom.

It took them half an hour to get out of the house, and the only thing that really got her there was the thought of Mrs. Gerald's hot chocolate. And giving her parents a huge, gigantic hug. But she knew exactly what was going to come with that hug. An earful of advice.

"Is there anything I should know about your mom and dad before I meet them?" Noah asked.

She glanced at him, sitting behind the wheel. "My mom is your typical first-grade teacher. She's soft-spoken. Kind. Worries far too much but has a solution for everything. Although, that solution can offer differ from mine...she errs on the side of caution."

Noah's lips twitched. "And your dad?"

"You know that saying, acts tough but he's really a big softy?"

"Yeah?"

"Not the case for my father. He acts tough because he *is* tough. But he loves me, something I remind myself of when he gets overbearing."

"So he's going to hate the thirty-five-year-old boyfriend who doubles as your boss?"

"Well, he hasn't liked a single boyfriend of mine yet but… you're a Marine, so there's hope."

He chuckled. "Sounds like I have my work cut out for me."

"Fortunately, not much scares you. Anyway, I'm hoping the second they see how much you mean to me, they'll love you." Not likely though. Telling them how much she loved Amber Ridge had not warmed them up to the town.

Noah pulled into the parking lot beside The Tea House, and she immediately spotted her parents' black RAV4. A smile curved her lips, almost making her forget about the pressure she was about to face to move back home.

Noah climbed out first and set his hand on the middle of her back as they made their way to the door. She spotted them in a booth by the window the second she stepped into The Tea House. Her mother looked up first, a large smile spreading across her face, then her dad. Although, his smile was more of a lip twitch. The second they stood, she ran into their arms and hugged them both at the same time.

God, they smelled like home—a mix of cinnamon and coffee and something else that was so infinitely them.

When she pulled back, tears gathered in her eyes. "Hey, Mom and Dad."

Her mother wiped a tear from her own cheek. "Addie, we've missed you, darling."

"I've missed you both so much."

When Noah stepped beside her, she turned and smiled up at him before looking back at her parents. "Mom, Dad, this is Noah Hayes. Noah, meet my parents, Mark and Diana."

Her father held out a hand. "It's nice to meet you, Noah."

"You too, sir."

His mother stepped forward. "In this family, we hug." She wrapped her arms around Noah's shoulders, and Noah returned the hug. When she pulled back, she clenched his shoulder. "Thank you for keeping our girl safe."

He dipped his head. "Of course."

* * *

NOAH FELT the frustration radiating off Addie beside him. Her thigh muscles were tense beneath his palm, and she'd barely touched her drink.

He didn't blame her. It had been thirty minutes of her parents telling her to go back to Bozeman and thirty minutes of Addie saying no. Every time she tried to change the subject, that new subject would last for a couple of minutes at best, before someone, usually her mother, drew the conversation back to Bozeman and all the reasons she should return home.

"Darling, I'm not saying you can't take care of yourself. But this is a unique situation. Someone has gone so far as to *kill* someone to send you a message." Her mother grabbed her chest like saying the words out loud caused her pain.

Her father leaned forward. He had a bushy white beard that matched his white hair, and he hadn't smiled once. "Someone wants you gone, Addie...so leave."

"But who?" Addie asked. "And why? This is information I need to know, but I won't if I run away."

"Your *life* is the priority right now," her mother gushed.

"And the sheriff will get that information eventually," her father added. "You just won't be here to watch them escalate."

Addie's chest rose and fell on a deep inhale. Noah tightened his fingers around her thigh.

Jesus, her parents were really pushing it. Did they not respect Addie's wishes at all? She was an adult, for Christ's sake.

"Mom, Dad, I really appreciate you coming to check on me," she started slowly. "I've missed you both so much, but my answer hasn't changed. There is nothing you can say that will make me leave."

Annoyance flared in her father's eyes, while her mother just looked ready to keep arguing.

"Hi, Addie. Noah."

Everyone looked up to see Jules by the table.

Noah frowned. The second Addie had told him that it wasn't her who'd told the deputies about his flashbacks, he'd pieced together that it had to have been Jules. It hadn't been Colt. And of course it hadn't been Toby. She must have overheard his conversation with Colt when she was looking for the photo.

Addie smiled. "Hi, Jules. How are you today?"

Jules's smile didn't quite reach her eyes. "Probably just as shaken as you."

Was it Noah, or was she avoiding looking at him?

Addie turned to her parents. "Jules, this is my mom and dad, Diana and Mark. Mom, Dad, Jules runs a food truck at the park. She was there when we found…Rhett yesterday."

Jules's brows shot up. "Your parents? I thought you lived in Bozeman."

"We're visiting," her mother said gently, still looking worried.

"Oh, okay." Jules tucked a piece of hair behind her ear. "It's nice to meet you both. You're a teacher, right?"

Addie's mother nodded. "I am. I managed to get some last-minute leave from work to come see Addie."

"What a wonderful job. I always wanted to be a teacher, but life got in the way." Jules cleared her throat, an emotion Noah couldn't place passing over the woman's face. "Well, I'll leave you all to it. Addie, let me know if you need anything, okay?"

Addie nodded. "Thank you."

"She seems nice," Diana said, once Jules left. "The poor woman though, finding that body with you."

"Cass is the one I'm worried about," Addie said gently. "She was dating Rhett."

That was a little fact that Noah still found interesting. Neither Cass nor Rhett had mentioned anything to him or Colt. And there was still the fact that Cass had neglected to tell Jesse that Rhett had been left alone with the equipment. When Jesse had questioned her about it, she'd told him she'd just forgotten, but that was bullshit. She had to be covering for him.

Noah couldn't trust her anymore, and a part of him wanted to let her go from the park for the omission, but they had time to think about it because obviously the park wasn't reopening today like they'd planned.

Her father leaned forward. "Addie, I'd really like you to think about what we're saying."

Jesus Christ, they weren't going to stop.

Addie climbed out of the booth. "I'm going to the bathroom, then I might need to go. I've got some work to do."

Her mother stood too. "I'll come with you, honey."

If the expression on Addie's face was anything to go by, she'd have preferred to go alone. Still, the two women crossed the café to the bathroom together.

Noah looked back to Addie's father. "With all due respect, sir, I think this is Addison's decision to make."

Mark looked at Noah, expression unreadable. "Addie told me you're a Marine."

"No longer serving, but yes."

"Why'd you leave?"

A sudden band tightened around Noah's chest. "It was time."

"As in your enlistment was up?"

Shit. Most people didn't ask for specifics. But a man like Addie's father? He should have expected this. "Medical retirement."

Mark's frown deepened. "Physical injury?"

"No."

Mark leaned back, expression still unreadable. "You getting help?"

"Yes, sir." Although, lately, Toby hadn't felt like he was helping in the way Noah needed. Progress had stalled. Sure, Noah hadn't had any more flashbacks, but that was because nothing had triggered him.

Mark leaned forward. "I'll be honest with you, son, I'm apprehensive about my daughter dating you. The combination of your age and you being her boss isn't sitting well with me. There's also the military stuff. I know the kind of holes that can form after spending years on active duty. I've spent a lot of time patching mine, but there are still some that sit wide open."

"You think they'll ever close?"

"No. But I've learned to live with them. That only came with time."

Time...time that Noah hadn't given himself before dating Addie.

Mark met Noah's eyes coolly. "I just need you to answer one question—is my daughter safe with you?"

He almost flinched. Every part of him wanted to say yes. He was a protector. It was why he'd become a Marine. And out of every person in his life, he wanted to protect Addie the most.

But could he honestly say she was safe with him a hundred percent of the time?

"Protecting your daughter is my priority." It wasn't a complete answer to Mark's question.

And by the look on the older man's face, he knew it.

CHAPTER 20

*A*ddie snuck a peek at Noah from beneath her lashes. He'd had a therapy session that morning, and since then he'd been...distant. Barely looking at her, giving one-word answers. And every time she touched him, his muscles did this thing where they clenched, like he didn't want her hands on him.

Wasn't therapy supposed to have the opposite effect? Shouldn't he return to her a bit more healed each time instead of looking like his wounds had been pulled wide open?

She cleared her throat. "I'm excited to meet your aunt Pam."

His fingers visibly tightened around the wheel. "She's amazing, and she'll love you."

"I hope so. And I hope she gets along with my parents too." She smiled. "I think Dad will like being surrounded by so many vets." There were a hell of a lot of them, with Jesse, Becket, Holden, Colt, and Noah.

Noah dipped his head.

See...*that*. *That* was what she was talking about. Where was the conversation? Where was the Noah who used actual words to agree with her and ask questions?

"Do you think therapy's helping?" The question burst out of her.

His brow furrowed, and there was a short silence before he answered. "I don't know."

At least he was honest.

She picked at a thread on her jeans. "Every time you come back to me from a session, you seem…"

"Worse."

Her head whipped toward him, surprised at his choice of words. "Do you *feel* worse?"

"Yeah, I do, but I'm not sure why. The first few sessions seemed to help. But now I feel like every part of me rebels against the advice he gives me."

"What advice does he give you?"

Noah's jaw clenched before he pulled up in front of a house. "Come on. We don't want to be late."

He wasn't going to tell her. Why not? Because she wouldn't like the answer? Because at least part of that advice involved her?

She climbed out to find Noah already by her side. After grabbing the potato salad from the back, they headed toward the house, but she couldn't just leave it like this.

"Noah, if this is going to work between us, we have to be honest with each other." When they reached the door, she stepped closer to him. "Trust me with the truth, even if you think I won't like it."

"The truth is, I'm falling in love with you, Addie."

Her jaw dropped, her heart taking off in a gallop. Love…he was falling in love with her. She'd known she was in love with him for weeks, but to know the feelings were reciprocated made a million emotions ripple through her body.

He inched closer and gripped her hip. "But as much as that makes me happy, it also scares me."

"Why does it scare you?"

"Because I want to do this right. I don't want to mess everything up."

"How would you mess it up?"

"By rushing it. By not giving you the best version of me to love."

She could have laughed. "Noah, I'd choose the worst version of you over the best version of anyone else, every day."

His eyes darkened, and he lowered his head and kissed her. The kiss wasn't desire or need—it was filled with emotion, and it consumed her.

When he lifted his head, he didn't step back, instead touching his temple to hers. "This is why I need you, Addie. You make me feel like my flaws aren't things I need to hide."

"They're just a part of you," she whispered, still breathless. Then she smiled. "Like how my chocolate addiction is a part of me."

He chuckled, and God, the sound was good to hear.

A car pulled up on the street, and Addie turned to see her parents climbing out. Her mother smiled, while her dad watched them closely.

She wouldn't say her father disliked Noah, he just wasn't overly warm or affectionate. In fact, she would say her father seemed to like Noah more than any of her previous boyfriends. But then, that shouldn't be a surprise. None of them had meant anything to her.

"Hi." When they reached the door, she hugged them both. Noah shook their hands, then opened the front door for everyone. He led them straight through the house and into the backyard, where they found the rest of the party.

Noah slipped an arm around her waist, and they walked around to say hi and introduce her parents. When they reached an older woman with graying hair and a wide smile, she pulled Noah right into a hug. "Noah, sweetheart, it's so good to see you."

"Hey, Aunt Pam."

When she pulled back, it almost looked like there were tears in the older woman's eyes. She might only be an aunt, but it was clear she loved Noah like a son.

Noah turned to Addie and her parents. "Aunt Pam, this is Addie, and her parents Mark and Diana."

Pam held out a hand to her mother and father. "Welcome to my home. It's nice to meet you both." Then she turned to her. "Addie." She tugged her into an embrace. "I've heard so much about you."

Her brows rose. "You have?"

"Of course." She pulled back, still smiling. "I make it my mission to learn everything I can about the partners *all* my children have their eye on."

"Pam…" Noah started.

Her smile widened. "I'm really looking forward to chatting with you today." She patted Addie's shoulder before turning to her parents. "Come, let's get you both a drink."

When her parents and Pam had left, she looked up to see Noah had his eyes on Jesse. "Go."

He looked back at her. "What?"

"You want to talk to him about Rhett and see if he's made any progress on the case. Go. I'll be okay."

"You don't want to come?"

She shook her head. "I could use a break from that today."

His brows flickered but he pressed a kiss to her forehead. "I'll be right back."

The smile slipped from her lips the second he turned away. She hated that so much was going on for him. How was he supposed to focus on his own mental health with a murder at his workplace, someone sabotaging his rock-climbing equipment, and the threats that kept being sent her way?

And why the heck was his therapist not helping him?

"Hey."

She jumped and spun to see Indie behind her. "Oh, hi!"

"Penny for your thoughts?" She rubbed her small, rounded pregnant belly.

Addie looked back at Noah, who was now deep in a conversation with Jesse. Neither of them looked happy. "I hate that what's going on with me is affecting Noah and Colt's new business."

"It's not your fault. You didn't ask for any of this."

"I know. But they're targeting *me*, not them. It's because I work at the park that it's affecting them. And now someone's dead—"

"That is *definitely* not your fault."

"The park has to remain closed now."

"Addie, listen to me."

She took her eyes off Noah to look at Indie.

"Everything that's happened is because some nutcase has decided they have nothing better to do than scare you. That has nothing to do with you. And you have been the most amazing thing for Noah's life."

She snorted. "I'm not sure about that."

"I am. I've never seen him look at anyone the way he looks at you. It's like you've put new life into him. Yes, right now, that comes with a bit of other stuff. But you are exactly what he needs."

Addie's lower belly did a little somersault. Because he was what she needed too. "Thank you. I'm not sure *he* agrees that he's what I need, though."

"Well, that's because boys can be both wrong *and* stubborn. Sometimes they just need a bit of convincing from us women."

She chuckled.

"You know what *you* need? A drink. I brought some amazing strawberry lemonade that would probably taste great spiked with a bit of vodka or rum."

"Actually, strawberry lemonade sounds really good, no alcohol needed."

"Wait here, I'll get you some."

Indie had just walked away when Addie's phone vibrated with a text.

Jules: Hey. I'm worried about you. Can I make you a meal? Or can we grab a coffee?

A smile curved Addie's lips. Jules had not stopped with the meals, the check-ins, the kind gestures…it was amazing. *Jules* was amazing.

Addie: I would love that. Coffee tomorrow?

She hit send and had just locked her phone when it vibrated with a text.

That was quick.

But when she looked at the screen, it wasn't Jules.

Unknown: You think I'm fucking around? I'm not. Just wait and see.

Fear fisted in her chest, but it was quickly replaced by another emotion…anger.

She was so mad. Mad that this asshole was messing with her life. That he'd *killed* someone. And he still wasn't even telling her why.

Addie: Tell me why you're doing this. What have I done to you?

Unknown: It's too late to start asking questions, Addie. You've already overstayed your welcome.

Her fingers were moving before she could stop them.

Addie: Fuck you.

* * *

"You think *I* did it?"

Jesse sighed. "Of course not. My deputy was just doing his job asking those questions."

Noah gritted his teeth as he looked around the yard.

"You didn't tell me things had gotten so bad," Jesse said, voice hushed.

"I'm seeing a therapist. I'm doing everything I'm supposed to do."

"I'm sure you are. I'm sorry you're going through that. I'm also sorry I can't share more of the case with you. I wish I could."

"You can't even tell me if you have any suspects?"

Jesse swallowed. "I can tell you that we found prints on the battery acid...Rhett's."

So he *had* done it. Asshole.

"Yet I'm still a suspect," Noah said quietly.

Jesse stepped closer. "You threatened to kill the guy. Less than a week later, he turns up dead. I'm doing everything I can to steer this case away from you and find the person who actually did it." He glanced around the yard before looking back at Noah. "Some of my deputies want me to get a court order to get any information your therapist has on your mental health."

Jesus Christ.

"But I told you, I'm fighting for you," Jesse pushed. "Because I know it would be a waste of time. You didn't do anything."

Noah spotted Addie across the lawn. Her head was down, and she was looking at her phone, but the second she glanced up and her gaze caught on his, he saw it. The fear. The anger.

"Something's wrong." He stormed across the yard. "What is it?"

She handed him her cell, and he took it just as Jesse came to stand beside him. Noah's gaze ran over the texts, and suddenly he wanted to punch something. Ram his fist into a fucking wall, he was so frustrated.

"He texted back," Jesse said, sounding a hell of a lot calmer than Noah.

"Yeah, but not to my last text," Addie said, shaking her head. "I'm so angry. And frustrated. Why won't they leave me alone?"

Noah tucked her into his chest. He wished he could stop this for her. He needed this to end.

The day went slowly after that. Too slowly. He tried to concentrate on the conversations around him, but he was giving a fraction of the attention that his family and friends deserved.

Even when they sat down to eat, he could barely stomach anything.

The only true smile that curved his lips was when his phone rang and Bonnie's name flashed across the screen. He leaned down and touched his lips to Addie's ear. "I'll be back in a minute."

He didn't answer the call until he was in his aunt's living room.

"Hey, Bon-Bon."

"Hey."

His brows flickered at his sister's mellow tone. "Everything okay?"

"Actually, no. Remember how I told you that I was scared about losing my job?"

"Yeah. Funding being cut at the shelter, right?"

"Yep. It happened. I lost my job last week."

Shit. "I'm sorry, Bonnie."

"Thanks. I've been looking for new jobs, but so far, there hasn't been much."

"Nothing?"

There was a small pause. "Actually, I found one job advertised. It's kind of perfect. Exactly what I'm doing now."

"That's great. Where is it?"

Another pause, this one heavier. "Amber Ridge."

He straightened. There was a job for Bonnie right here in Amber Ridge? Bonnie hadn't been home for thirteen years. No one had even *seen* her since she was eighteen.

"It's a stupid idea, isn't it?" she rushed when he was silent for too long. "It's been so long. Everyone probably hates me for running out of town—"

"Bonnie—"

"I should go. I've got food in the oven. We'll talk soon, Noah."

She hung up before he could get another word in.

Shit. He tried calling her back, but she didn't answer. He quickly typed out a text.

Noah: You caught me off guard. This is what I should have said— yes, come home. We all want to see you. This is where you belong.

Technically, he couldn't speak for everyone. Indie and Bonnie had always had a rocky relationship, but even though Indie was mad at her sister for leaving, she still loved her. Coming home now was better than never.

There were other people who were also angry at Bonnie, the main ones being the White family, who'd lost their son the night of their high school graduation party. Bonnie and Dean White had been dating. He'd gotten drunk, she'd left, and he'd then tried to drive himself home. He'd crashed the car and died at the scene.

His family blamed Bonnie. But it wasn't her damn fault.

The back door opened and Becket and Sky stepped inside. Becket held a couple of glasses in one hand and plates in the other, while Sky held her dog, Bella. Bella wasn't a typical cute dog. But Sky and Becket were infatuated with her.

"What are you doing in here?" Becket asked when he saw Noah.

"Just sorting some things out." He wouldn't be sharing anything about Bonnie until he knew for sure what her plans were. He looked at Sky. "Is that dog allowed in here?"

"That dog," Sky said slowly, "is part of the family. Pam agrees."

Noah chuckled. Of course she did. Pam loved all her family, fur or people.

Suddenly, Bella lunged for a piece of bread on a plate. Sky gasped, her elbow hitting a glass on the counter. It hit the floor and shattered.

Darkness squeezed around Noah like a wet blanket, the stench of blood and sweat thick in the air.

Dead. Boone was dead. And now they thought they could make him talk?

The blood around his wrists had long since dried. Physically, he felt numb. Like he couldn't move or breathe.

A glass shattered. It was the asshole trying to get his attention, threatening to cut him. It wouldn't work. Nothing would.

"Tell me if it was preparation for a larger raid."

He looked up at the asshole who'd given the directive to kill his teammate. "I'd prefer to just see you in hell."

"Noah."

He flinched at the weight of Becket's hand on his shoulder.

Then he turned to see Sky looking at him, worried. But she and Becket weren't the only ones in the room.

Mark stood in the open door, a frown on his face as he watched, like he knew exactly what had just happened...and he didn't like it.

CHAPTER 21

Addie rolled from her belly to her side. Why was she cold? She was never cold with Noah in the bed. Heck, usually, she was on the verge of overheating.

She reached for Noah…but he wasn't there.

Her eyes popped open. The room was dark. So dark, she could barely see a thing. It had to be the middle of the night. But then, why wasn't he here?

Quickly, she turned on the bedside light before tapping the screen of her phone.

Three in the morning.

Concern wiped away any thoughts of going back to sleep, and she slipped out of bed. On the floor, she found a discarded shirt of Noah's and pulled it over her head before moving out of the room.

Everything was dark in the hall. She'd expected a light on somewhere. Maybe he'd gone to the bathroom in the hall to avoid waking her. But it was empty.

Had he slept somewhere else?

She stepped into the living room, almost expecting to see him asleep on the couch. He wasn't. He stood facing the window, the outline of his body stark against the moonlight.

Slowly, she crossed the space between them. "Noah—"

He moved so quickly she didn't have time to react. One second, she was behind him, the next, her back was pressed to his chest, his arm around her throat.

Air stalled in her lungs and panic surged through her veins.

"Noah…" she breathed, forcing calm into her voice when calm was the last thing she felt. "It's me…Addie."

The muscle in his arm tensed.

"You're safe," she whispered.

"Addison?" Shock, fear, panic…it was all tangled together in his voice.

"Yes." Gently, she touched the arm that was wrapped around her neck and swiped his wrist with her thumb. "You're in your home in Amber Ridge."

"Addie…"

The arm suddenly dropped and the warmth disappeared from her back.

She turned slowly, and the pain on Noah's face…it killed something inside her. He looked pained and angry and frustrated, and he searched her body like he was looking for injury. An injury he'd inflicted. He wouldn't find one.

"You didn't hurt me," she whispered.

"I could have." He scrubbed his hands over his face with shaking fingers. "Are you okay?" he asked when his hands dropped.

"I told you, you didn't hurt me. How are *you*?"

She stepped forward, but Noah mirrored her move, stepping away from her, keeping that space that felt too big between them.

She hated the distance. It felt like a wall she couldn't cut through. An immovable barrier between them. "Noah—"

"I should have trusted my gut. Even Toby agreed with me."

She frowned. "Toby?"

"I'm being selfish by keeping you. I'm thinking about me, not you or your safety."

"Hey." Another step forward, but again he backed away. "You're *not* being selfish. We're in this together. I want to go through this with you."

"I'm dragging you into my shit. I'm trying to have you before I've done the work and made sure I'm okay. And if I'm not okay, you won't be either. You won't be safe around me."

Fear started to weave through her bones. Fear of what was about to come. That he was going to hurt her, hurt *them*, before they'd even given this relationship a chance.

"You're not dragging me anywhere," she pushed. "We're both adults. We're both making the choice to be here. To love each other."

"It hasn't been equal though. I'm your boss. I'm older than you. There's a power imbalance."

They were back to that? "I'm not a child. I'm an adult."

"And I've come close to hurting you so many fucking times."

Four. He'd come close to hurting her four times. Because he was struggling.

She wanted to fight for him, for *them*. To tell him he would never hurt her…but he was right. It wasn't an impossibility. And what if one day he did? What if one day he didn't snap back to the present in time?

It would destroy him. And that would destroy her.

He rounded the couch so that it sat between them, big and immovable. "I need to go."

"Go where? This is your home." Her words were barely a whisper.

He turned.

"Noah, please stop." The rational part of her brain told her to let him go. He needed space and time, and trying to keep him would be for her. It would be selfish. But there was also this ache deep in her belly…one that told her to grab onto him and not let go. One that felt completely empty without him.

"No, Addison. We can't do this anymore."

And there it was. The words she'd been waiting for. The words she'd feared. They sat in the air, and she was too scared to touch them.

"You're breaking up with me." She wasn't sure if it was a question or a statement. It didn't matter. The pain that burned inside her was the same either way.

And it all amounted to the same thing—she needed to let him do what he thought he needed to do…and trust and hope that he returned to her.

But it still hurt. God, it hurt.

* * *

THE PAIN and sadness on Addie's face almost made him want to take it back. All of it. To close that distance between them, take her into his arms, and assure her that everything would be okay.

But that would be a fucking lie. He didn't know if it would be okay. He'd almost hurt her again. And unless he did something, it would just keep happening and she'd never be safe with him.

He stepped away, afraid her proximity might push him to make the wrong decision.

Another flash of pain in her beautiful blue eyes. But it would hurt more if one of these times he used his strength, the skills he'd learned in the military, to hurt her. Neither of them would come out of that unscathed.

"I'm sorry, Addison." So sorry that his heart felt like it was fucking bleeding.

Tears welled in her eyes, almost breaking him. "I get it. I wish things were different but…I get it. I just want you to be okay."

Somehow her understanding made it worse. He had no fucking idea how, but it did. "Just until I know that you can touch me and no part of my body will confuse you with a threat."

She nodded, a single tear falling down her cheek.

He wanted to tell her that it would be soon, but that would be an empty promise he couldn't keep. He had no idea how long it would take to fix himself or how the fuck he was supposed to get there.

His fingers twitched to swipe the tear away. He turned before he could. Walking away was hard. Maybe one of the hardest things he'd ever done.

In the bedroom, he pulled on jeans and a T-shirt.

He felt her behind him. "I'll call someone to watch the house."

"*I'll* leave," she pushed. "You stay. It's your home."

"No. Stay here. Lock the doors. It's safer than your place. I'll talk to Jesse about what we can do to ensure your safety." Whatever it was, it had to keep her safe from him as well.

Once he was dressed and his bag packed, he moved to the door, every step feeling hard and heavy and wrong. He grabbed his car keys from the hall table and flicked off the alarm. He'd just put a hand on the door when he felt it.

Addie grazed his arm, her warm, gentle touch surging into his bloodstream. "Noah, I'm not going to try to stop you. I just need you to know…I'll be waiting for you."

His fingers tightened on the knob, his eyes squeezing closed in pain. He couldn't trust himself to turn to her. To look at her. Because then he'd back out of this. And he couldn't afford to do that.

He stepped outside and pulled the door closed behind him. Then he had to physically force himself to move. To put one foot in front of the other. When he slid behind the wheel, he didn't leave right away. Instead, he sent a text to Becket asking him to watch the house until Jesse could sort out some protection.

Twenty minutes later, his cousin pulled up, and finally he drove away, but not before making himself a promise. This was it. This was when the healing began. For Addie. For their future.

"Oh, my darling girl, I'm so sorry."

Addie dug her fingers into her thighs beneath the table, the bite of pain helping to hold off the tears. Jules didn't need to see her cry. "It's been three days since I moved out. And three days since I've heard his voice. I hate it."

She'd left because she had to. Packed up her things that same morning and moved back home. She hadn't been able to stay. Everything had smelled like him. A constant reminder that he was gone.

Her parents were still at her house, and she'd craved their comfort. Plus, it meant her house didn't feel too quiet. And she had people to pretend she was okay in front of. Not that she'd been very good at pretending.

Of course, Noah had texted that same night asking where she was. A part of her had hoped that he'd reply asking her to come back. That he'd made a mistake.

He hadn't.

Jules reached over the table and grasped her hand. "Your parents are still in town?"

"Yeah, but they're leaving tonight. Mom has to get back to

work. Dad offered to stay. Well, less offered and more pushed. But I don't want him here. I want him away from me and in Bozeman where it's safer. He's not a young Marine anymore. Plus, I seem to always have a deputy on me watching my back."

She glanced out the window, and sure enough, the patrol car was in the lot.

Jules nodded slowly. "It's good you have such great parents. But can I give you my two cents on this whole Noah stuff?"

"Of course."

"This might be for the best. You've only known him for a short amount of time. He's been through a lot. It sounds like he needs a bit of time to work through some things before he gets into a long relationship."

Addie frowned. "I wish I could be there for him while he works through it. I wish I could help him."

"Sometimes people need to figure stuff out on their own." Jules suddenly coughed, and when she brought her hand up to her mouth, her fingers were shaking.

"Jules, are you okay?"

"Yes, I'm fine. Just a cough."

Addie studied the older woman, suddenly noticing how pale she looked.

Jules lifted a hand to her forehead and massaged her temple.

"Do you have a headache?" Addie asked.

"Yes, it comes and goes."

"Are you sick?"

Jules lowered her hand and smiled, but it looked forced. "I'm okay. In fact, I feel better than I have in a long time."

"Why's that?"

"Because I'm sitting here, in this beautiful small town, talking to you. I'm happy."

Addie tilted her head. "That's great, but if you're sick—"

"I'm fine. Really."

Addie wanted to push. She'd become so fond of Jules these

last few months, and she wanted her to be okay. But now that she thought about it, she barely knew anything about the woman. They always spoke about *her*.

God, she was the worst. Yes, Jules asked a lot of questions, but Addie should have asked more questions back. "I'm sorry, I should know this already, but do you have family close by?"

"Oh, my husband and I divorced a long time ago, and he's since passed. But even before he died, he was a narcissist, so no tears shed there. And I have one daughter who I don't see nearly enough of."

One side of Addie's mouth lifted. "She's lucky to have you."

"No, *I'm* the lucky one." She coughed again.

This time, Addie reached over and placed her hand on Jules's arm. "You should go home and rest."

"Yes, I might do that. But I've actually got an appointment in twenty minutes." She checked her watch. "I should get going. Thank you for the visit. Again, I'm sorry about Noah, but I'm glad that you're safe. Do you want me to walk you to your car?"

She shook her head. "I'm in the parking lot and the deputy's car is right there."

"Okay. Keep safe, dear." She climbed out of the booth but pulled Addie into a hug before she left.

Addie hugged her back, loving that she'd developed such a good friendship with the older woman. She'd learned quickly that very little matched a big bear hug from Jules.

The second she left, Addie's mind went back to Noah. A part of her had expected—well, hoped and prayed—that he'd call in the last three days. Had he not because it was too hard for him? He needed to cut as much contact as possible?

She shook her head. She needed to stop. She was being selfish in trying to keep him. If he needed space to heal from his trauma, then she needed to give him that space.

Pain cut through her chest at the thought. All she wanted to do was help him. It was all she'd *ever* wanted.

With a small sigh, she rose from the table.

She'd just stepped outside when she almost ran straight into someone. She frowned when she realized she recognized him. Although, she'd only met him once.

"Toby."

The therapist's brows rose. "Addison, right?"

"Just Addie's fine."

He smiled. "It's nice to see you again."

"You too." Well, not really. She'd been angry at the guy since Noah's revelation the other night.

"How are you?" Toby asked, his smooth voice strangely calming.

"I'm fine." She had the notion that she was treading water without knowing if she was going to sink or swim.

"That's good. Well, it was great to see you." He stepped around her.

Go to your car, Addie. Leave it be.

Did she listen to the voice in her head? Absolutely not.

She turned back toward him. "You agreed that he should leave me."

Toby faced her again. "Excuse me?"

"Noah. He came to you for help, and you encouraged him to leave me."

"I'm sorry, I can't disclose what's discussed between me and my patients."

"You don't have to disclose anything; he already did. And I'll give him space if he wants it. I would give that man anything he asks. But just so you know, you're wrong."

Toby's brows lifted. "Wrong?"

"We're stronger together, both of us, and his healing doesn't have to happen in isolation."

"Addie—"

"I know you meant well, but love isn't something you earn

once you're 'fixed.' It can help us mend. And I should be with him, walking with him through the darkness."

Before he could reply, because there was nothing he could say to change her mind, she turned and headed toward her car. She didn't feel bad about what she'd said, but she didn't feel good either. There was just this hollowness inside her where Noah had been. She missed him. She missed him so much, and knowing that he loved her but was hurting alone made it all worse.

When she pulled into her drive, she took out her phone and sent him a text for no other reason than she needed to tell him.

Addie: I miss you.

Three words. That was it.

He might not write back, but at least he'd read what she'd written.

She climbed out of the car, grabbed her bag from the back, and moved into the house.

"It's too hot, Mark. Here, let me cool it down."

Her father whipped his coffee mug out of her mother's reach. "I like my coffee hot."

When the door closed behind her, they both looked up.

Her mother's brows pinched while her father's jaw locked.

Could they see her sadness? The same sadness she'd been trying to hide for days?

Her mother crossed the space between them and pulled her into a hug, and that was when she let the tears fall.

She *was* sad. And in the safety of her mother's arms, she couldn't hide it.

* * *

Noah punched the bag so hard, it rattled under the impact. His arms ached and his ribs hurt. He'd lost track of how long he'd been here.

But he didn't stop. Not yet.

Three days. Three entire fucking days of no Addie, and it was killing him.

Coming home to Amber Ridge was supposed to be the answer. It was supposed to stop the nightmares. Stop him from waking with trembling limbs. He'd done everything right. Gotten out. Come home. Immersed himself in civilian life and started therapy.

So why the fuck wasn't he getting better?

He punched the bag harder, feeling the impact run up his shoulders. Each hit came harder...faster. Air whooshed in and out of his lungs.

He'd always thought he was a strong person. But wouldn't a strong person have been able to process what had happened by now and move on? Why wouldn't that period of his life leave him the fuck alone?

"Hey."

He spun around, his fist flying back like he was going to punch the guy.

The man didn't so much as flinch.

Noah's chest heaved as he lowered his fist. There was something familiar about the man. He was tall and muscled, with dark hair and eyes. "You shouldn't sneak up on people."

The guy's brows rose. "It's my gym."

His gym... Then he remembered where he'd seen the guy—in The Tea House the day Rhett had approached Addie.

"You're the UFC fighter who opened the place?"

"Former UFC fighter. And former Army Ranger."

So the guy was a high achiever.

"I'm Zane."

"Noah."

Zane gestured toward the octagonal ring in the center of the room. "Want a round in the ring, Noah?"

He glanced at the ring. He'd been here so long, his muscles

ached. But they also craved the exhaustion that would come from a real fight.

Zane must have seen it, because without a word from Noah, he tilted his head. "Come on. One round. I'll go easy on you."

Noah could have laughed. He didn't want the guy to go easy on him. He wanted to hit someone. To feel the impact of someone hitting *him*.

Zane pulled on the same type of gloves Noah wore. They had padded knuckles but open fingers to allow grappling. They also had secure wrist straps.

"You need to warm up?" Noah asked.

"Nope. I'm good to go."

They touched gloves before Noah stepped back and centered his weight on the balls of his feet. Then they circled each other slowly, eyes locked.

Noah threw the first jab. Zane dodged it easily. Next Noah tried a sharp left hook. Again, Zane avoided it, the hook missing his cheek by an inch.

The guy had good reflexes. But then, Noah expected that from a former UFC fighter.

A minute in and Zane hadn't made a single offensive move.

"You gonna throw a punch?" Noah asked, arms up.

"When I need to."

Noah jabbed again, followed by a low kick to the leg. Zane absorbed it, barely flinching before finally throwing his own jab-cross combo. Noah avoided the first hit, but the second caught him in the shoulder.

Pain flared through his body—and it was exactly what he needed.

He retaliated with a kick to Zane's ribs that landed hard.

The two of them continued like that for another twenty minutes, each hit coming hard and fast. Noah put so much focus on the fight that everything else in his world blanked, and for the first time in days, he could breathe. It was the fresh fucking air that he needed.

By the time they finished, Noah had nothing left. The taste of blood tinged his tongue and exhaustion pulled at every limb.

Zane straightened, not looking tired at all. But then, he hadn't spent an hour at the bag before the sparring match. He nodded. "That was good. Feel better?"

"Tired."

"It's when we're tired that we stop focusing on the petty bullshit that doesn't matter." Zane tapped his shoulder. "Anytime you want another round, shout out."

"Thanks. You've opened a good place here."

"So far, it's proven to be a good decision. We'll see if it remains that way." He pulled off his gloves and left the ring.

Noah had a quick shower before leaving the gym. He was almost back at his truck before he noticed Addie's father's car beside his.

He frowned. "Mark, what are you doing here?"

"I went to your house, but you weren't there. A neighbor said you've been getting home late with a gym bag. This is the only gym in town."

Jesus. He was like a detective. Either that, or his neighbors had big mouths. "Everything okay?"

"No."

His muscles locked, panic hitting him square in the chest. "Is it Addie? Is she all right?"

For a moment, Mark was silent, taking Noah's measure. "My daughter is a strong woman. Some people think that because she's young, she doesn't know what she wants, but they're wrong. She's always known. And she wants you, Noah."

He swallowed, his throat suddenly dry. "I need to work through some things first."

"I know. That's why I'm here. To tell you that I've been where you are. I had some shit to work through when I got out, and I had to decide whether I was going to work through it alone or with Diana."

"How did you decide?"

"I didn't. I just couldn't stay away from her."

"So she helped you heal?"

"I'll never fully heal. What I went through, what a lot of people in the military go through, is nothing that can be *recovered* from. But it *is* something we can learn to live with. And I wanted to live with Diana…just like you want to live with my daughter."

"Sir—"

"Take this." He held out a piece of paper.

"What is it?"

"It's the number of my therapist. I know you've got a guy you're seeing, but my guy's better. I can say that because I truly believe he's the best. And I guarantee you'll see progress by the end of the first session."

Noah took the paper from Mark's fingers. He still had the card Addie had given him with the same name and number.

"Diana and I are leaving tonight. I hope that I see you again, son." He took a step away before turning back to Noah. "We gave a lot of ourselves to our country. Now it's time to live on our terms."

Noah didn't move. Not while Mark climbed into his car or while he drove away. He stood alone in the parking lot for another minute before finally glancing down at the number.

Then he cursed before dropping into his truck and pulling out his cell. That's when he saw the text.

Addie: I miss you.

He closed his eyes, the sound of her voice in his head before he responded.

Noah: Are you okay?

Addie: Are you?

No. He wasn't. And because of him, she wasn't either.

He looked back at the piece of paper and without hesitation, called the number.

A female voice answered. "Hi, this is the office of Dr. Ted Burton, Teresa speaking. How can I help you?"

"Hi, my name's Noah Hayes, and—"

"Noah. Mark told us you might call. What can we do for you?"

Noah ran his fingers through his hair. "I'd like to make an appointment with Dr. Burton."

CHAPTER 23

"It's nice to meet you, Noah."

Noah dragged his gaze from the small rectangular window to the older doctor with the silver hair. Noah had made the one-hour drive from Amber Ridge to Bozeman for this appointment because he'd wanted to meet the doctor in person.

His office was different from Toby's. There was more stuff in the room—books filled the shelves. Photos and knickknacks sat on the desk. Throw pillows filled the worn leather couch.

"It's nice to meet you too," he finally answered.

The doctor pushed his black-rimmed glasses up his nose before lowering a pen to his notebook. "Can you tell me why you're here?"

"Because I feel like I'm trapped between two places. One minute, I'm in Amber Ridge, the next, something snaps and I'm back in Iraq, being held prisoner in a concrete cell."

"What happens in the cell?"

"I have to watch my teammate die. I have to feel that same helplessness in my bones."

"Is this just during the day?"

"No. Night too."

"That sounds terrifying." He cocked his head. "Did you have a nightmare last night?"

"I have nightmares every night. The only time I don't is…"

The doctor waited a beat, then asked, "The only time you don't is when?"

"When Addison's with me." The second he said her name, he felt that familiar ache in his chest. The same one he felt any time he thought about her.

His bushy white eyebrows pulled together. "Who's Addison?"

"Mark's daughter."

"No, who's Addison to *you*?"

Noah looked out the window again, focused on a branch that was blowing in the wind. He didn't even know how to answer that question. "She works at a park that my friend and I run. And I love her."

"She's your girlfriend?"

"She was. I told her I needed a break."

The doctor tilted his head. "Why would you give someone up who was helping you? She *was* helping you, wasn't she?"

"She was the *only* thing that helped. But it wasn't fair to her. I'm not in control when I have flashbacks, and if I ever hurt her…" The muscles in his forearms tightened.

Dr. Burton leaned forward slightly. "Do you know what your nightmares and flashbacks are?"

"A hell I can't escape?"

"They're your brain trying to process an experience that you didn't know if you'd survive. Your brain is trying to make sense of what happened to you and find safety again. But right now, you're stuck in a loop."

"So how do I get out of the loop? Because I'm going to be honest, I've been in this seat before, and it didn't help."

"Yes, I'm your third therapist," the doctor said quietly. "But you're here anyway, which means you must have *some* faith I can help you."

Either that or he was desperate.

"I'm going to make you a promise right now, Noah. You *will* feel safe again. The nightmares might feel real, but it's *you* who's in control. It's always been you." He slid a piece of paper across the wooden coffee table between them. "In a second, I'm going to ask you to write down your last nightmare. Then read it. Then re-write it, but in a safer, more empowering way."

"How will that help?"

"It will help teach your brain that it's not happening anymore. You're not in danger. You survived. It's going to make you feel more in control and reduce the power that nightmare has over you."

He stared at the piece of paper, white and empty. He wanted to believe it would help, but he was almost scared to believe that he could get better, in case that hope crashed and died.

"But first"—Burton sat back—"tell me more about Addison."

His gaze shot up at the mention of her name. "I already told you, I asked for a break."

"Did she want the break?"

"No. It hurt her." The pain on her face flashed through his mind. Hell, it had been damn near all he could think about for the last week.

"But you did it anyway."

"To protect her."

"From you?"

"Yes." *Fuck yes.* "From the person I become when I have no control."

"Have you ever hurt her?"

Noah swallowed the lump in his throat. "No, but there have been a few close calls."

The doctor nodded slowly. "Do you want to know what I think?"

"Isn't that why I'm paying you?"

A half smile curved the doctor's mouth. "I don't think these nightmares and flashbacks make you dangerous. I think perhaps you tell yourself that as a form of punishment. Maybe because *you* survived what happened in Iraq…and someone else didn't."

Noah inhaled sharply. The guilt of Boone's death sat on his chest, so fucking heavy he couldn't breathe. It could have been him. It *should* have been him. "I don't know how to live with the guilt."

"You carry the guilt because you care. Because you loved your teammate. But that doesn't make his death your fault. Punishing yourself doesn't bring anyone back. It just buries you right alongside them. Just like suffering by yourself doesn't make you stronger. It just makes you more alone." The doctor cocked his head. "If you love her, it should be *her* choice whether she wants to sit with you in this tough time."

Noah's heart started to beat faster, the idea that he could have her while he wasn't fixed or healed or whole so enticing that his fingers ached to reach out and grab it.

"Remember, the best way to honor the ones we love is to live a *life* that honors them." Burton set a pen on top of the paper. "I'd really love to learn your story."

With shaky fingers, Noah lifted the paper and pen. This was it. This was the start of the end of his hell.

It had to be.

An hour later, Noah stepped outside and breathed a lungful of fresh air. He felt raw and vulnerable, but there was also a hope inside him that hadn't been there before.

Hope for him and Addie.

Hope that there was a way forward for them together.

As he drove home, he told himself not to get too excited. He'd felt good after his first appointment with Toby too, but progress had stalled, then stopped pretty damn quickly.

When he reached Amber Ridge, he didn't go straight home. Instead, he went to the adventure park as a way to fill his time and not obsess about Addie the entire day.

In the parking lot, he climbed out and headed down the path, only to frown when he saw Jules inside her van.

What was she doing here?

Her back was turned, and she looked to be digging through her small fridge.

"Jules."

She screeched and spun before grabbing her chest. "Holy cheese balls, Noah, you scared the life out of me!"

"Sorry, I thought you heard me coming."

She shook her head. "Nope. I was reading use-by dates. What are you doing here?"

"I'm going to clean some equipment."

She nodded, not even a glimpse of a smile on her face. "Okay."

"Did you ever find that photo you were looking for?"

Pain etched her features, but then she blinked and it was gone. "No. Hopefully it turns up."

She started to turn.

"Jules."

There was the smallest tensing of her shoulders before she turned back. "Yes?"

"I know it was you. And it's okay."

For a moment, her eyes flared, but then she blinked. "You know what was me?"

"You told the deputy what you heard me talking to Colt about the day we found Rhett."

She shuffled her feet, her cheeks going red. "I just thought they should know."

"Do you think I killed him?"

There was a short silence before she answered. "Honestly? I don't know. Probably not. But I've come to care about Addie. And I don't want her getting hurt."

"I feel the same way. If you're not comfortable working here anymore—"

"No, I want to work here."

"Good."

"I'm—" She stopped and touched her head, her brows drawing together like she was in pain.

He frowned. "Hey, are you all right?"

"Just a headache."

"Maybe you should go home and lie down."

"When I'm done here."

Noah nodded and stepped back. "Okay. I'll leave you to it. Come find me if you need anything."

He turned and headed into the mountains. He waited until he was a good distance from the food van before pulling his phone from his pocket and calling Jesse.

"Noah, hey. What's going on?"

"Have you looked into Jules at all?"

"Just a basic background check. Why?"

"She touched her head and…I'm ninety-nine percent sure her hair's a wig."

"Noah, wearing a wig is hardly against the law. There could be a whole number of reasons for it."

"I know. I just…let's keep an eye on her. Please."

* * *

ADDIE CHECKED on the patrol car through her living room window. It was almost always there.

It made her feel safe but also guilty as hell. This was a small town. There weren't a huge number of law enforcement officers to go around.

In the kitchen, she set her hot chocolate on the counter to call the sheriff's station.

"Amber Ridge Sheriff's Department, Janet speaking."

"Hi, Janet, this is Addison March. I was wondering if I could speak to Jesse."

"Is this an emergency?"

"Well, no, but—"

"He's very busy. If this isn't—"

"Please, can you just tell him it's me? I guarantee he'll take the call." Okay, she couldn't guarantee it, but she was hopeful.

The woman sighed. "Please hold."

There was a faint click, and the line went quiet. Ten seconds later, Jesse's voice came over the line. "Addie? Is everything okay?"

"Jesse. Hi. Yes, it's fine, but I just wanted to tell you that you don't need to waste your resources by putting a deputy on my home."

"Addie, someone was murdered. And they left you a direct threat with the body."

She swallowed, her gaze going to the window again. "I know, but I've got an alarm on my house now, and new locks."

"It's not enough. Look, we've got a new lead we're following up on. And there's at least *some* good news...the coroner has given us a time of death, which was early hours of the morning. That rules Noah out as a suspect."

Thank God.

"We're doing everything we can to get to the bottom of this," he continued. "For now, I'm going to keep the deputy outside your house. Noah would kill me if anything happened to you."

Was that the same Noah who hadn't talked to her in days? "Okay." She lifted her warm drink again. "I really appreciate everything you're doing."

"It's my job. Nothing new I should be aware of?"

"No."

"Good. Call if you need anything."

"I will."

She hung up and set the phone back on the counter. Then there was silence. The same silence that had surrounded her since her parents had left. She hated it. The home that had once felt warm and cozy now felt empty and lonely.

Maybe that was because she was bored. She'd done everything that could possibly be done work wise, and she was trying to minimize her time out of the house.

But she *did* need some groceries.

She nibbled her bottom lip.

Screw it. Grocery store, then straight home.

After pouring the rest of her hot chocolate down the drain, she grabbed her phone and keys and headed outside. But she didn't go to her car. She crossed the street, and the deputy immediately rolled down his window.

She frowned when she realized she recognized the guy. "Ellis?"

He grinned at her. "Hey, Addie."

"What are you doing in Amber Ridge?" He was a deputy from the Gallatin County Sheriff's Office in Bozeman. They'd also gone to school together.

"Your sheriff asked us to loan an officer because they're running short. So, here I am."

Great. She wasn't just inconveniencing her own town; she was taking resources from Bozeman too. "I'm sorry."

"Why? It's the easiest job I've ever taken."

"You're not bored?"

"Bored of getting paid to eat pretzels, watch your house, and listen to true crime podcasts? Hell nah."

She chuckled. "Okay, well, I'm just running down to the grocery store."

He straightened. "Great. I'll follow you."

"When do you finish?"

"I'm assigned to watch you until six."

Yep, she felt like a huge, mammoth inconvenience. "Okay. I'll see you there."

She climbed into her car and drove to the grocery store. She'd just pulled into a parking spot when her phone vibrated with a text.

Noah: Hey, Addison. How are you?

She stared at the text for a full thirty seconds.

It was so formal. A stranger could have written it.

Addie: I'm fine. Running into the grocery store.

As she walked toward the entrance, she noticed that Ellis wasn't far behind. Her phone buzzed with another text.

Noah: Are you alone?

He should already know the answer to that because both he and Jesse had decided.

Addie: There's a deputy with me.

Noah: Good.

She grabbed a basket and was about to push her cell into her pocket when the next text came through.

Noah: Have you been spending much time with Jules?

Her brows drew together. Where had *that* question come from?

She stopped in the bread aisle.

Addie: She brought over some food this morning, and we had a chat yesterday. Why?

Jules was probably the closest thing she had to a friend in this town. If she called Indie, the other woman would probably hang out with her. But she was Noah's sister, so it felt strange right now.

Noah's name popped onto the screen as the phone rang.

Her heart did a little skip. She hadn't heard his voice in days. And she missed it. God, she missed it so much. She missed all of him.

She put the cell to her ear. "Noah?"

"Hey, Addison."

She closed her eyes, letting the deep rumble of his familiar voice roll over her skin. "Is everything okay?"

"I need you to do something for me."

"What?"

"Stay away from Jules. At least for the moment."

She frowned. "Why?"

"I just need you to take my word for it."

Frustration tangled with the anger that was already sitting in her chest. "No. Unless you tell me why, I'm not doing it. She's my friend. She's been looking after me. So you need to give me a good reason if you want me to give her up."

"Addie—"

"Unless you have something new to tell me, I'm hanging up." She started pulling the cell from her ear when Noah spoke quickly.

"She wears a wig."

Addie froze. "What?"

"I saw it move. It could be nothing, but I just...I have a bad feeling. She works at the park, so she's had access to things like your key *and* Rhett. She's had ample means to get close to you. She arrived in town at the same time all of this started. Please."

Jules wore a wig? Addie never would have guessed.

She didn't want to agree to not seeing Jules. But what if she *was* involved? Then the question became—why? "Okay. I don't think she has anything to do with this, but to err on the side of caution, I'll stay away from her for now."

"Thank you."

She nibbled her bottom lip. "How have you been?"

"Good. I actually saw your dad's therapist this morning."

"You did?"

"Yeah." There was a small pause. "He thinks I made a mistake pausing things with you."

Tears Addie hadn't expected gathered in her eyes, but she blinked them away. She was about to ask him what *he* thought— then Jules stepped into the aisle.

Crap. "Noah, I need to call you back."

"Is everything okay?"

"Yes. Everything's fine." She hung up before he could get another word in.

Jules smiled when she saw Addie and closed the distance between them before pulling her into a hug.

"Addie, hi, honey." When she pulled back, she frowned. "Is everything okay? You feel tense."

She was probably stiff as a board. "I'm fine." She cleared her throat. "Doing some shopping?"

"Restocking some things for the van in the hope that the park opens in the next week or so." She tilted her head. "Should you be out by yourself?"

She opened her mouth to tell Jules she had a tail but stopped herself. If Jules was a suspect, she should say as little as possible. "It's just a quick trip."

"Okay, as long as you're keeping safe. How about a coffee tomorrow?"

Oh, man. She wanted to say yes. She enjoyed her catch-ups with Jules. It was strange, actually. She felt a connection to the other woman that she hadn't really experienced with anyone else, friends or strangers.

But she'd made a promise to Noah. "The guys have actually given me a bit to do on the park's website. Rain check?"

"Oh. Sure. I'm also happy to come over with my laptop and keep you company too. I have admin to do, and it must be lonely at your house. I—" She stopped and winced, grabbing her head.

Addie touched her shoulder. "Hey. You *still* have a headache?" It seemed to be constant. Every time they met lately, Jules looked to be in some sort of pain.

She smiled but it looked forced. "I'm okay. I'll text, okay? Let me know if you need anything before then."

Addie nodded and watched the older woman walk away.

No. Jules couldn't possibly have anything to do with this… could she? She seemed so kind and genuine and always wanted to help. There didn't appear to be a bad bone in her body.

Or if there was…she hid it well.

CHAPTER 24

Addie jogged from her car to the door of The Tea House. It was raining and cold, and she needed a hot chocolate in her belly as fast as humanly possible. It wasn't even a want anymore. It was an if-she-didn't-get-it-she'd-die kind of need.

Okay, maybe not die, but life would be tough.

A sigh slipped from her lips when she stepped inside the café. It was warm. Warm and dry. Two things that felt pretty dang good.

She'd run out of chocolate powder at home. Who knew how that had happened—she usually had a backup for her backup container, but she'd been distracted at the grocery store last week.

Mrs. Gerald smiled at her from behind the counter. "Addie, good timing. I just received an order of salted caramel hot chocolate."

"Oh my God, Mrs. Gerald, I could kiss your feet."

The café owner chuckled. "No kisses needed. A large?"

"The biggest to-go cup you have. And a cappuccino, please."

"Won't be long."

The cappuccino was for Ellis. She glanced over to see him

"

standing outside the café, under the small shade. They'd gotten into a good routine this last week. He tailed her. She bought him coffee, sometimes pie, and all was right in the world. He'd even given her some true crime podcast recommendations. Not that she'd be listening to them anytime soon—it wasn't really her thing.

Not only had she felt safer with Ellis this last week, but she and Noah were also making progress. He was calling more. Texting every day. She hadn't seen him, but it was progress.

When the drinks were done, she paid and turned, only to almost stumble straight into a woman.

"Cass. Hey." Since Rhett's death, she'd texted Cass a couple of times and even tried to call her once, but she hadn't received a response. "How have you been?"

Cass's brows lifted. "How have I been? We found Rhett's dead body at the park. *Then* I got a warning from the sheriff's department for not disclosing all of the information from the day of the climb."

Addie glanced around, noticing people at the nearby tables staring at them. Not a surprise, considering the volume and harshness of Cass's voice. "I'm sorry. But why didn't you just tell them what you knew?"

"Because then they'd think it was Rhett, but he had nothing to do with what happened on the wall."

Addie felt like telling her that his prints were found on the container of battery acid. She just stopped herself. And in any case, it didn't excuse lying to the authorities.

"It doesn't matter anymore though, does it?" Cass continued. "Because he's dead."

Addie swallowed hard. "It was also hard for me and Jules—"

"Oh, was it? Were you both in a relationship with him too?"

She frowned. "So you were actually dating?"

"Yes. Why is that so hard to believe?"

Maybe because originally, she'd called him a man-child, then they were sleeping together, but now they'd been dating? "Look, I'm sorry. I didn't realize you two were so close."

"Are you sorry because I lost him or sorry because you're responsible for his death?"

She flinched but didn't have time to respond before Cass bumped her shoulder hard and stepped to the counter.

Addie turned, wanting to say more. Wanting to defend herself. But what was the point? Cass obviously believed what she wanted to believe.

With a sigh, she walked around her. That's when she realized Ellis had stepped inside and was only a foot away.

"Everything okay?" Ellis asked when she reached him.

"Not really. But she's just angry." She handed him a coffee. "Here you go."

"Ah, the best part of my day. Thank you."

"How else am I supposed to thank you for babysitting me?"

He chuckled as they stepped outside. "No thank you needed. I told you, it's easy."

Easy or boring? Because it looked boring. But she was glad he didn't hate it.

She climbed into her car, and on the drive home, her thoughts went back to Cass. Had Cass spoken to Noah or Colt about how she felt? And did she really blame Addie, or was she just upset right now?

When Addie pulled onto her street, she saw the car outside her house. Jules.

She pulled into her driveway and turned off the car, and yep, Jules stood by the front door under the porch, dish in hand.

Oh no. Addie had successfully avoided Jules for the last week, always coming up with excuses as to why they couldn't catch up —some believable, some not so much. It had been hard.

Holding her hot chocolate, she climbed out and headed toward the front door.

Jules straightened. "Hi, Addie. I hope it's all right that I dropped by."

"Is everything okay?"

"I was worried about you. I haven't seen you in a week."

Addie held back a frown. "You don't need to worry about me. I've just been taking a few days to myself. So much has happened with Rhett and Noah that I thought it was needed."

"I understand that." Jules's gaze shifted to the door, then back to her. "Can I come in? We can have a chat."

Crap. She didn't want to be rude, but she'd made a promise to Noah.

But then...what exactly made Jules a suspect? She glanced at the woman's hair before moving back to her eyes. A wig? There could be plenty of reasons for it. Still...

"I'm actually expecting someone. Maybe next week?"

Jules's frown deepened. "It's my wig, isn't it?"

Addie's eyes widened. How did she know? "Um—"

"I know Noah saw it the other week. And when I saw you at the grocery store, you glanced at it a few times, and again just now."

Dammit, she was too obvious. "Jules...I'm sorry. I don't know what to think. I'm just trying to stay safe."

Jules bit her bottom lip before resignation washed over her face. "I have brain cancer."

Addie's stomach dropped like she'd been punched. "*What?*"

"I have terminal brain cancer." Jules swallowed. "I wear the wig because my hair fell out, and now it's short and patchy, and I don't look like the person I used to. I wear the wig to feel just a little bit more like my old self."

Tears welled in Addie's eyes. "Oh, Jules, I'm so sorry."

"Thank you. It's been hard. Really hard. But this friendship between us has helped me."

Addie didn't know what to say. She wanted to cry for Jules. "I've really enjoyed our friendship too."

Jules nodded. "Good. I won't force myself on you. I know you're doing what's best for you, which is exactly what you need to be doing, so I'll go. Hopefully when this is all over, we can resume our friendship." Jules handed her the dish before walking back to her car.

Addie opened her mouth to call her back but stopped. She believed Jules, but at the same time, she didn't have any proof... and Jules was right. She had to protect herself.

God, she hated this. All of it. Not taking Jules into her home and wrapping her in her arms felt wrong.

As Jules drove away, the same words repeated over in her head—terminal cancer. It made Addie want to cry, and she hadn't even known her for that long.

She just had to pray that they found the person doing all this. It wouldn't be Jules. *Then* she could be the friend Jules needed her to be.

* * *

NOAH PULLED INTO HIS DRIVEWAY. It was midafternoon, and the drive from Bozeman had taken longer than usual with construction slowing him down. He didn't care. The session had been another good one. Hell, he'd only had four sessions with the new doctor and already he felt different. Lighter. The nightmares had still come, but not every night...and the biggest difference was, he didn't wake up in a cold sweat. His heart didn't race. He was able to open his eyes and breathe.

Was it possible there was another side to this PTSD? A side where he could function again? Sleep and have a healthy relationship? A few weeks ago, he wouldn't have believed it. Now? Now there was this light at the end of the tunnel, and every therapy session brought him closer.

He was about to climb out of his truck when his phone lit up with a call from Toby.

Shit. He hadn't called the other therapist since canceling his last appointment. Did he owe Toby more than that? Probably a conversation. But not right now, while he was feeling good. He'd do it later.

He climbed out and walked to the front door.

Jesse had run another background check on Jules, but again, nothing had shown up. She'd lived her entire life in Missoula before moving here to work at the park. She'd worked in a café for the previous five years. She was also divorced.

Inside, he turned to his alarm, only to stop.

It was off.

The *fuck?* He never left home without turning it on.

Quietly, he slipped into his bedroom and took the Glock out of the bottom drawer beside the bed. Then, slowly, he crept back into the hall. He kept his back close to the wall and the Glock to his chest.

Someone had accessed his home. Who? Were they still here? And how the fuck had they turned off his alarm?

He stepped into the kitchen, only to stop at the crackle of plastic from his walk-in pantry.

What the hell were they doing?

With silent steps, he inched closer. When he reached the pantry, he spun, Glock raised and aimed.

The second he saw her, he lowered his weapon. *"Indie?"*

She didn't turn. It was like she didn't hear him.

Was she…organizing his pantry?

He tapped her on the shoulder, and she screeched, a packet of noodles flying into the air as she spun around. She pressed one hand on her pregnant belly and the other to her chest. "Noah! I think you almost sent me into labor." She yanked out an earbud and glared at him like *he'd* done something wrong. "Do you *know* how dangerous it is to sneak up on a pregnant woman? Do you want to deliver a baby right now?"

"Indie…you broke into my house."

"I did not. You gave me a key and the code for the alarm. I didn't break anything."

He scrubbed a hand over his face. *Jesus Christ.* "Next time…text."

"I was going to, but then I got hungry. I came in looking for a snack, but your pantry looked like a war zone, so I got distracted."

She'd broken into his house in an attempt to get a snack, only to reorganize his pantry? "Is this a pregnancy thing?"

She rolled her eyes. "It's a my-brother's-a-slob thing." She lifted a bag of candy and stepped into his kitchen. "I found these. Since when do you eat candy?"

"I don't. Addie bought them. She's more of a chocolate person, but she switches to candy every so often."

Indie glanced at the candy, then back at him. "Does that mean I can't have any?"

He chuckled. "Open them. I'll replace them."

"Thank God. Last time I was denied candy, I cried. Apparently, pregnancy makes you irrationally emotional." She ripped the bag open and popped a Swedish Fish into her mouth.

"Indie…what are you doing here?"

"I'm here to see *you*." She dropped onto a stool and patted the one beside her.

He put the Glock on the counter before sitting. "I didn't see your car."

"Colt dropped me off."

"So he witnessed you breaking in?"

"Again, there was no breaking involved. But yes, he came in with me before I told him he could go while I reorganized the pantry." She lifted another candy but didn't put this one in her mouth. "How are you doing?"

Noah ran a hand through his hair. "Better."

"I've been wanting to talk to you for a while." She paused, her expression softening. "Something happened on your last mission, didn't it?"

He should have told her. He knew he should have told her. She was his sister. His closest family member. And she'd shared so much about her fertility struggles, he should have let her into his darkness too. "There was an ambush. My teammate and I were captured. They killed him in front of me in an attempt to get information out of me."

Tears immediately filled Indie's eyes.

Shit. "See, this is why I didn't tell you."

She scrubbed her eyes. "No. They're just pregnancy hormones. I told you, I've been emotional." She reached over and squeezed his leg. "I'm so sorry you went through that, Noah."

"I'm working through it. I've found a great therapist and I'm making progress."

"Why didn't you tell me?"

"You've had your own stuff going on." Not just the infertility she'd grappled with for years. She'd also been separated from Colt. She'd had issues with his mother. Not to mention her struggles with her mental health.

Indie tilted her head. "You need to tell me these things. I know you're good at taking care of everyone else. But we want to take care of you too. I love you, Noah. I need you to be okay."

His heart gave one of those big fucking thuds. "I love you too, Indie. And I should have told you."

"What can I do to help?"

"You're already doing it by being here. And growing my niece or nephew in your belly."

One side of her mouth lifted but then lowered again. "What's going on with Addie?"

"I fucked up. I've *been* fucking up."

"Tell me about it."

"I was having flashbacks. Sometimes while I was awake, sometimes asleep. I didn't like her being around me when I had them. They were unpredictable...so I decided she just shouldn't be around me at all right now."

She seemed to take a second to process that. "I'm going to tell you what I think."

"Of course you are."

"You love her. I can see it. And I'm certain she loves you too, because who wouldn't? And if what you say is true, then she's already seen the worst parts of you. She's seen your demons, and she hasn't run from them."

"But what if I hurt her?"

"Do you think you're capable of that?"

"A year ago, I would have said no."

"Ask me."

He frowned. "What?"

"Ask me if you're capable of hurting her."

"Indie—"

"The answer is no. I *know* you. I've known you my entire life. There is not a bone in your body capable of hurting a woman. Especially her. Maybe sometimes you feel like you lose control, but you'll always come back to the light before it's too late. I don't need to be a licensed therapist to know that."

He swallowed hard. Even if she was right, he was still scared, which was a new emotion for him, because not much scared him. At least, not much *used* to scare him.

Indie leaned closer. "She makes you happy and she wants to support you...so let her."

It was exactly what Dr. Burton had said. And hell, it was exactly what every part of him had been screaming to do.

So what the hell was he doing *here*?

CHAPTER 25

The doorbell rang at exactly five-fifty p.m. Addie's stomach grumbled. Pizza. Thank God. Although, she hadn't heard the best things about Burt's Pizza.

Ha. That was an understatement. She'd been flat-out warned against the place.

But there'd been nothing else that delivered around here on a Sunday night. She'd called half a dozen places and every one of them told her it was pickup only, and she was already comfy and warm with the heater on and wearing her best sweats. The last thing she wanted to do was change and tackle the wind and cold outside.

She grabbed some money from her purse and opened the door to a kid with shaggy bleach-blond hair who wore a name tag.

She smiled warmly. "Hi, Pete. You have one pepperoni and one cheese pizza for me?"

"Yeah. Here you go." He didn't smile. Not even a hint of a smile.

Okay, not the warmest delivery. Odd, considering he was the

nephew of the infamous Burt, apparently both the friendliest and worst pizza maker in Amber Ridge.

"Thank you." She took the pizzas and handed him payment with a tip. He didn't even say thank you. Just turned and left.

Bad pizza *and* poor service? How was this place still in business?

She closed the door and moved to the kitchen, where she set the cheese pizza on the counter before heading back toward the door. The pepperoni was for Ellis. He finished his shift in less than ten minutes. Although, she might need to warn him about the quality before he took a bite. The pizza in Bozeman was good, so this might be a shock to his system.

The second she stepped outside, wind hit her in the face. Argh. Cold. She hated the cold.

She jogged across the lawn…only to frown when she got closer to the patrol car.

It was empty.

Where was he? Was he doing a perimeter check? He'd told her he did them hourly, so maybe.

She turned and scanned the street, then her house, but she saw no one.

Her pulse picked up speed, and suddenly the need to be back in her house with the door locked almost suffocated her. She was halfway up the drive when she spotted something.

An arm. It was poking out from the side of the house, not visible from the street because her car was parked in the drive.

Oh, God…had Ellis fallen?

Quickly, she ran to the side of the house—only to freeze, every inch of her skin turning to ice.

At first it didn't seem real. His stillness. The red soaking the back of his shirt.

But it *was* real. Someone had stabbed him.

No.

She shot forward, closing the distance between them before tumbling to her knees, the pizza dropping to the side. "Ellis?"

Nothing. Not even a flicker of movement.

Oh, Jesus. Her fingers shook violently as she checked for a pulse.

Dull thumps hit her fingertips.

He was alive! Thank God.

Help. She needed to get him help! An ambulance. Medical care. *Something.* But her cell was inside.

Her knees shook as she pushed to her feet, almost giving out on her. She didn't let them. She forced her feet to move, ignoring the buzzing between her ears that competed with the sounds of her ragged breaths as she sprinted into the house. She was about to leave the door open, then stopped. Someone had stabbed Ellis. That someone could still be out there. She turned and flicked the lock.

Her chest heaved in panic.

Phone. Where had she left her phone?

After her shower, she'd texted Jules. It was in the bedroom.

She sprinted to the bedroom. The second she stepped inside, someone grabbed her arm from behind and threw her to the floor.

She cried out but didn't have time to push up before a heavy body dropped onto her back, preventing her from moving.

Fear locked her muscles. She opened her mouth to scream, but a sharp blade suddenly touched her throat.

Air stalled in her lungs, fear catapulting her into stillness.

A mouth touched her ear, warm breath skittering over her skin, making nausea crawl up her throat. She wasn't sure if they were about to say something—but a knock on the front door suddenly banged through the house.

A hand quickly covered her mouth, the knife pressing so hard to her skin she felt a slice of pain.

"Addison?"

Noah! He was at her door!

Her breathing quickened, the need to get free, to scream his name, consuming all the terrified parts of her.

"Addie, are you okay? I came to talk to you but saw the patrol car's empty." There was a small pause. "Can you let me in?"

The hand on her mouth tightened, fingers cutting into her cheek.

A few seconds of silence passed. Then the asshole loosened their hold. Not just the hand at her mouth, but the knife too.

Did they think Noah had left?

It didn't matter.

Quickly, she tucked her chin hard to her chest, which both protected her neck and caused his hand to slip from her mouth—then she screamed.

* * *

NOAH PULLED up in front of Addie's house. The need to see her consumed him. Everything Indie and his therapist had said was true. Addie hadn't wanted to be separated from him, so he shouldn't have made that choice for her. But he'd panicked.

He wasn't sure what had changed. Maybe his therapy sessions. Maybe just the time apart from her. But now he knew he wouldn't hurt her. And with each day, after every session with his therapist, he trusted himself more.

He parked in front of her house and climbed out of his truck, only to narrow his eyes at the empty patrol car across the road. Where was the deputy who was supposed to be watching her place? Was he inside *with* her? Was he checking the exterior?

He scanned the front of the house and the yard. He wasn't within sight.

When he reached her front door, he knocked. "Addison?"

A second of silence passed. Nothing.

"Addie, are you okay? I came to talk to you but saw the patrol car's empty." More silence. "Can you let me in?"

There wasn't even the sound of movement on the other side of the door.

His gaze shot back to the empty patrol car, a bad feeling crawling through his gut.

What the hell was going on?

He was about to check the back of the house when a scream pierced the air.

His heart slammed into his fucking ribs, fear blackening the world around him.

Addie!

Without thought, he pulled off his jacket, wrapped it around his elbow and smashed the glass beside the door. Then he reached inside and flipped the lock.

It took him less than five seconds to gain entry. Despite his speed, when he stepped inside, there was the crash of the back door slamming against a wall and a small, feminine groan from the master bedroom.

He had to choose—chase the asshole or go to Addie.

He chose Addie.

He sprinted into the bedroom, and his heart stopped at what he saw.

Addie lay on her side, hand on her neck, a hint of blood between her fingers.

"Addie!" He dropped down beside her.

Her gaze shot up, the terror in her eyes shifting to relief. "Noah."

"How bad?"

She shook her head. "I'm fine. Just a nick from his knife touching my neck." She removed her hand and, sure enough, the cut was small.

Relief had the world graying around him.

"Go," she pushed. "See if you can still catch him."

He didn't want to leave her. He wanted to stay here. Hold her. Protect her. But she was right. He had to find the asshole.

He sprinted through the house and crashed out the back door.

There was no sign of anyone, and the neighboring fences were so low, the person could have easily jumped any one of them.

The asshole could be anywhere. *Fuck!*

He stepped back inside and pulled his phone from his pocket to call Jesse.

"Noah."

"Addie was attacked. I need you at her house *now*." Footsteps sounded from the other room, and he raced into the hall just as Addie went out the front door, towels in her hands. He cursed. "I need to go." He raced outside after her. "Addie!"

She didn't stop at his call, just continued to run around the house.

What the hell was she doing?

He reached her, and that's when he saw it—the deputy.

He dropped beside Addie and placed his hands over hers as they pressed towels against the wound.

"I've called an ambulance," Addie said quickly, her voice shaking.

He glanced at her, hating how pale she was. "I've got this," he said quietly.

She shook her head. "No. I need to help him. He was protecting me. And he…he…"

"Hey." He waited for her to look up at him, and he saw pools of tears in her eyes. "This isn't your fault."

"I don't want him to die. I don't want another person to die because of me!"

"The paramedics will be here soon. They'll take care of him." He couldn't promise the deputy would live, but fuck, he wished he could.

She nodded slowly, a tear slipping down her cheek.

The sudden high-pitched wail of an ambulance pierced the air. The second the paramedics got there, Noah lifted his hands and stepped back, but Addie remained where she was, hands on the man's wound.

"Addie, you can let them take care of him now."

She shook her head, tears still in her eyes. "He can't die."

"Addie." Gently, he gripped her wrists and tugged her back.

As soon as she was on her feet and away from the deputy, he pulled her into his arms. She fell against him, holding him as tightly as he held her.

But the entire time, the same thing ran through his mind.

What if he hadn't come? What if he'd been too late?

<h1 style="text-align:center">CHAPTER 26</h1>

Addie ran her finger along the small bandage on her neck, her gaze stuck on her reflection in the bathroom mirror. Her skin was still damp from the shower, and a towel was the only thing that covered her body.

She'd been attacked. Attacked in her own home. And Ellis had been stabbed.

Would he be okay? He'd been hurt protecting her. And the guilt… God, it ate at her.

She closed her eyes and breathed, but her lungs felt tight.

Voices sounded from somewhere else in the house, probably the living room. Were the deputies still out there? Or was it just Noah and Jesse? The second she'd been cleared, she'd given her version of events to Jesse, then come into the bathroom to shower. The need to wash the blood from her fingers had been so strong it was all she'd been able to think about.

She doubted she'd sleep here tonight. The glass beside the door was broken. But even if it wasn't, her home didn't feel safe right now. If she was honest, it hadn't felt safe since her parents left.

In her bedroom, it was easier to hear. Hushed voices came

220

from the other side of the closed door, and she could just make out what they were saying.

"We've taken prints. We're interviewing neighbors. We'll find something."

It was Jesse. He sounded angry. But then, of course he did. It was his job to find this person. And not only had he not managed that yet, they'd attacked again.

"I *need* this to be over, Jess. Tonight could have been so much fucking worse."

She dug her nails into her palms at Noah's words. If she'd thought Jesse sounded angry, that was a drop in the ocean compared to Noah.

But he was right. Tonight could have gone differently. She'd had a *knife* pressed to her *throat*. She could have been killed if Noah hadn't shown up when he did.

She took a quick step back.

It wasn't just herself and Ellis she was worried about. Noah didn't need to be dragged into this. He was already dealing with enough. Too much. And now her problems were weighing on top of his own, and she had no idea if he could carry it all.

She'd just opened the top drawer of her dresser when a knock thumped on the bedroom door. Before she had a chance to say anything, it opened and Noah stepped in. And God, there was something fierce about him tonight. The way his eyes were narrowed, as if he expected danger. The fisting of his hands like he was ready to jump into a battle to save her.

"Hey."

She swallowed hard. "Is Jesse still out there?"

"He just left. They're all gone. It's just you and me."

She nodded and looked back to her drawer, searching for her fluffy llama pajama top. "I'm sorry I bailed. I really wanted a shower." Her finger trembled as she dug through the tops. Where was it?

"Are you okay?"

That quiet question made fresh tears gather in her eyes. She hated them. She didn't want to cry. She wanted to rage and shout. God, she was tired of this. "I'm not sure. I wasn't the one stabbed in the back, so I should be."

"You still went through a lot, Addison."

She pushed more clothes aside, noticing from her peripheral vision that he was moving toward her, closing that small bit of distance between them. "I'm sorry I've dragged you into this. I'm sorry that you have to deal with this and me and all my problems when you have enough on your plate. I'm sorry…" She couldn't catch her breath, the air whipping in and out of her lungs.

Strong arms suddenly wrapped around her body from behind and covered her hands. "Addie, it's okay to not be okay. You shouldn't have gone through what you went through tonight."

"You were part of it too."

The muscles in his arms tensed. "If the asshole were here right now, I'd kill him."

The quiet fury in his voice made all the fine hairs on her arms stand on end.

She closed her eyes, allowing the feel of his body surrounding her—his warmth and strength—to soothe some of the panic that had been sitting in her chest since she'd found Ellis.

"What can I do?" he whispered.

She shook her head and turned before pressing a palm to his chest. She meant to push him away, but for some reason, couldn't. Maybe because she liked his closeness. Maybe because he made her feel safe, something she hadn't felt in hours.

"Nothing. This is my problem."

"Addie—"

"You were right to break up with me." Jesus, the words hurt. Like razor blades against her throat. "You need to focus on you and your healing. I'm setting you back." *Selfish.* The word flashed in her mind. He wasn't just protecting her…he was protecting himself. And by fighting it, she was setting him back.

His hands went to her hips. "That's *not* why I did what I did."

"It should have been. And I should have left Amber Ridge after the first warning. Maybe then, Rhett wouldn't have gotten involved with this guy and been killed, and Ellis wouldn't have been hurt. Tomorrow, it could be you." Her heart jackhammered at the thought.

"Addie—"

"But I can't go back to Bozeman, in case he follows me and puts my parents in danger."

"Addie—"

"I need to go somewhere else. It will give you the time you need to work through what happened. And maybe this person will forget about me."

She'd thought there was no space between them, but he stepped closer. "Look at me."

She didn't want to, because he had the power to make her forget everything she needed to focus on. Getting out of Amber Ridge. Keeping those she loved safe. But when his thumb slipped beneath her shirt and grazed her skin, she inhaled sharply and looked up. And those intense eyes made her feel everything she knew they would.

"You're *not* going anywhere." He said the words slowly. Firmly. Like that was the only way she'd hear or understand. "I made a mistake. I shouldn't have asked for a break. I got scared, and I'm sorry. But I'm hoping like hell you'll forgive me."

She searched his eyes. "I don't want anyone else to get hurt." Her voice cracked in the middle of her words. "I don't want *you* to get hurt." Physically. Emotionally. Hurt in any way. She *loved* Noah. And if anything happened to him…

"The only thing that will hurt me is losing you." His hand slid up her side before cupping her cheek. "Don't leave me."

She closed her eyes and leaned into his palm.

"I missed you." Her quiet words slipped into the air, soft but also so incredibly heavy.

He lowered his forehead and touched it to hers. "These last few weeks have been hell without you."

His warm breath whispered against her skin, making her tingle. It had been so long since she'd touched this man. Kissed him. Let him chase away the world around them.

He lowered his head to the crook of her neck, and his lips grazed her skin. "God, I've missed kissing you."

She closed her eyes and tangled her fingers through his hair. The next graze of his lips was higher.

"Noah…kiss me."

He lifted his head, fire burning in his eyes before his mouth crashed to hers.

The groan that tore from her lips was loud, and even though it was just a kiss, she swore she felt him everywhere.

She parted her lips for his tongue and curved it around hers. Then she was tasting him. He was mint and warmth, familiar and safe.

Needing more, she reached for the base of his shirt and tugged it over his head. The second it was off, she worked on his jeans. He stepped out of them before lifting his head.

She wanted to groan and plead for his mouth to return to hers. But then she looked up and saw the way his chest heaved. The way he looked at her with quiet awe, as if she was something he'd never quite get used to seeing in his arms. "I love you, Addison."

Her heart squeezed, the words sinking deep inside her, filling every inch of space, even space she didn't know was there. He loved her…and that meant everything.

"I love you too." Her words were barely a whisper but sounded loud in the quiet room. "I love you so much, Noah Hayes, that I ache for you."

* * *

Noah wanted to fucking drown in those words. Love. She loved him, and he loved her.

His mouth crashed to hers a second time, this kiss a slow invasion of her mouth. A taste of the sweetness that was Addie.

She was all he wanted...and she was *his*.

He reached for the knot in her towel and undid it, letting the material drop to the floor. Then he was lifting her into his arms, but she was only there for a second before he set her on the low dresser behind her.

He stepped between her thighs, and she widened for him, welcoming him.

This...this was where he wanted to be. Where he'd clawed his way back to ever since leaving her.

She wove her fingers into his hair and tugged him down. He kissed her before shifting to her cheek, then her neck. He kissed all the way down her chest until he reached one perfect nipple and took it between his lips.

Addie gasped, and the sound gutted him.

He swirled the hard bud in a circle with his tongue before sucking it deep inside his mouth. Fuck, she tasted good. And every sound she made, every groan, every whimper, felt like a reward.

He switched to her other breast and did the same, but this time grazed his teeth against the nipple before flicking it back and forth. He continued to suck her like candy as he trailed a hand down her stomach, reaching her core.

Slowly, he ran his thumb over her clit. Her entire body jolted as if struck with a bolt of electricity.

So damn sensitive.

He did it again, this time rolling the small bud.

Her breathing grew choppy, her fingers tugging at the strands of his hair, lifting his head up until she was kissing him again, her tongue diving straight into his mouth.

She shuffled closer and wrapped her legs around him, his cock fucking stone as it pushed against her, only the thin barrier of his briefs between them.

The need to plunge inside her tore at him, so fucking desperate that it took every scrap of self-restraint to remain exactly where he was.

Like she could read his mind, she reached between them and freed his cock.

His breathing stopped. It just fucking halted. Because her fingers were around him. Holding him. Driving him fucking wild.

She slid her hand up and down his cock before pressing the tip to her entrance.

He hung his head. It was the best kind of torture.

She urged him closer with her legs.

"Addison." It took everything inside him, every scrap of willpower, to grip her hips and still them both. "Wait. I'm not wearing anything."

She gasped, like she couldn't believe she'd forgotten. And yeah, he'd almost lost his damn mind too.

She reached down and opened a drawer before rummaging to the bottom to find a foil. He had it open in two seconds. As he rolled it over his cock, Addie's mouth was on him again. His shoulder, then his neck. Kissing and sucking. Toying with him.

When he was finally covered, he gripped her hips and pulled her to the edge of the dresser, his tip once again at her entrance.

Her eyes flared as she cupped his cheeks and tugged his head down, and the second their mouths met, he slipped inside her. And fuck, she was tight.

Her moan cut into the air, making blood roar between his ears. For a second he didn't move. He barely breathed.

But then Addie nipped his bottom lip before whispering, "I love you so much, Noah Hayes."

Her legs tightened, pushing him deeper, and he completely lost himself. He started to move, falling into everything that was Addie as he thrust in and out of her.

It was ecstasy. This woman and everything she did to him was exactly why he'd been fighting his way out of his head and back to her.

For this…for her.

He lowered his head and sucked her neck, tasting her skin. It was as sweet as every other part of her.

She latched onto his shoulders, her nails digging into his skin. The bite of pain competed with the waves of pleasure.

He lifted her and turned to press her against the wall. Then he was deeper, her walls clenching his cock, tipping him closer to the edge.

He continued to thrust, deeper, faster, reaching for her nipple and rolling it between his thumb and forefinger.

Her breathing grew louder. More ragged. She was close. And he wanted to nudge her over the fucking edge.

He hooked her thigh higher around his waist, and her breathing hitched, then she cried out. And he lifted his head to watch her fall. Her head flung to the side and her lips parted as she cried out his name.

Fucking beautiful. All of her.

He kept thrusting, kept moving in and out of her, until that last bit of restraint snapped and he shattered. Broke into a thousand fucking pieces and lost himself inside her.

Then he couldn't move. He just held her, touching his forehead to hers as they sucked in long gasps of air.

"I think," she whispered, heaving breaths cutting into her words, "make-up sex is my favorite."

He laughed. That…that was just one of the reasons he loved her. Because she made him laugh when laughing was the last damn thing on his mind.

Eventually he'd need to move. They had to pack up and go to his place. But right now, he couldn't. All he could do, all he wanted to do, was hold her as they stayed connected in the most intimate way.

CHAPTER 27

Addie watched the trees outside the car, anxiety tingling her spine. Maybe it shouldn't be, but the closer they got to the park, the higher her nerves crawled up her throat.

"Hey."

Her gaze swung to Noah behind the wheel. His brows were drawn together like he was worried.

How long had he been watching her?

It had been a week since the attack in her house. A week since she and Noah had found their way back to each other. It had been a quiet week…which was good, right?

He looked at the road before glancing back at her. "What's wrong?"

"I haven't been back to the park since we found Rhett."

The image of his dead body in the small kitchen flashed in her mind, making her skin crawl.

Noah reached out and gripped her thigh. "It's safe. We've got the silent alarm on the cabin that only you, me, and Colt know about, so we know no one's been in there. And I'll be by your side the entire time."

229

She nodded quickly. "I know. I guess I'm also a bit worried about Cass."

"What about Cass?"

Crap. She hadn't told him. "I guess with everything going on I forgot to mention that I ran into her at The Tea House last week. It was the same day Jules told me about her cancer."

She swallowed hard, still feeling sad whenever she thought about that. She *had* told Noah about Jules because it had been a constant on her mind.

"What happened?" he asked.

"She was angry."

"At you?"

"Yeah. She confirmed she and Rhett were in a relationship and said his death was my fault."

Noah's fingers tightened around the wheel. "She really said that?"

"She sure did." Addie lifted a shoulder. "She was hurting."

"It doesn't matter. Nothing about what happened to Rhett was your fault. He obviously got mixed up with the asshole who's harassing you and paid the price. Have you spoken to Cass since?"

"No. I texted once or twice to check in, but she hasn't responded. And I'm not sure if she'll be too…friendly toward me today." Would she spew more accusations about Rhett's death being Addie's fault? Or would she keep it to herself because they were going to be at work?

"If she says anything to hurt you, she's out," Noah said quietly.

"Noah, you don't have the staff to be letting anyone else go."

"She's already had a warning for covering for Rhett the day of the climb. And we're already advertising for new employees. We can replace her too if we need."

"She's good at her job. Besides, I'm sure everything will be fine. I *am* looking forward to checking in on Jules though." She glanced behind her at the pot of soup she'd made. After everything Jules had done for her, it didn't feel like enough.

"Hm." That was all Noah said. He didn't have to say it out loud for her to know that he still thought Jules was involved in what was going on. And that was despite the second, more in-depth background check coming up clear and Jules giving them no indication that she had anything to do with this.

Another reason she knew it wasn't Jules was because her attacker had felt like a man. His strength, the hardness of his body…there was no way it had been Jules. Something she'd told both Noah and Jesse.

When they reached the park, there were already five cars in the lot—Colt's, Jules's, Cass's, Buck's, and Flint's, which meant they were last to arrive.

She grabbed the soup, and the second Noah was around the car, his hand went to the small of her back as they headed toward the log cabin.

Inside, Colt, Buck, and Flint were talking, while Cass and Jules stood together.

Addie walked to the women, offering Cass a small smile and a hi before looking at Jules. "Hey. I made this for you."

Jules gasped. "Oh, Addie, you didn't need to do that."

"I know. I wanted to. It's my mother's famous chicken soup."

Jules took the dish and set it on the desk before giving Addie a hug. "You are so beautiful, my darling."

"Jules, you've made me a million meals in the last few months. It was the least I could do." She pulled back. "How are you doing?"

It felt like a stupid question. The woman had terminal brain cancer. Although, she didn't want to be too specific, because she was aware of Cass's presence.

Jules nodded. "I'm doing really well."

"Good." Addie stepped back.

"That was kind of you," Cass said.

Addie turned to look at her, nerves once again rattling her rib cage. "Just being nice. How are you, Cass?"

Something flared in the other woman's eyes. It came and went so quickly that Addie almost thought she'd made it up in her head. "Better. I took Noah and Colt up on the therapy they suggested and offered to pay for. It's helping." Then she smiled slightly, and it actually looked genuine.

"That's great." *Really* great. Addie didn't want things to be weird or awkward between them if they were going to continue working together.

Noah cleared his throat, and everyone turned to look at him. "Thanks for coming to the team meeting. I see everyone's gotten coffee from Jules. Thanks, Jules."

The older woman smiled before reaching for a to-go cup on the desk and handing it to Addie. "Mexican hot chocolate. I think you'll like this one."

Her mouth salivated. "Thank you."

"We still don't know when the park will reopen because they haven't found Rhett's killer," Noah continued.

There was the smallest flinch from Cass beside her.

"But they will soon," he continued. "Until then, everyone will continue to be paid as promised. And the offer for company-paid therapy is also still there."

Addie snuck a peek at Cass beside her. She seemed okay. But then why did she flinch every time they mentioned Rhett?

Was therapy really helping? Or was at least part of it for show?

* * *

HE SHOULD FEEL GOOD. The team meeting had gone well. Buck was doing better. And everyone was happy that they'd continue to be paid.

So why did it feel like a rock was sitting in Noah's gut?

Because Jesse didn't seem any closer to finding the guy? Because they didn't know how long the park would be closed or how much longer Addie would be at risk?

Addie touched his arm. "Are you okay?"

He looked down at her as they walked down the path through the park. "Yeah, just stuck in my head." A damn understatement.

A gust of wind blew over their faces. Colt and Flint were checking one side of the park while he and Addie checked another, just to make sure all the lockboxes and equipment were still okay.

"You know," she started slowly, "I'm pretty good at sorting out head thoughts."

His lips twitched. "Is that right?"

"Mm-hmm. I've even been called a brain wrangler before."

He stepped over a tree root before turning to help her. "Really? Who called you that?"

"My dad. I'm pretty sure I was six and giving him advice about our dog. Poppy kept eating his socks, so I told Dad to give him his own. Pretty good advice."

He chuckled. "It sounds like great advice, but I'm fine." He shot a look at her. "Cass seemed okay."

"Yeah, she did." Addie frowned. "It was a complete one-eighty from the last time I saw her. She said the therapy's been helping."

"Well, at least Toby's helping *someone*."

"You offered Toby's services?"

"She asked if we knew anyone, and we gave her a list of local therapists. Cass was the only one who took us up on the offer, and she chose Toby."

Addie kicked a stone. "When's your next session with Dr. Burton?"

"Tomorrow. It's strange, I've actually started looking forward to the sessions."

"You didn't look forward to them before?"

Noah laughed, but the sound was almost hollow. "I dreaded

every one of them. I had to force myself to go. But Burton's different. His sessions don't feel painful—they feel like progress. He's the first therapist to stop the nightmares. And I don't feel scared about having a flashback anymore. I feel more in control."

"Noah, that's wonderful."

He glanced at her. "I also like him because he encouraged me to make things right with *you*."

"I should get him a Christmas present."

They stopped at Jules's food truck, and Noah rounded it and checked that the doors and windows were locked. When he returned to Addie, her smile was gone and she was frowning at the vehicle, arms wrapped around her waist.

He touched her hip. "What's wrong?"

"I hate that Jules is sick. She's such a beautiful person."

"Sickness doesn't discriminate."

"I know. It just sucks."

He squeezed her hip before turning, giving her a moment to gather herself. They were just starting back toward the path when a gasp and a thud sounded from behind him. He spun to see Addie on the ground.

Fuck! He dropped beside her. "Hey! What happened?"

Her cheeks turned a pretty pink shade as she pushed up into a sitting position. "My lack of coordination in combination with my complete inexperience with hiking led me to trip over a stupid tree root."

He didn't even crack a smile. He wanted to kick his own ass for not sticking right by her side. "Are you hurt?" Gently, he lifted her hands and studied them.

"No. I'm okay. Just a wounded ego." She started to stand... only to frown, glancing to the loose soil near her feet. "What's that?" She lifted a piece of paper that was just poking out of the dirt.

Not a piece of a paper. A photo. The edges were frayed and

the print dirty, but he wasn't sure if that was from the dirt and any recent rain, or the age of the photo.

Addie ran her thumb over the photo to brush off some of the dirt. "Is that Jules?"

It was hard to tell with it being so scuffed, but maybe. "It kind of looks like her, doesn't it?"

"Yeah, but much younger."

Jules looked to be maybe in her twenties in the photo, with long dark hair. She sat in a hospital bed, holding a baby. "She was looking for a photo the other week. This must be it."

"She was?" Addie frowned. "It must be her and her daughter."

"She doesn't have a daughter."

Addie frowned up at him. "Yes, she does. She told me she has one daughter that she doesn't see nearly enough."

What the hell?

Raindrops suddenly hit their shoulders.

Shit. He wrapped an arm around Addie. "Come on. Let's get back. I'll ask Colt to check the rest of the equipment boxes."

But even as they jogged back to the cabin, his mind was still on the photo. This entire time, his gut had told him that Jules was somehow involved in whatever was going on. And now, he was even more certain.

CHAPTER 28

Addie leaned over the kitchen counter and studied the old photo. The tiny size of the baby. The grief on Jules's face. She'd wanted to call Jules when they'd found the photo yesterday and ask her about it, but Noah wanted Jesse to look into it first.

She lifted her hot chocolate and sipped the warm liquid before glancing toward the hallway. Noah was in the shower. He'd tried to get into *her* shower, but she'd all but pushed him out. They needed to get to the bottom of this Jules stuff today—*now.*

Her phone vibrated with a text.

Cass: Hey. I just finished another therapy session, and I was wondering if I could come over and talk to you about the other day? Toby encouraged me to apologize in person.

Her brows lifted. Well, Toby may not have had an effect on Noah, but he seemed to be doing wonders for Cass.

If she was home by herself, she would have said no, but since Noah was here...

Addie: Sure. Stop over whenever you're free.

She texted Cass Noah's address, then her attention shifted

back to the old photo. Why was Jules so sad? Did something happen to her baby? Is that why Jesse's background check hadn't found a child?

Regardless of why Jules looked sad in the photo, Addie was upset that the thing had gotten so damaged in the weather. The photo was obviously old and valuable. And if Jules didn't have a digital copy, it made it irreplaceable.

Hang on, was it dated? Her parents always dated photos.

She turned it over.

No date. She was about to turn it back over when her thumb ran over a light indent in the paper. She paused before running her finger over the same place again.

Something had been written there. Maybe the rain had washed it away.

She needed a pencil.

She pulled open Noah's junk drawer and started rummaging through it. Pens. Scissors. A ball of rubber bands in a knot. Her gaze landed on a lead pencil.

Gotcha.

She returned to the photo and gently shaded over the indentations.

It was a name...Alison. Then numbers. No, not numbers—a date.

Two, slash, four, slash...

She gasped at the last number.

The pencil dropped from her fingers, and she took a big step back, her hip hitting the counter behind her.

"Hey, I'm still waiting for Jesse's call."

She jumped at Noah's voice and looked up to see him walking into the kitchen.

"She might have put the baby up for adoption," he continued. "I can't think of any other reason she'd have that photo and would have told you that she still has a daughter, when Jesse's check came up with nothing."

Adoption…the word made another rock drop in her belly.

Noah stopped in front of her, finally studying her face. He frowned. "What's wrong?" He cupped her cheek, concern darkening his eyes.

"There was a date on the back of the photo. Noah…it's my birth date."

He glanced at the photo.

"There was also a name," she continued. "Alison. And a few months ago, Jules called *me* Alison by accident."

Noah's eyes flared. "And you were adopted."

The air suddenly felt thick in her lungs. "Do you think—"

"I think we need to find out what the hell is going on."

Addie looked at the back of the photo. At her birth date. At a name that perhaps had been meant for her.

"Addie." The softness of Noah's voice combined with the warmth of his hand on her cheek had her looking back at him. "Are you okay?"

"I never looked into my birth mother because I never felt the need. I love my parents. I had a great childhood. If this is true, why wouldn't Jules tell me?"

"We don't know anything yet. I'm going to call Jesse and get him to organize a meeting with her. We'll all be there. Okay?"

She nodded quickly, but a numbness had settled deep into her bones. Was Jules her birth mother? If she was, why come here, form a relationship with her, and not tell her? And was she involved in what was going on? None of it made sense.

"Addie—"

"Go. Call Jesse. I'll wait here." She needed a second alone to process everything.

Maybe he saw that on her face, because he nodded before kissing her forehead. "I'll be right back."

The second he was gone, Addie lifted the photo again. There was a shake in her fingers now, and it took her a moment to turn the picture back over. And the second she saw it again, unexpected tears blurred her vision.

The photo looked different now. *Jules* looked different.

Addie had always felt so grateful to her birth mother for choosing her parents to adopt her. And because of that, her reasons for giving her up had never really mattered before. But now? Looking into Jules's eyes? She suddenly wanted to know everything.

If it *was* true, it explained the instant connection. The motherly feel, like they were old friends.

A text came through on her phone, and she had to blink tears away to unblur the words.

Cass: Hey. Just coming to the door now. I'll be holding brownies otherwise I'd knock.

Quickly, she scrubbed at the tears that fell from her eyes. Her head was a mess, and she barely processed what she was doing as she left the photo on the counter and moved to the door to find Cass approaching the other side.

"Hi." She stopped at the door, a glass dish of brownies in her hands. "Are you okay?"

"Yeah. You've just caught me at a crappy time."

"Oh. Is Noah here?"

"Yeah, he's in the bedroom on the phone. Is it okay if we rain check?" Jules took up every inch of brain power she had. Addie needed to call her. Talk to her. Find out what the hell was going on. And until she did, she couldn't focus on anything else.

"Oh. Okay. Um, is it all right if I use your bathroom though? I left Toby's office so quickly I didn't think to make a bathroom stop."

"Sure. Of course." She turned…

And that's when she thought about the brownies.

If Cass had only decided to come here *after* her therapy appointment, how did she already have something baked?

She started to turn back, but something hard suddenly

slammed into her head. Arms wrapped around her waist, catching her before she hit the floor, as her world turned black.

* * *

"SHE WAS ADOPTED."

There was a pause over the line before Jesse spoke. "Who?"

"Addie. She was adopted. And on the back of that photo, we found a date and a name… Jesse, the date is the day Addie was born, and the name was Alison, something that Jules has called Addie before."

Jesse cursed. "That matches."

"Matches what?"

"I was just about to call you. We found hospital admission papers. Twenty-two years ago, Jules Faber had a baby girl."

"What happened?"

"At the time, she was suffering from significant mental health issues, the main one being schizophrenia. It was so severe that she'd been admitted into institutionalized mental health facilities three times before giving birth. Her medical notes say that on day two in the hospital, she had a delusion and almost killed the baby. I'll save you the details, but if nurses had been a second later, the baby wouldn't have lived."

Jesus Christ. "So she gave the baby up for adoption?"

"Yeah."

"Now Jules has found Addie. And it looks like maybe she's having more episodes."

The rustle of movement sounded. "I'm going to her place now."

"When it's safe to do so, Addie will want to talk to her."

"I'll keep you updated."

Noah hung up, fingers tight around the cell. He ran his fingers through his hair, giving Addie a few more seconds alone, knowing she needed some time to process what she'd learned.

Why? Why hadn't Jules just been honest when she'd met Addie? And how was she involved in everything that was going on?

He took a breath before stepping out into the hall.

A cool breeze brushed over his face before he saw the open front door.

The fuck?

He sprinted forward, only to stop at the drops of blood on the wooden floorboards. He followed the drops outside. Addie wasn't there. No one was.

No. "Addie?"

Nothing. Fuck!

Fear clawed at his chest, helplessness choking him.

He ran outside, following more drops of blood right to the empty street before grabbing at his hair. Gone. She was gone.

He pulled out his phone again. Jesse answered on the first ring. "Noah—"

"She's gone."

"What?"

"The door was open when I got off the phone, and now she isn't here, Jesse. Addie's gone! We need to find Jules, *now.*"

CHAPTER 29

A voice pulled Addie from her sleep, making her eyes scrunch. A familiar voice. But one she couldn't quite place. Not yet. Because her head…God, it hurt.

She reached up and touched her skull, only to flinch at the sharp pain.

What happened?

"That was my intention, but things changed."

Addie froze at the voice. A familiar voice. Cass. But she wasn't the only thing Addie heard. The deep rumble of an engine vibrated beneath her. She was in a car.

She cracked her eyes open, but everything was so blurred she couldn't make anything out.

One blink. Two. But even when her vision started to clear, she had no idea what she was looking at.

The back seat of a car? No, not even the back seat. She was on the floor, facing the space beneath the driver's seat.

"I didn't…no, that's not…"

Who was Cass talking to? And what the hell was going on?

She closed her eyes. *Think, Addie. How did you get here?*

Her eyes flashed open…the bathroom. Cass had arrived and

asked to use it, Addie turned, then…nothing. Cass had done something. Hit her? Maybe with the glass container of brownies?

Her heart beat faster. She was part of it. Cass was part of whatever was going on.

"I *know* drugging her would have kept her out for longer, but like I told you, she asked me to leave. What was I supposed to do, shove them down her throat? My choice was knock her unconscious or walk away. I chose to hit her. And trust me—it felt *good.*"

The brownies had been laced…Jesus.

She had to attack Cass. Yes, it would be dangerous while the other woman was driving, but what was the alternative? Wait for her impending death or whatever the hell was about to happen?

"The trunk?" Cass gasped. "Are you kidding? I could barely drag her limp body to the car. And I already risked a neighbor seeing *and* Noah coming out and witnessing what I was doing. I got her out of there as quickly as I could."

Noah…oh, God, he'd know she was gone by now and he'd be losing his mind.

Stupid. She was so stupid for opening the door while she was by herself. But she'd been so distracted with the photo of Jules that she hadn't been thinking.

"Look, I'm just pulling into the park now, then she'll be all yours."

Addie's heart gave a giant thump. All *whose?* Who the hell was behind this? And they were at the park?

She tried to push up, but a wave of dizziness had her falling right back down. The second she hit the floor, nausea coiled in her belly.

No. She couldn't be sick. Not now.

"What do you *mean* you're not here yet? I've done my part— I've gotten her here. Now you have to take her so I can get the hell out of Amber Ridge. And when the money comes, you give me my cut."

Money? What money?

The car suddenly stopped.

Shit. She needed a weapon. She lifted her head, grateful the upper half of her body was behind Cass's seat so she couldn't see her.

But there was nothing. The floor was completely bare.

"No. I'm not waiting in this fucking parking lot with the woman I kidnapped in the back. I may as well call the sheriff to arrest me. I'm dragging her ass out, hitting her a second time so she *stays* unconscious, then getting my ass the hell out of town. You'd better hope you get here before she wakes up."

Addie didn't have a weapon and she was out of time. It took every ounce of strength she had to remain perfectly still as the front door opened.

A second later, *her* door opened.

Breathe, Addie. Just breathe.

Hands slipped beneath her arms and dragged her out of the car. Her lower body hit the ground with a thud, but still, she made sure to remain limp. Then Cass let her upper body go, and her head hit the ground. This time, it was hard not to wince at the bite of pain.

Footsteps sounded beside her. She took a deep breath before opening her eyes to see Cass walking back toward the car.

Addie lifted her leg and kicked the other woman in the calf as hard as she could.

Cass cried out and dropped, and the second she hit the ground, Addie pushed up. For the second time, the world tilted, dizziness trying to press her back down. She refused to let it and forced herself to her feet.

"You fucking bitch," Cass growled as she jumped up.

Addie had just straightened when a kick caught her in the stomach. She cried out and fell to the ground.

"You really thought you could get away with murder?" Cass growled.

Addie tried to suck in air. "What are you talking about?"

"He *told* me what you did to Rhett. You slept with him, and when he cut things off, you lost it and killed him. You're crazy! He even told me how you made all that shit up about a stalker to gain sympathy."

Another kick caught her in the ribs. She gasped for air as pain cut into her airways.

"I don't know who told you those things," Addie gasped. "But they're lies!"

"You think I'd believe *you* over him?"

"Him *who*?"

Cass pulled her leg back to kick Addie again, but when she flung it forward, Addie grabbed her ankle and rolled, pulling the other woman to the ground. Cass's head slammed into the asphalt with a thud.

Addie didn't give her a chance to recover before she turned and kicked, getting Cass right in the face.

The crunch of Cass's nose was loud, but her scream was louder as she grabbed her face.

Addie didn't stick around to see what happened next. She shot to her feet and ran. She wanted to jump into Cass's car and drive, but there was no guarantee the key was in the car and not on Cass, and then Addie would be cornered.

And what if the second person showed up and blocked her leaving? She'd be outnumbered, and there was every chance that person would have a gun.

Addie ran straight to the cabin, but not to the door. She lifted a rock and threw it through the window. The glass shattered, but she didn't attempt to get inside. Because again, she'd be cornered. Instead, she cut into the trees behind the cabin.

The broken window would have set off the silent alarm, alerting Noah and Colt. Which meant someone would come. She just had to hide until they did.

She rounded trees and jumped over roots. Jules's food truck came into view ahead. She was just reaching it when a shout sounded behind her.

"I'm going to kill you, Addie! And I know these woods far better than you! You can't hide from me."

Too slow. She was moving too slowly. But with the rippling pain in her ribs combined with the pounding of her head, she couldn't run any faster.

Suddenly, she tripped over a rock and hit the ground hard. Her ribs cried out in pain and when she tried to push up, the pounding in her head swayed the world around her.

"You really think you can outrun me?"

Oh, Jesus… Cass was so close.

Quickly, Addie crawled toward the vehicle, but instead of hiding behind it, she crawled beneath it. There was barely any space, and she just fit. It was a risky hiding spot. If Cass checked there, then she was as good as dead.

The pounding footsteps grew closer. When they stopped at the front tire, Addie covered her mouth to silence any sounds trying to escape. Then she watched Cass's boots circle the tires.

Don't look underneath. The quiet words whispered in Addie's head.

Cass cursed and started jogging away.

Addie was just breathing a sigh of relief when a new voice sounded.

"Cass!"

Addie's heart stopped. She knew that voice.

But, no, that didn't make sense. It couldn't be him…could it?

Three words slipped from his mouth. "Where is she?"

* * *

NOAH COULDN'T BREATHE. He wanted to punch the fucking wheel, do something, *anything*, to drown out the helplessness.

She was gone. Addie was fucking gone, and he'd been right there when she was taken. He couldn't wrap his damn head around it.

He pushed his foot harder to the floor of the truck.

Was it Jules? Had she somehow instigated this?

Jesse hadn't wanted him anywhere near Jules's house, but nothing and no one could have stopped him. He wasn't just letting Jesse and his team handle this search. He was a damn Marine, and he was going to find Addie.

When he pulled up in front of the ranch-style home, Jesse and a female deputy were already on the lawn.

"Where is she?" Noah asked, before he'd even closed the door to his truck.

Jesse stepped forward. "Not home."

"What do you mean, not home?"

Jesse touched his shoulder. "I've got deputies patrolling the streets. We'll find her."

"You'll *find* her? This *could be* her. *She* could have taken Addie."

"I know. And we're doing everything we can to find out if she did." Jesse glanced behind him. "Did you check her phone? See if there were any hints of where she might be?"

A breath hissed out of him. "Yeah, I grabbed it before leaving the house." He stormed back to the truck and grabbed her cell from the middle console.

On his way back to Jesse, he unlocked the phone and went into her recent calls, but there were none from today. Then he opened her texts. "Shit."

"What?" Jesse stepped closer.

"Cass was at my house…"

"Cass?"

"Cassandra Ainslee, from the park. She texted Addie to ask if she could come over, then again to say she was there."

"What time?"

Noah looked up. "The same time she disappeared."

The woman behind Jesse touched her radio. "Dispatch, this is Deputy Claudia Russell requesting an address and plates for a Cassandra Ainslee. She's a suspect in the disappearance of Addison March. Over."

A red convertible suddenly pulled into the drive.

Jules.

Noah tried to step forward, but Jesse put a hand on his chest. "Stop. As far as we know, she hadn't broken the law yet."

"Stop? She's part of this, Jess!"

"You *think* she's part of this. We need to find out if that's the case."

Noah fisted his hands, every fucking part of him wanting to storm forward and question the woman until he had answers.

Jules climbed out and pressed a hand to her chest. "Oh my... have I done something wrong?"

"Jules Faber, I'm Sheriff Hayes, and this is Deputy Russell. We need to ask you a few questions."

She rounded her car. "What's this in regards to?"

"Addison March."

Jules's eyes widened, panic suddenly taking the place of every other emotion. "Is she okay?"

"Before we disclose anything, we need to ask you some questions. We can do that inside your house or down at the station."

The station? Fuck that. They didn't have time. Every minute— hell, every *second*—mattered.

"Where is she?" Noah growled.

Jesse turned. "Noah—"

"I know you're her birth mother. And I know you're somehow involved in everything that's happened to her."

Tears formed in the older woman's eyes, her mouth opening and closing. "You know?"

"Jules—"

"Wait." She stepped forward, cutting him off. "What do you mean, where is she? Is Addie missing?"

"Miss Faber, *please*," Jesse pushed.

She swallowed before nodding quickly. "Okay. I'll tell you everything, but I have to say, I don't know where she is right now or what's going on." Jules crossed to her front door and stepped into her house.

Noah was the last in. He'd barely stepped foot inside the living room before he demanded, "What's going on, Jules?"

The older woman lowered her grocery bags to the counter and visibly took a breath before turning. "I can tell you what I'm doing here, but I'm not sure where Addie is. I would never hurt her. Because, yes…she's my daughter. Or at least, my biological daughter." She shook her head and frowned. "I've, um, struggled with my mental health for most of my life. When Addie was born, it was the worst it had ever been. Pregnancy hormones and everything. So much so that I…I had to make the difficult decision to give her up for adoption."

Tears welled in Jules's eyes, but she blinked them back before continuing.

"Two years ago, I was diagnosed with brain cancer. That's when I started searching for her. I knew I had to find her before I died. I needed to at least meet her and confirm that I made the right decision in giving her up. I found someone who was good at locating people and they did exactly that. I didn't know how to approach her…but then, I saw the ad for a food vendor at the park. It had her name on it. So I applied."

She lifted a shoulder, like that was it. That was the end of the story.

No. That told them *nothing* about what was going on. There was more. There had to be more.

"Does anyone know you're here?" Jesse asked. "Would anyone have an issue with you being here?"

"I don't have many people in my life. Well, except my therapist. But in the eighteen months I've been seeing him, he's become more like family."

Noah's brows flickered. "Who's your therapist?"

Jules's smile softened. "You've met him. I encouraged him to come down from Billings and check out the park. He liked it so much, he decided to stay and set up an office here. Tobias Thacker."

Something hard formed in Noah's gut. "Toby? *He's* your therapist?"

"Yes. He's wonderful. We've grown close over the past year or so, and honestly, I have nothing but wonderful things to say about him."

"I was seeing him for a while too," Noah said to Jesse. "I felt like he was pushing for me to break up with Addie." Did that have something to do with all of this?

Jesse looked back at Jules. "You said you've become close with him. So he knows you have no friends or family. He also knows you have brain cancer. And when you told him that you had a daughter you wanted to reconnect with, he came down here too."

Jules frowned. "Yes. I told you, we've basically become family. What are you getting at?"

The deputy's phone rang, and she stepped outside to answer it.

"Do you have many assets, Miss Faber?" Jesse asked.

"Assets?" Jules asked. "I mean, I inherited a bit from my own parents when they passed on a few years ago. A house, some shares. A lump sum of money that I haven't touched. I live pretty frugally because that's what I'm used to. Why?"

It finally made sense. "He wants your inheritance. But then he found out about Addie, and she threatened that. He tried to scare her away before you two got close. But now…" He couldn't finish the sentence.

Jules shook her head. "No. He wouldn't do that."

The deputy stepped back into the room and looked at Jesse. "Sheriff, that was the station. Cassandra Ainslee's car was caught on a few street cameras moving west."

Noah looked at Jesse. "The park is west, but she wouldn't—"

Suddenly, Noah's phone dinged. He glanced down.

Shit. "That's the silent alarm at the park…someone broke into the office."

CHAPTER 30

"*Y*ou lost her?"

Toby's voice rang in Addie's ears. Toby…all this time.

Was *everything* Toby? The texts. Rhett's murder and Ellis's stabbing? All to scare her out of town? But why?

"She pretended she was unconscious and *attacked* me. Do you see my nose? I'm lucky she didn't have a weapon!"

Addie touched a hand to her chest, trying to remain calm as she watched Toby's shoes close the space between him and Cass. "We need to find her *now*, before any of those soldiers show up."

"No." Cass stepped back. "The deal was, I deliver her here to you and then I leave."

"I know this is scary, Cass. But if you don't help me, and they find her, you'll be arrested anyway." His voice was soft now. Gentle. "She *murdered* Rhett. You loved him. Help me make sure she can't hurt anyone else."

Jesus, had he been using his training as a therapist to manipulate Cass?

There was a pause before Cass spoke. "Thirty minutes. And if we don't find her, I need to go."

"Thank you. Call me if you find her. I'll take care of her."

"Good. Because I can't kill anyone."

"I know. It's okay. That's why I'm here."

Addie's belly rolled at that gentle, I-care-about-you fakeness. He was using Cass. Lying to her. And she was buying all of it.

Cass and Toby both walked away in opposite directions.

For a few minutes, Addie didn't move. She wasn't even sure if moving was the best option. She could wait here for Noah or Colt, because one of them had to arrive soon.

But there was a chance Cass or Toby would return, and she was vulnerable under this food truck. They'd probably already checked the cabin, so maybe they didn't plan to return there? Plus, there were knives in the kitchen. A phone to call Noah, in case he hadn't connected her with the alarm.

Move. Every part of her screamed that she needed to get out from under this vehicle. Run.

She closed her eyes and drew in a deep breath.

You can do this, Addie. Survive until help comes.

One more deep inhale and she slipped out from under the chassis, her body hurting from all the injuries. Her pulse galloped in her veins and her legs felt like rubber. But she moved. Slipping through the trees, trying to run quickly while keeping her steps as quiet as possible.

Her eyes scanned the forest around her, searching. Making sure she was alone. Every step had her breathing quickening and the fear in her chest squeezing and expanding.

When the office came into view, she almost sighed in relief.

So close.

It wasn't until she reached the window that she realized she'd have to crawl through the broken shards of glass that bordered the frame.

Crap.

She turned and searched for a rock. When she found one, she used it to break the remaining glass off. Every time she hit a new shard, she cringed. After three hits, she couldn't risk the sound anymore.

Someone would hear. She just needed to get inside.

She grabbed the edge and hauled herself up. Small fragments of glass cut into her palms, shooting pain into her hands. But she ignored it. She had one focus, find a weapon.

She dropped to the other side. She was in. Now she needed a knife.

In the kitchen, she searched through the drawers, finding the long butcher's knife. She wrapped her fingers around the handle and turned. But the second she stepped into the office, she stopped.

Because there, standing in front of her, was Toby—and he had a gun aimed straight at her chest.

"Put down the knife, Addie."

She swallowed, every part of her wanting, *needing*, to keep the knife firmly gripped in her palm. But she didn't have a choice. The knife dropped with a clatter.

"How did you know I was here?"

"I saw you. I could have taken a shot but I'm not the best distance shooter, so I followed instead."

"Why?" The single word was coated with confusion and disbelief. "Why have you done all this? What money is there to gain from chasing me out of town?"

"You still haven't worked it out?"

"Worked *what* out?"

"Jules."

She frowned. "What does Jules have to do with any of this?"

His step forward was slow and predatory. "Every so often, I get a golden client. Someone who's nearing death, but with no family to leave any inheritance to. Usually, it's the elderly. But it could also include the sick…like Jules."

Finally, she understood. And it made *her* sick. This guy didn't want to help people—he wanted to take from them. Steal.

"So she started seeing you for therapy, you learned that she had no one to will her money or assets to, and that she was going to die, so you took advantage of her."

"I made myself important. Home visits. Late-night calls. I spent *eighteen months* investing in Jules. We both benefited. But then, she suddenly reveals that she has a daughter! She didn't even tell me she was looking for you, and suddenly she calls me from fucking *Amber Ridge* to tell me what she was doing. And I knew if I didn't act quickly, everything I'd worked so hard for would be taken from me—by *you*."

Everything he'd worked hard for? Was he serious? He hadn't worked hard for anything. He'd lied and taken advantage of Jules, only showing her kindness so he could steal from her.

"You're a terrible person," she whispered.

"No. I'm smart. But clearly, *you're* not. I tried to scare you away. I even tried to break up you and Noah because I knew if you two started dating, you were never going to leave. Once you were gone, I could keep getting closer to Jules. Reaffirm to her that *I* am the closest person to her. But you just wouldn't heed my warnings. You just kept getting closer to Jules."

"Why did you kill Rhett?" The question burst out of her.

"The sheriff was onto him. I couldn't have him ratting me out for paying him to tamper with the rock-climbing gear and steal your house key." He frowned. "I'd actually planned to kill him when he turned his back to me, but he was so cocky and made me so damn angry. He started yelling, saying I was a psycho and he was going to tell everyone what I'd done."

He'd lost his temper? How was this guy a therapist? "And now you plan to kill *me*?"

"I do. And then Cass. I'll put her prints on the gun, and everyone will think she did it. Jules will be so upset that she'll lean on me. And everything will go back to the way it was."

Something flickered outside the window. It took everything

inside Addie not to look. But she didn't need to. She knew what it was.

"There's something you don't know," she said quietly.

He lifted a brow.

"There's a silent alarm on this cabin. It alerted Noah and Colt the second I broke the window. And I think they just arrived."

A crunch of what sounded like glass beneath feet came from the other room.

Toby moved so quickly that she didn't see him coming. He yanked her in front of him and pressed his back to the wall.

Then Noah stepped into the room, gun raised, eyes narrowed on Toby.

* * *

NOAH PRESSED his foot to the floor, his truck well exceeding the speed limit. He'd run out of Jules's house so fast that Jesse hadn't been able to stop him. Not that his cousin would have. Jesse and his deputy were behind him.

Cass had headed west. The park was west and the alarm had gone off…it meant she was there. It *had to* mean she was there.

He checked the rearview mirror to see Jesse's patrol car close on his tail. Colt would be on his way too. His friend knew Addie was missing. Noah had no doubt that the second the alarm went off, he'd have connected it to Addie.

Noah's fingers tightened around the wheel. He wanted to kick his own ass. This entire time, it had been Toby. Noah had sat in the man's office and asked for his help while telling him things he'd never told anyone. And the asshole had used that information against him. Pushed him to break things off with Addie, likely to leave her unprotected.

Noah was going to kill him. And if the asshole had touched a fucking hair on Addie's head, he was going to tear him apart with his bare hands.

He pulled into the driveway of the park but didn't go all the way to the parking lot. He couldn't risk Toby or Cass realizing he was here before he wanted them to know.

Cass…fuck, he'd basically handed her to Toby on a silver platter. But she'd made the choice to work with him. And now she needed to be stopped too.

When the truck was parked, he took his Glock from the middle console and climbed out.

Jesse and his deputy were already out of their patrol car.

"Claudia, I want you to search the forest. When backup gets here, they can do the same." Jesse turned to Noah. "Let's go check out the office."

Noah nodded before jogging down the drive. He moved quickly, scanning the trees as he ran, looking for threats.

When he finally reached the cabin, he remained low, moving quietly. He didn't bother with the door. It was closed and didn't look broken. So where had they gained access? What had set off the alarm?

He rounded the cabin and spotted the shattered window.

He was about to haul himself inside when he heard her voice.

"There's a silent alarm on this log cabin. It alerted Noah and Colt the second I broke the window. And I think they just arrived."

His heart stopped. Addie. She was alive!

Quickly, he leaped through the window and ran into the office. What he saw made his blood run cold.

Toby had his arm around Addie's throat and the muzzle of a gun to her temple.

Noah's eyes narrowed. "Put down the gun, Toby."

He growled. "No. I'm calling the shots here. *You* put down the gun or I shoot her."

"You don't want to die today."

The therapist's jaw visibly tightened. "I'm holding a gun on your woman. If you want her to live, then you need to unlock the door and let me leave."

"You expect me to believe that you'll just let her go?"

"What's the alternative? Wait for me to shoot her?"

"The alternative is for you to release her and put your hands up so no one gets hurt."

Toby laughed, but the sound was almost manic. "I'm not going to prison."

"I'm afraid that other than a bullet to your head, that's your only option."

A single second passed before Toby suddenly pulled the pistol from her head and started to point it at Noah.

Addie immediately shoved his arm straight up into the air and dropped.

That's when Noah fired, hitting Toby in the skull.

Jesse appeared in the window, gun raised, but he wasn't needed.

Toby crashed to the floor and Noah was across the room in seconds, wrapping Addie in his arms.

"Shit, Addison, you scared the hell out of me! Are you okay?"

She dug her head into the crook of his neck. "I am now."

He tightened his arms around her. She was alive. Safe. He wasn't too late.

Finally, he could breathe again.

CHAPTER 31

$\mathcal{A}$ddie sat still at the desk in the office as the paramedic did all his checks. Every so often, he asked her a question or directed her to look somewhere or take a deep breath. She was so distracted, he often had to ask twice.

All she could think about, all she *wanted* to think about, was Noah.

He stood near the doorway in the front area, talking to Jesse and Colt. Every few seconds, his eyes found her, running over her body, like he was checking to make sure she was okay and safe.

The day was a blur, everything from finding her birth date on the back of that photo to Toby pressing the muzzle of a gun to her head...none of it felt real.

"Okay, all done."

She looked at the paramedic. "Can I go home?"

Noah appeared beside them, his intense gray eyes flicking from her to the paramedic. "Finished?"

The paramedic stood. "Yes. A mild concussion and some bruising and scratches." He looked back at her. "You need to be woken every couple hours throughout the night, just to make sure symptoms aren't getting worse."

Noah nodded. "I can do that."

"Good. If symptoms worsen—like nausea, severe headache, or confusion—please go to the emergency room."

She swallowed. "I will."

The second the paramedic left, Noah crouched in front of her. "How do you feel?"

"Tired." Ha, tired barely touched the surface of how she felt. She was *exhausted*. The adrenaline crash had hit her about thirty minutes ago, and it had hit hard.

He slipped a piece of hair behind her ear. There was pain in his eyes. And anger and frustration and so many other emotions. "I hate what happened today."

"Me too. And there's still so much to sort out. Jules. Cass. Oh God—Cass." She straightened. "Did anyone find her?"

"Just now. They're bringing her up to the parking lot to take her down to the station. We can wait until we know she's gone before leaving, if you want?"

Addie shook her head. "No. I just want to go."

Understanding darkened his eyes. He looked like he wanted her out of here as much as she did.

As they stepped out of the office, she studied the broken window. "I'm sorry I dragged it all in here."

"I'm not. You breaking that window alerted us that you were here. You saved yourself."

"Thank God for the silent alarm."

"Thank God for *you*." He kissed the top of her head and they stepped outside.

When a female deputy walked out of the forest with Cass beside her in handcuffs, Addie stopped.

Then Cass met her gaze, and the other woman's eyes flared in anger. "You're still here?" She turned to the deputy. "She killed Rhett! Why isn't *she* in cuffs?"

Noah took a step toward her, but Addie held him back. "No. I need to say something to her."

"Are you sure?"

She nodded before crossing the lot.

"You're a murderer!" Cass spat.

"I didn't kill Rhett," she said carefully, when she reached her.

"You *did*. Toby told me everything."

"He lied to you. Just like he lied to everyone else. *He* killed Rhett because Rhett became a liability after he paid him to tamper with the rock-climbing gear, the day Buck fell. He also paid Rhett to steal my house key."

Cass paled before vigorously shaking her head. "No. That's not true. Toby told me—"

"Toby only cared about getting his hands on Jules's money. After killing me, he planned to kill *you*, then frame you for my murder."

Cass blinked, the last scrap of color leaving her face.

"Come on." The deputy pulled her away.

The second Addie was in Noah's truck, she closed her eyes and leaned her head back.

"You're safe to sleep," he said quietly as he started the engine. "I've got you."

She turned to look at him, a soft smile curving her lips. She loved him. An entire-body, didn't-know-what-she'd-do-without-him kind of love.

She reached over and placed a palm on his knee. "I know you do."

He'd just pulled onto the road when she saw the phone in the middle compartment...her phone.

"That's how I knew Cass had you," Noah told her.

Addie lifted her cell to see a missed call from her parents. They couldn't know what had happened today. They would have just been checking in. But the second she told them, they would lose their minds.

That was a call that could wait until tomorrow.

She was about to set the phone back down when a text came through from Jules.

Jules: Addie, I need to know if you're okay. Please tell me you're safe.

She stared at the text for an entire minute, not sure how to respond. There was so much that needed to be discussed.

Noah shot a couple of glances her way but didn't ask anything until he pulled into his garage. Then he turned to her. "What's going on?"

"I think I'm going to call Jules."

"You sure you want to do that now?"

"I don't think I'll be able to sleep if I don't."

His gaze shifted between her eyes before he nodded. "Okay. I'll wait in the house for you." He squeezed her thigh before climbing out.

Her finger hovered over Jules's name for a few moments before finally, she squeezed her eyes closed and dialed the other woman.

Jules answered immediately. "Addie? Are you okay? Are you safe?"

It was strange, but even her voice sounded different. Or maybe Addie only heard it differently because everything about Jules had changed. "Is it true?"

There was a small pause. "Yes. I...I'm your birth mother."

Unexpected tears filled Addie's eyes, and she wasn't quite sure why. She'd never felt the need to find her birth mother, but now that she had? It was like this piece that she'd never known was missing just slotted back into her life.

"Why didn't you tell me?"

"I was going to. There were so many times the words were right there on the tip of my tongue. But you've told me how great your parents are and I just...I always got scared. That you had them, so you wouldn't need or want me. I have so little time left, and I didn't want to risk you not wanting to be a part of that time."

And that was the added pain…that Jules didn't have long.

Addie swiped a tear from her cheek. "You should have told me."

"I should have. I'm sorry. And I'm sorry about Toby. I didn't know. You're safe now?"

"Noah and Jesse got there in time."

"Thank God."

Addie ran her finger down a seam in her jeans. "I need some time to recover from today and get used to this new information, but after that I'd like to see you."

There was a small pause. "Really?"

"Of course."

"I-I would love that." Emotion clogged Jules's voice. "You rest now, honey. Talk soon."

Even though the other woman couldn't see her, Addie just nodded before hanging up. Then she leaned her head back. So much bad had come from today, but learning that Jules was her biological mother? That felt like a small bit of good.

* * *

HE'D ALMOST BEEN TOO LATE. The thought was on repeat in Noah's mind, taunting him. Making him sick to his fucking stomach. A few more minutes and he might have been. Hell, even getting there to find the gun against Addie's head made it hard for him to breathe.

A text came through on his phone, and he lifted it to see his sister's name.

Indie: Colt just got home and told me she's safe. But I need to hear it from you. Is she okay?

Noah: She has a concussion and some scratches.

Indie: And what about you?

How was he? He was in a world of fucking pain and what-ifs.

Noah: It will be a while before I'm okay.

Indie: What can I do?

Noah: You're already doing it by checking in.

Indie: I'm leaving food on your doorstep tomorrow. And I'm making chocolate pudding for Addie. Let me know if you need anything else.

Noah: Thanks, Indie.

He lowered his phone and ran his fingers through his hair. What he really needed, the only thing he needed, was Addie.

He looked in the garage to see she wasn't on the phone anymore. Her head was back and her eyes closed. But it was the track of tears down her cheeks that had his heart tearing in two.

Quietly, he crossed the space between them and opened her door. "Hey. How'd it go?"

She turned and looked at him. "Jules is my biological mother."

"She is."

"I wish she'd told me from the start."

He reached up and brushed a tear from her cheek. "Me too."

"How are you feeling after today?"

"Angry that you were taken from me. Furious that Toby was behind it and I didn't see it. I want to kill him all over again for putting a gun to your head."

"That's a lot of anger."

"Fortunately, I've got a great therapist."

Addie's brows flickered. "I hate that Toby used you."

"But he's gone now."

"Thank God."

Gently, he slipped his arms beneath her legs and back and lifted her.

She gasped. "Noah! I can walk."

He didn't care. He needed her close. As close as damn possible.

She sighed before leaning her head against his chest.

Inside, he lowered her to the couch. "I need to feed you and we both need a long-ass shower."

Addie grabbed his arm before he could go. "That stuff can wait." She tugged him down and there was no part of him capable of saying no.

He lowered to the couch beside her, and she immediately nestled into his chest.

"I'm sorry she took you," he whispered.

Her head lifted. "Why are *you* sorry? It wasn't your fault."

"You should have been protected in my home."

"*I* opened the door. *I* let her in. I'd just learned about Jules and I wasn't thinking clearly."

"But—"

"No. No buts. It wasn't your fault. If we're going to blame anyone, let's blame Toby. With Cass's help." She cringed. "Another staff member we need to replace at the park."

"The park is the last thing I'm thinking about right now." He pulled her closer, his arms wrapping tighter around her. It still didn't feel close enough, but he had a feeling nothing would.

He wasn't sure how long they sat like that. At some point his phone rang. He wrestled it out of his pocket to see that it was Bonnie. He needed to talk to his sister. Since she'd told him she lost her job, they kept missing each other's calls, and Noah had gotten preoccupied with everything going on.

He'd call her back tomorrow. He needed to make sure she was okay.

He shoved his cell back into his pocket and closed his eyes, so fucking grateful that Addie was safe. That she'd survived. That she was *his*.

CHAPTER 32

A smile tugged at Addie's mouth as she watched her father across Pam's backyard, talking to Noah. As expected, both her parents had shown up the next day, a couple hours after she'd called them. They hadn't stayed in town that time, but they'd been making the one-hour drive down to Amber Ridge as often as possible since.

She loved it. Having her parents here was like bringing everyone she loved together.

She nervously checked her watch.

"Not here yet?"

Her gaze flew up at her mother's voice. "Not yet, but she's only ten minutes late."

"I'm nervous too."

Not a surprise that her mother could tell she was nervous. She knew her better than anyone. "We've both already met her. We shouldn't be nervous."

Her mother shook her head. "No. This is different. She's not my daughter's coworker anymore—she's the woman who gave me the gift of my child. I have a lot to thank her for."

Addie's skin tingled. She wasn't sure she'd ever get used to the fact that Jules was her birth mother. "I'm sure she wants to thank you too, for giving me the best upbringing."

"I hope we did."

Addie hugged her mother tightly, so unbelievably grateful that she'd been gifted such amazing parents.

"Hey, why aren't I included in this family hug? What am I, chopped liver?"

Addie laughed at her father, pulling back to see him now beside them.

Her mother jokingly swatted her father on the arm. "Mark, you get far more hugs from our daughter than I do."

"Doesn't mean I can't have more."

Addie hugged her dad. "I love you too, Dad."

He grunted but also wrapped a firm arm around her waist.

God, she loved both of them so much.

When she stepped back, her mother touched her shoulder. "Are you sure you're okay? You've been through so much since moving here."

"I have." She scanned the yard for Noah, finding him with his aunt and sister. "But I've also gained so much too." Noah. His family. Jules. A great job. An entire life.

Her father glanced over his shoulder before looking back at her. "He makes you happy."

"No. It goes far beyond happy." It was a combination of peace and joy and this new vision for her future.

Her father nodded. "He's a good man. I approve."

She chuckled, knowing that would have taken a lot for her father to say. "Really? I thought no one would ever be good enough for me."

"They won't be. But he's probably as close as you'll get."

She grinned at him.

"All we've ever wanted is for you to be happy, darling," her mother said quietly.

"I'm so lucky to have you both."

"No, *we're* the lucky ones." Her mother squeezed her hand.

When her phone vibrated with a text, she looked down.

Jules: Hi, honey. I'm at the front door.

Addie glanced up, not sure why she was so nervous for Jules to meet her parents again. "Jules is here."

Her mother nodded. "We'll wait here."

Addie cut across the yard and hurried through the house. When she opened the door, her pulse sped up. She'd only seen Jules once since finding out she was her birth mother, and she'd been nervous as heck that time too.

Jules had shared so much during that visit. The heartache of giving up her only child for adoption. The long road to stabilizing her mental health.

Jules's lips curved. "Hi, Addie." She lifted the tray in her hands. "I made chocolate chip cookies."

Addie chuckled. "Jules, you know I'm going to have to try one of them before the main meal."

"I won't tell anyone." She stepped inside. "How have you been?"

"Good. Great, actually. Noah's really been looking after me. And my parents have made the drive here a few times. It's been nice. It's also nice to feel safe again. How are *you*?"

Jules had trusted Toby. Not just trusted—he'd been like family to her.

She frowned. "The shock is still there. It will probably be there for a while. I knew him for eighteen months, and he seemed so genuine. He always said exactly what I needed to hear. He was my only friend for a long time. I never would have suspected that his motives were anything but genuine. But I'm trying to forgive myself for bringing him into your life."

"Jules, there's nothing to forgive. He knew how to deceive you because he'd done it before."

Jesse's team had done a lot of digging and learned that Toby had inherited huge sums of money from three different patients. *Three*. The man had been a skilled con artist.

"Still, I hate that he tried to hurt you," Jules said quietly.

"He hurt you too. And I'm glad he's gone."

They were about to step out the back door when Jules touched her arm. "Wait, before we go out there, I want to say something."

"Anything."

"I don't want you ever to feel like you *have* to have me in your life. If you ever want me to leave Amber Ridge—"

"Jules. I may not have looked for you, but I'm glad you found me. I am so grateful that you chose the best parents for me. You gave me a gift, and I have lived the happiest life. I want to get to know the woman who gave me that life."

Tears gathered in Jules's eyes, then she wrapped Addie in a hug. "Oh, that makes me happy."

When they separated, Jules scrubbed her eyes and headed into the yard. Addie watched her parents walk straight up to the woman and embrace her. For a moment, Addie didn't move. She just watched as the woman who'd given her life hugged the parents who'd raised her.

She blinked back her own tears before shifting her gaze and finding Noah across the lawn. He was already looking at her, his eyes dark and intense. Then he started toward her. Her heart beat a little faster with each step he took. Because she loved him. He'd become her safety. He'd become home.

* * *

NOAH WATCHED as Addie embraced her parents. The old strain around her eyes was gone. The visible tension in her muscles. All because the asshole who'd been gunning for her was gone.

When she started toward the back door, he was about to follow her when a hand touched his shoulder.

"You look happy."

Noah dragged his gaze from Addie to Jesse, and Holden and Becket on either side of him.

He dipped his head. "There's a lot to be happy about. Addie's safe. She has Jules in her life. And she and I are good." Good? That didn't even begin to describe how they were. The woman was his entire world.

"That's great." Jesse clenched his shoulder.

"And did I hear you're reopening the park?" Holden asked.

"In two weeks. We just have to train the new staff." They'd found some great people to work for them. People with more experience, who'd be a hell of a lot better than Rhett and Cass.

"How are Addie and Jules doing?" Becket asked.

"Really great, actually. Addie still wishes she'd known the truth from the beginning, but she's happy Jules found her." And Jules had actually apologized to Noah for not trusting him, and he apologized to her for doing the same.

"You trust her?" Jesse asked.

"I trust that she came here to get to know Addie, and her only crime was trusting that con-artist therapist." No part of Noah felt bad that Toby was dead. The asshole had killed Rhett, stabbed the deputy, and had intended to kill Addie.

Becket frowned at him. "I know I don't ask enough, but have you heard anything from Bonnie?"

Noah's fingers tightened around his beer. "I've tried her a few times this week but haven't gotten through. I'll try again later today."

"It's good you're back in contact," Jesse said. "After a thirteen-year absence, I wasn't sure we'd *ever* hear from her again."

"I wondered too. I know people are angry that she left. Indie really struggles with it. And I get it—her leaving hurt everyone, particularly because of her timing. But I forgive her for leaving, and I need her to know that she's always got a home here in Amber Ridge."

Becket nodded. "Agreed. She may be a cousin, but she's more like a sister."

Exactly why Bonnie should come home. Despite what she may think, she was loved here.

When Jules stepped into the yard, Noah's gaze shifted to see Addie standing by the back door, watching all three of her parents embrace. There was a hint of tears in her eyes.

He was moving before he could stop himself. Crossing the yard and jogging up the steps so he could pull Addie into his arms. "Hey."

Her smile softened as she splayed her fingers over his chest. "Hey. I missed you."

She had no idea. Even the smallest distance felt too much ever since Cass had taken her. "Everything okay with Jules?"

"Yeah, it is. I'm so glad she found me." Her smile widened. "A bit like you."

"Technically, you found *me* when you applied for the job at the park."

"Thank God I lied about having rock-climbing experience."

"You know I saw right through that lie, right?"

She shook her head. "I don't think you did. I think I was pretty good at pretending. Why else would you have hired me?"

"I can think of a few reasons."

"Really?"

"Mm-hmm."

"You don't think I'm too young for you anymore?"

"Do you think I'm too old?"

"Nah, I'm so wise, people wouldn't even realize there's an age gap."

He laughed.

The smile on her lips grew serious. "Your sessions with Dr. Burton still going well?"

"The man's a miracle worker. The work he's done has changed everything for me."

Addie cupped his cheek. "No. *You've* done the work. It's all you."

"God, I love you, Addison."

"I've loved you since the day I interviewed for that job."

His eyes darkened, and he lowered his head and kissed her. He didn't care who was watching. He just needed to feel this woman against him and get lost in her.

The sudden ringing of Noah's phone made him want to growl and ignore it. He didn't because, if it was who he thought it was, he couldn't miss her again.

He looked at the phone screen.

Bonnie. Finally.

Addie glanced at the cell before stepping back. "Talk to her."

He lowered his head and kissed her one more time. "I'll be back."

He moved into his aunt's living room and took the call. "Hey, Bon-Bon."

"You answered."

"Yeah, sorry, it's been a crazy couple of weeks."

"Is everything okay?"

"It is now." He shoved his other hand into his pocket, not wanting to go into everything, because he wanted to find out how Bonnie was doing. "How have you been?"

There was a small pause. "Actually, I did something."

Noah frowned, his fingers tightening around the phone. "What? Is something wrong?"

Silence stretched over the line, making anxiety pool in Noah's gut.

"Bonnie, you're scaring me."

"I'm in Amber Ridge."

Another entire ten seconds of silence passed, where Noah had to repeat the words in his head to make them make sense. But even when he did, the shock ensured he didn't have words. Not a single one.

"You're *here?*" he finally choked out.

"I applied for that job at the women's shelter. I didn't think I'd get it but…I did. Although, now that I'm here, I'm not sure if I made the right decision. I feel nervous and sick. Have I made a mistake?"

His sister was home. After thirteen years away, she was finally here. "You didn't make a mistake, Bonnie. You're exactly where you're meant to be."

"I've been gone for so long. So many people are angry at me. I don't know how to build a life here. I should have thought about that before taking the job."

"You're here. That's the first step."

There was another pause. "I know you've been great to me, and I'm so grateful for that. But…what if she doesn't forgive me?"

Bonnie didn't need to say the name for him to know she was talking about Indie. "There's only one way to find out."

"And then there's the White family."

His chest tightened. "Dean's death was *not* your fault. He was eighteen, and he made his own choices that night."

"I left him at the party."

"He *chose* to drink. *Then* he chose to get behind the wheel."

"But his family—"

"Were hurting. It's been thirteen years. They should see things clearly by now." Or at least, he really fucking hoped they did. "Where are you staying?"

"I'm renting a place."

"Where? I'll come see you."

"I'll text you the address."

He nodded, even though Bonnie couldn't see him.

Footsteps sounded behind him. "Good. This is *good*, Bonnie. I'll see you soon."

"Yeah. And Noah…thank you."

"For what?"

"Not giving up on me. Seeing past my mistakes."

"You'll always be my little sister."

He hung up and turned to see Indie a few feet behind him, a deep frown on her face. "That was Bonnie?"

"Yeah."

Another step forward. "You said you'd see her soon. Are you going to visit her?"

"Actually, she's here."

Indie blinked, then her eyes flared. "Here? As in, she's in Amber Ridge?"

"Yeah. Bonnie's come home."

CHAPTER 33

Half a dozen people were in Zane Merrick's gym. All men, but that wasn't because it was an all-male gym. Not many women had visited since opening. Half the men were hitting bags, two were in the ring, and one was warming up with a jump rope.

The place had enjoyed a constant flow of people since he'd opened. It was good. *Being* here was good. The fresh start he'd needed. Somewhere no one knew the shit he'd been through.

"You going to lunch?"

He turned to look at Stetson, one of his young employees. The kid was only twenty and not great in the ring or at a bag, but he was keen to learn. "You got things handled here?"

"Absolutely. Don't need to worry about a thing, boss."

He bit back a laugh. The kid's enthusiasm was why Zane liked him. "Be back soon."

The second he stepped outside, cool afternoon air ran over his skin. Fuck, it was cold here. But then, Billings, the town he'd come from, had been cold too.

As he walked, an elderly couple smiled and said hi as they passed. Another thing he was learning about small towns—

people were friendly. The other day a couple had stopped and asked if he'd dropped a five-dollar bill. The week before he'd received three *hellos* along one damn street.

He wasn't used to it.

He turned right onto Fifth Street to see The Tea House up ahead. The first few weeks living here, he'd gone to the diner for his coffee. A big fucking mistake *that* had been. The stuff tasted like watered-down dirt. Combine that with Burt's Pizza and he'd assumed this town didn't have good coffee *or* pizza.

It had damn near been a deal breaker.

Then Stetson had told him to try The Tea House, and fuck he was glad he had. Good coffee. Good pie. And Mrs. Gerald reminded him of his late grandmother, who'd not only raised him but was the best woman he'd ever known.

He stepped inside The Tea House to see most of the tables taken. Which was fine. He wasn't staying.

Mrs. Gerald stopped in front of him on the other side of the counter, a warm smile curving her lips. "Zane, dear, how are you today?"

"I'm good. How are you?"

"Busy. But I would never complain about that because there was a time not so long ago when I was close to shutting the place down because we weren't busy *enough*."

"With coffee like yours?"

"Oh, our coffee wasn't what it is today." She frowned. "You look tired. Are you doing okay?"

He could have laughed. He'd been tired since all the shit that had gone down in Billings. It was only recently that he'd finally been able to sleep again. "I'm doing all right."

"How about an extra shot in your coffee?"

"I would never say no to an extra shot."

Her smile widened. "Coming right up."

The café owner had just turned when a woman by the

window caught Zane's attention. She sat at a booth, the weak sun shining on long brown hair with blond streaks.

It was his military training that had taught him how to read body language. Little things gave people away. Nervous touches to the face. Visibly tight shoulders. Even the flickering of eyes. Right now, the woman was doing all of that. Her knuckles were white around her coffee and her gaze was sweeping the street outside. But not like she was waiting for someone. More like she was afraid she'd *see* someone.

Who? And who was she?

He hadn't seen her before, which was strange in a town the size of Amber Ridge. Everyone here seemed to look at least somewhat familiar, like he'd run into them at the grocery store at some point.

He turned back to the counter. Not his business.

When Mrs. Gerald set his coffee in front of him, he thanked her and paid, leaving a generous tip before heading out.

The nervous woman had left too and was heading toward a car...but it wasn't just Zane who was watching her. Two men a few cars away had their eyes on her—and not in a good way.

Zane stopped because even though he liked to mind his own business, his gut told him that those guys were about to cross a fucking line.

He waited, and like clockwork, the assholes moved toward her. Zane's eyes narrowed, then *he* moved toward her.

One of the guys stepped in front of her, blocking her way to her car. He said something Zane couldn't catch, and the second guy behind her blocked her from walking away.

The woman looked over her shoulder before the guy in front of her spoke again. Zane stopped close enough so he could hear the conversation. If one of them so much as raised a hand, he was stepping in.

"You think you can just stroll back into town like everyone forgot what you did?"

The woman straightened. "Respectfully, get out of my way, before I make you."

They both laughed, but it was the guy in front of her who responded. "You'll make us? What will you do? Leave us at a party to *die?*"

She glanced behind her, and that's when Zane saw her eyes harden. "Last chance."

The guy at her front grabbed her arm and yanked her forward.

Zane cursed and stepped toward them—but she was faster than Zane. She stepped *into* the movement, then with her free arm, she reached over the guy's shoulder and tugged him forward. At the same time, she hooked her foot behind his leg, and in one swift maneuver, she shoved his upper body while sweeping her leg.

The asshole lost his balance and fell sideways.

The second guy cursed and went to grab her, but Zane grabbed *him* before he could do anything.

"Don't even think about it," he growled.

"Don't touch me *ever* again." Her voice was low and angry.

The jerk on the ground got up, his cheeks red. He looked like he wanted to lunge for her, but then Zane stepped behind her, and the guy froze.

Yeah, the asshole knew exactly what would happen if he made another move.

The jerk swallowed and stepped back. Maybe he was smarter than Zane had given him credit for.

"Come on." His friend grabbed his arm. "She's not worth it."

Finally, they both turned and headed toward The Tea House.

Zane looked down at the woman, but she was still watching the closed Tea House door. "Are you okay?"

"I'm fine." Even though she said the words, there was an underlying shake in her voice.

Finally she looked up at him, and *fuck*, her eyes were beautiful. A mixture of brown and hazel. They were like pools of emotion.

She lifted a shoulder, and the sadness…damn, it just leached out of her. "It's nothing I can't handle."

She shouldn't *have* to handle an asshole grabbing her. "What was that about?"

"You don't want to know." She swallowed before stepping back. "Thank you for the backup. I should go."

She turned and had only taken a step before he spoke.

"Hey."

She glanced back at him.

"You handled yourself well. You ever want a bag to hit or a ring to have a round in, I run The Pit, a gym here in town. You're welcome anytime."

Her brows flickered. Like she was surprised he was being nice to her? "Thanks. I'll keep that in mind."

Then she climbed into the car.

And for some fucking reason, he *really* hoped she took him up on that offer.

Order book six, Zane and Bonnie's story, UNFINISHED, now!

Declan

Cole

Ryker

BEAUTIFUL PIECES

Erik's Salvation

Erik's Redemption

Erik's Refuge

SHORT CHRISTMAS STORY

Hidden Shadows

RECKLESS SERIES

Reckless Hope

Reckless Trust

Reckless Fall

Reckless Faith

Reckless Love

AMBER RIDGE SERIES

Unafraid

Unraveled

Untouched

Unbroken

Unchained

Unfinished

JOIN my newsletter and be the first to find out about sales and new releases! CLICK HERE

ABOUT THE AUTHOR

Nyssa Kathryn is a romantic suspense author. She lives in South Australia with hubby and two daughters and takes every chance she can to be plotting and writing. Always an avid reader of romance novels, she considers alpha males and happily-ever-afters to be her jam.

Don't forget to follow Nyssa and never miss another release.

Facebook | Instagram | Amazon | Goodreads

www.ingramcontent.com/pod-product-compliance
Lightning Source LLC
Chambersburg PA
CBHW050557190726
48283CB00007B/2170